# NOBLE FALL

*A JAKE NOBLE THRILLER*

# WILLIAM MILLER

Noble Fall

Copyright © 2023 by Literary Rebel, LLC

All rights reserved.

No part of this publication may be reproduced, distributed, or transmitted in any form or by any means, including photocopying, recording, or other electronic or mechanical methods, without the prior written permission of the publisher, except as permitted by U.S. copyright law. For permission requests, contact LiteraryRebel.com.

The story, all names, characters, and incidents portrayed in this production are fictitious. No identification with actual persons (living or deceased), places, buildings, politicians, and products is intended or should be inferred. Any similarity between characters in this book and evil investment bankers is entirely coincidental.

Book Cover by LiteraryRebel.com

1st edition September 2023

Also by William Miller

**THE JAKE NOBLE CHRONICLES:**
NOBLE MAN
NOBLE VENGEANCE
NOBLE INTENT
NOBLE SANCTION
NOBLE ASSET
NOBLE STORM

**THE MACKENZIE AND COLE MYSTERIES:**
THE DEVIL HIS DUE
SKIN IN THE GAME

**NON-FICTION:**
CRAFTING FICTION VOLUME ONE: HARD-BOILED OUT-LINES

## Special Thanks

This chapter in Jake Noble's life is dedicated to the early readers who help catch the pesky typos that somehow manage to slip past three drafts and two line edits. I'd especially like to thank Ken Friedman and Cathy Sable. The pair of them were invaluable in the editing process.

# Chapter One

Jacob Noble was a wanted man. He'd been on the run for over forty-eight hours. He was being hunted by CIA, MI6, and the London police. He was tired, hungry, and his feet slipped around inside construction boots that were two sizes too big. Breath steamed from his lungs, misting up in silver clouds that broke apart on a cold breeze. The shoulder seams on his rented tuxedo had split and a half healed cut above his left eye was weeping blood again. Soft white flakes swirled down from a black vault overhead, collecting in small white carpets between cold metal tracks.

Less than a mile south and west of Clapham Station in Battersea there is a railway switching station. It was originally built in 1872 and continually improved upon over the years. As the industrial revolution took hold, the switching station grew like a cancer over the surrounding neighborhoods, driving out poor and lower class residents. Large warehouses were erected where tenements used to be. The switching station was blown up twice during the blitz and rebuilt in the early sixties. It remained in near constant use until the mid-eighties when Margaret Thatcher's party passed a bill that financed a larger, more modern switching station north and west of London. Now the South Chapel Station is used mostly as a collection point for rusting old box cars and decrepit locomotive engines in need of repair.

Ice formed atop the abandoned hulks as Noble picked his way quietly along, searching for someplace to hide. His oversized boots crunched in the snow and cold cut through his second-hand tux.

"Noble!" Gregory Hunt's voice echoed across the quiet yard. "It's over, Noble. I don't know what game you're playing but it ends here. Stop right where you are and put your hands up."

Noble spun around, one hand going automatically to the gun in his waistband. Hunt, along with a pair of goons from the CIA's Office of Security named Dunlop and Simms, stood at the vast turn junction. The security guys already had their weapons out and trained on Noble, hoping for an excuse to pull the trigger. Noble relaxed his hand away from the gun. "Hunt, you have no idea what you just walked into. If you're smart, you'll turn around and walk away."

"I know perfectly well what's going on, Noble." Hunt didn't bother to bring his gun out. He was content to let the Office of Security people do the heavy lifting. He stood there in a five-hundred dollar camelhair coat with his blond hair blowing in the wind and his hands stuffed in his pockets. "I told the Company it was a mistake to trust you. You finally outed yourself, Noble. Got caught with your hand in the cookie jar."

"I'm innocent." Noble backed away. He was in an alley formed by rusting box cars. "If you give me a chance, I can prove it."

"You're all out of moves, Noble." Hunt and his goons slowly advanced. "You're a traitor and the CIA knows it. They're turning you over to the Chinese. With any luck, I'll get to be at the exchange and watch you take the walk of shame. Now turn around, get on your knees, and put your hands in the air."

"You know I'm not going to do that," Noble said, looking for an opening between the cars.

Hunt shrugged, as if it was all the same to him. "We're taking you in dead or alive."

"You'll have to kill me."

"Have it your way."

The sharp *thwap-thwap-thwap* of suppressed weapons shattered the winter air.

# Chapter Two

*48 hours Earlier*

NOBLE CARRIED A CUP of steaming coffee to a table in the corner and sat with his back to the crowded buffet, using the reflection in the glass to study his fellow passengers. He paid particular attention to hands and feet. Faces can be deceiving, but hands and feet often give an operative away. While he sipped his coffee, Noble eyed an Asian at the far end of the car. He wore rugged hiking boots and his hands were stuffed in the pockets of his overcoat. He was a small bulldog with a wide face and a mouth that turned down at the corners. One foot danced under the table and he kept throwing nervous glances around the buffet car.

The InterCity 225 hurtled through the English countryside. The carriage rocked to the steady *clickity-clack* of the wheels on the tracks and rolling farmland slipped past rain-streaked windows. Noble peeled up the plastic lid and blew on his coffee while he waited to see if the Bulldog would make a move.

The man opened his mouth in a silent grimace, like he was working up his courage, then pushed to his feet in one quick motion. His mitts came out of his pockets. He was clutching a pack of smokes in one hand and a lighter in the other.

Noble was already halfway out of his seat, heart grinding in his chest. He stopped, breathed a sigh, and lowered back down. The Bulldog was just a smoker trying desperately to resist the urge. Noble shook his head and grinned. The cargo was making him nervous. He was jumping at shadows.

The Bulldog headed for the smoking car. Noble watched him go and then pulled out his cellphone. His Citizen Nighthawk told him it was just after seven P.M. in London. It would be early afternoon in Saint Petersburg, Florida. He dialed and his mother picked up after just three rings.

"Hello stranger. I was starting to think you'd forgotten about us."

"It's been four days," Noble said.

"It only took Jesus three days to come back from the dead," Mary Elise Noble said.

Jake smiled. He lifted his coffee to his lips and said, "I'll be back day after tomorrow."

"You'd better be, buster. That beast of yours is a real handful. Barks every time I come back from the store."

"He's just happy to see you," Noble said. "When he barks, you're fine. When he growls, you should be nervous."

The Czechoslovakian wolfhound had been bred and trained for war, disciplined not to bark from the time he was a pup, but living with Noble aboard *The Yeoman* had brought out a playful side. Gadsden now had a mangled rubber squeaky-duck which he guarded jealously and a blanket he wouldn't allow Noble to wash. They played tug-o-war and Noble had even taught the dog to bark. That had been the most difficult part of Gadsden's training to overcome. It required Noble to sit on the deck of the ship, barking at the moon every night for weeks until Gadsden finally joined in. Noble's neighbors in the marina must have thought he was a lunatic. Now Gadsden gave a single short bark anytime he saw someone he liked, mostly Noble and his mother. Occasionally he'd give a bark for Ruby, the jazz singer who owned Noble's favorite watering hole.

"Well, hurry back. I'm afraid the beast is going to bite my leg off," Mom said. "Or this tub of yours will flip over."

Noble heard the creak of a hawser line through the long distance connection. Despite her protests, his mother liked the dog and was coming to terms with the boat. A few days aboard *The Yeoman* meant autonomy and that was something she sorely lacked at the assisted living facility. Noble said, "Give Gadsden a scratch behind the ears for me."

"Will do," said Mary Elise. "You been reading your Bible?"

"When I have the time."

Mary Elise Noble was a Born Again Bible-quoting Christian and it was her mission in life to make her son a believer. Noble had scoffed at the idea of a man in the sky until he met a girl named Sam Gunn. When Sam prayed, things happened. It forced Noble to reevaluate everything he thought he knew. He said, "Been reading through the Old Testament. Some of it's a little confusing. God gets the Israelites out of Egypt and then they make a golden cow and piss him off. Not too smart."

"Buster, you just described the human condition. Sometimes God has to let us wander the desert for a while to smarten us up."

"Guess that's the moral of the story," Noble said.

"It's not allegory. It's historical, but the point is we're flawed and without God we make a mess of things."

Noble considered that a moment. "And a little time in a bad situation will force us to rely on God."

"I'll make a Bible scholar out of you yet."

"Highly unlikely." Noble chuckled. "I have to let you go, Ma. I'm on a train and we'll be going through a tunnel any minute."

"Good to hear your voice, Jake."

"You too, Ma."

He thumbed the disconnect button as the train hurtled into the tunnel. Darkness closed around the locomotive, causing the lights in the buffet car to stand out bright in comparison. An announcement came over the speaker system, letting the passengers know that they'd be disembarking at London King's Cross in less than an hour. Noble finished his coffee and made his way back along the train to his compartment.

He had placed a small piece of clear plastic tape at the top of the door frame. It was still attached but that didn't necessarily mean the compartment was safe. Skilled agents would search the door for tamper evidence before breaking in.

Noble rapped gently.

From inside he heard the first part of the coded exchange. "What do you want?"

"Change for the vending machine," Noble said.

The door slid open and Hap Chan peered out. He was short and bald, with thick glasses that magnified his nervous eyes, and a weak chin, making him look like an overgrown turtle. He craned his skinny neck to peer over Noble's shoulder and said, "I was starting to worry."

"Try to relax, will ya?" Noble slid past him into the compartment and closed the door. "We'll be in London soon. Tomorrow we'll be on a plane headed to Washington."

The compartment was a double sleeper with a pair of beds jammed together in a space not much bigger than an average sedan. The only luggage was Noble's sling pack and a briefcase that contained all Hap Chan's earthly belongings. The little guy plopped down on his bunk with a worried frown on his turtle face. "Why couldn't we fly out of Edinburgh?"

"Because the flights are cheaper from London," Noble told him.

Government agencies pick the strangest times to pinch pennies. Flying out of Heathrow would save the CIA five hundred bucks, so Noble and the Chinese defector would be staying the night at a CIA safe house in the heart of London. Noble wasn't worried. The hard part was over. He'd gotten Hap Chan out of China via Macau. It had been touch and go there for a few days but Noble and Hap Chan managed to book passage to India and from there to Edinburgh.

Chan knotted his hands together and stared out the window at the black expanse. Anxiety pinched his brow. His lips twitched. Most defectors would have breathed a sigh of relief the moment they landed in England, but Hap had been a bundle of nerves since they left Macau and seemed to grow increasingly anxious the farther they got from China.

Noble dropped down onto his own bunk, leaned across the space and fixed Hap with a look. "You're out, Hap. You're free. There's nothing to worry about. In a few days you'll start a new life in America."

Hap Chan took a shuddering breath and tried to relax but his shoulders were still pulled up around his ears and his hands tortured themselves into strange shapes. He said, "China has a very long reach, my friend."

Noble shook his head and picked up a dog-eared paperback. He leaned his shoulder against the bulkhead and tried to ignore the nervous little man while the train hurtled along the tracks. Thirty minutes later the speakers announced their imminent arrival at King's Cross Station.

Noble closed his book, reached across and used it to whack Hap on the knee. "Easy-peasy-lemon-squeezy."

"I'll feel much better when we land in America."

The hard clack of the tracks started to space out as the train slowed, making its long and winding way through the heart of London. Hap forgot to be scared for a few minutes as he gazed out the window at the lights and the crowds. The train swept around a curve, under an overpass, and then slowed even more as it chugged into King's Cross.

A low rumble of locomotives mixed with hissing air brakes and the chatter of waiting passengers. Noble stuffed his paperback into his bag and checked the hall before motioning Hap to follow. They stepped down onto the smooth concrete landing at platform 7 and, as they made their way toward the main terminus, Noble spotted the Bulldog trailing behind.

## Chapter Three

The club was a dark, smoke-filled cavern with a pulse in the heart of the Bijlmer neighborhood in Amsterdam. There was no name, just a sign over the door depicting a skull wreathed in flame. Haitian voodoo symbols had been spray painted on black walls and sputtering candles dribbled wax on the sticky floor. Tribal music blasted from the speakers at all hours. The cacophonous mix of bongos and synthesized base tracks had driven the last of the honest residents from the neighborhood, leaving a demilitarized zone within a two block radius.

The Haitian was twenty-nine years old, and rail-thin with knotted muscles and long black dreads. Voodoo symbols were inked on his bare chest and dark sunglasses hid a Devil's eyes. He lounged in a filthy leather sofa at the back of the club, flanked by pretty young girls bathed in candlelight. A thick blunt hung from his bottom lip. Curlicues of noxious smoke drifted up toward the ceiling. His name was Daniel Baptiste, but everyone called him The Haitian. He idly stroked one bare white thigh while he sorted baggies of black tar heroin on a low table littered with empty beer bottles.

The front door opened and a white man with an eye patch entered. He waited just inside for his eye to adjust to the darkness and, before he could get the layout of the place, was hemmed in by three men with bulging shoulders and python arms. He spoke to them. The Haitian was too far away to hear what was said, but watched the interaction with interest. One of the enforcers motioned for the white man to spread his arms. He was searched and then the enforcer turned and nodded.

The Haitian waved the white man over and watched as he crossed the club. He was a warrior. The Haitian could see it in his stride, in the way he moved. This man was no stranger to the dark and dirty places of the world. He was a shark swimming in dangerous waters and his one eye drank in the details, marking threats, planning his exit if things went bad. He was dressed in a leather sport coat and dark denims, and the patch over his eye was a new edition. The skin around the patch was still red and raw.

He stopped at the table, scanned the heroin and the empty bottles, and spoke in a British drawl. "Can we talk?"

The Haitian studied him a moment from behind the dark sunglasses, waiting to see if silence would make the white man nervous, waiting to see if he would start to fidget. He stood like a statue carved from marble. His hands were at his sides, dangling like big heavy weights and his eye stared back at the Haitian, as if he were prepared to stand there all day.

The Haitian passed each of the girls a small baggie of black tar and told them to get lost. They clutched at the drugs with the trembling fingers of junkies and hurried off to the bathroom. In five minutes they would be nodding on the floor. The Haitian motioned to the open seat across from him and the white man sat.

"I was told you were the man to see for delicate problems."

"Maybe." The Haitian shrugged. "Ya know my fee?"

He nodded. "I can pay in euros."

"What ya got for me, mon?"

He slipped a hand inside his coat and brought out a slim manilla folder which he passed over. The Haitian opened the flap and shook out a series of black and white surveillance photographs of an old woman on a boat in the tropics.

"What chu want kill an old lady for, mon?"

"We don't want her dead. We need her as leverage."

The Haitian grinned. "Putting the strong arm on somebody?"

"We need photographs so our target knows you are in control of the old bag," he said. "When it's over she dies, but it has to look natural."

"Ya said *we*. Who's your partner?"

The skin around his mouth tightened. "He'll remain anonymous."

"Not sure I like working with silent partners." The Haitian scratched his bare chest. "Makes me itch."

"We'll double your normal fee. You want the job, or not?"

"When?"

"Soon as possible. You in?"

The Haitian grinned, flashing gold teeth. "I'll ice the old woman for ya, mon. But I want half up front."

"The money will be in your account by the time you land in America," he said. "She lives in Saint Petersburg, Florida. She's currently staying on a boat called *The Yeoman*. The marina and slip number are in the file. Keep her alive until we tell you. Then I want the boat to burn, and I need proof of death."

"I always provide proof," the Haitian assured him.

"Call me when you land. My number is in the file." He stood up, tipped a nod, and headed for the door. The Haitian watched him go, then turned to the pictures of the old lady. Daniel Baptiste had grown up poor in Haiti. He'd joined a gang at the age of ten and killed his first man at twelve. Killing an old lady meant nothing more to him than swatting a bothersome fly. He picked up his phone and opened an app to search for flights.

# Chapter Four

Mary Elise Noble sat in a deck chair aboard *The Yeoman*, feeling the ship rise and fall on a gentle swell. She was small and frail, with skin like brittle paper and thinning white hair. A knobby yellow shawl hung loose around her boney shoulders and fuzzy house slippers protected her feet from the cold deck. She watched a squall line creep across the eastern horizon. If that line of dark clouds made its way any further inland, Mary was going back to the Wyndham Arms. She didn't mind watching 'the beast' but she didn't care to spend the night on this rickety old tub in a thunderstorm.

Mary was a survivor. She'd survived cancer and Vietnam and Watergate and the death of her husband. She'd survived that boob Jimmy Carter in the White House, witnessed a man walk on the moon, and lived to see the first black president. Sitting there on the deck of *the Yeoman*, listening to the creak of hawser lines and waves slapping the hull, Mary could feel the long years of her life winding down, coming to their inevitable end. She'd lived a good long life. She was closer to the end than the beginning, but she still had a few good years left. She closed her eyes and turned her face up to the last rays of the setting sun.

There was a party three boats down. A bunch of young people, younger than Jake, were dancing to music that Mary didn't care for. The girls wore tight little skirts and the guys were dressed in expensive silk shirts and sunglasses. Mary thought they might be drug dealers. She watched Miami Vice and knew drug dealers liked to party on boats.

She reached down one skeletal hand and scratched Gadsden behind the ears. His mouth dropped open and a banner tongue unfurled. It was his silent way of letting her know he enjoyed the attention. A salesman had come along earlier looking to sell something and 'the beast' chased him off with a menacing growl. Mary gave him a doggie treat as a reward.

The Yeoman was a forty-foot schooner of brass and wood with a bunk that Mary found surprisingly comfortable. It was docked in the basin across from Staub Park, in downtown Saint Pete. At first Mary doubted very much she'd get any quality rest on a boat, especially this boat, but the waves lulled her to sleep every night and sunlight through the port window nudged her awake in the morning. She had gone shopping yesterday. Jake's small refrigerator was stocked with leftovers and the galley cupboards were mostly bare. Mary bought enough to get herself through the week, along with a little extra for Jake when he returned.

Cooking for herself was a nice change of pace. She was treated like an invalid at the Wyndham arms. Everything was done for her. They cooked and they cleaned and a nurse even stayed in her room while Mary showered to make sure she didn't slip and fall. Mary enjoyed preparing little meals for herself aboard *the Yeoman*. She didn't make anything fancy, her tastebuds were mostly gone anyway, but just being able to cook and clean up after made her feel useful again. The assisted living facility had been a Godsend after the cancer, when Mary was too weak to scratch her own nose, but now she was strong again. And she wanted control of her life back. She wanted to enjoy the time she had left.

More and more Mary was thinking of finding a little apartment, maybe somewhere near the marina where she'd be close to Jake, although rent prices in this area were astronomical. She'd even toyed with the idea of asking Jake to take her out on the boat, maybe up the coastline so she could see Maine in summer.

Of course, that would have to wait until Jake returned from his latest 'business' trip. She certainly wasn't going to take this old tub out by herself. She wouldn't even know where to begin.

A brisk wind swept in off the bay, carrying with it the smell of salt water and a taste of brine. Mary shivered and tugged her shawl a little tighter. The sun would be sinking below the horizon soon, taking the last of the light along with it and the temperature would drop.

She gave Gadsden another scratch and said, "Guess you and I ought to take our evening stroll before it gets too chilly."

The beast was on his feet instantly, tongue hanging from his mouth in a big sloppy doggie grin. Mary changed into a pair of scuffed sneakers, picked up a mutilated tennis ball from the counter in the galley, and made her way carefully to the gangplank. Gadsden followed, watching her closely. Once she'd made it onto the dock, Gadsden trailed along beside as she walked across the street onto the green expanse of Straub Park.

"Ready?" she asked Gadsden and held up the ball.

He gave a single tail wag.

Mary tossed the ball. It didn't go far and the beast was on it before it even hit the ground. He caught it in his powerful jaws and carried it back to Mary, dropping it in her hand.

"Good boy," she told him and threw the slobber-stained tennis ball, trying to make it go further this time.

# Chapter Five

Noble steered Hap Chan along the concourse toward the main terminal and spotted two more Asian men. One closed in from the left, the other mixed with the crowd of passengers in front. Noble told himself not to panic, Great Britain is full of Asians, but something about these three set off alarm bells. As Matthew Burke always said; when there's doubt, there is no doubt. And the quiet alarm bell in Noble's brain kept telling him something was off. It's like wading in the ocean and feeling something bump your leg; you can't be sure it's a shark, but it's time to get out of the water.

As the throng pushed through the double doors to the terminus, the man in front glanced once over his shoulder and his eyes stopped briefly on Noble before settling on Hap Chan.

The warning bell turned to a whooping siren, telling Noble to get out of the water. He took Chan by the elbow and steered him toward the famous wall in King's Cross with *Platform 9 and ¾* emblazoned in gold paint on red brick. It's inside the main concourse rather than at the platforms, probably to avoid a traffic jam and risk some poor tourist falling onto the tracks. A knot of people, mostly kids in red and gold scarves, were queued and waiting to take pictures. Noble shoved Chan into the group.

"What is this?" Hap Chan asked, scanning the crowd.

"They're very famous books," Noble said.

Chan puzzled over the inscription on the wall and said, "I don't see any books."

"Don't you ever go to the movies?" Noble asked, marking the movement of the three Asian men. "It's platform 9 and ¾. You know? wizards."

"What wizards?"

"It's a tourist thing to do."

The Bulldog stopped at a newsstand and pointed to a pack of smokes. One man browsed a rack of t-shirts while other asked for directions from a uniformed railway officer.

The line of kids took their pictures. Soon Noble and Hap Chan had reached the front of the queue. The three Asian men were still hanging close. Bulldog haggled over the price of a magazine while number two browsed the sweaters and three took a call on his mobile.

Noble held out his phone to a pair of girls and asked them to take his picture. He and Hap Chan stood up against the wall. Noble slung an arm over Chan's shoulder and said, "Smile."

Hap Chan stood ramrod straight with a serious expression on his face.

The teen girl, wearing a Hogwarts sweater and pigtails, snapped a picture and handed the phone back. Noble pretended to inspect it and then said, "Can you get another? That one didn't get the sign in the background."

She smiled and obliged.

Noble forced her to take six more. She slowly lost her patience and her mouth formed a straight line as Noble rejected each new image. The crowd started to boil.

"Come on," someone shouted. "Other people are waiting."

"What are you doing?" Hap Chan questioned under his breath as the sour faced girl snapped picture number seven. "Are we in danger?"

The three Asian men were still hanging around.

The fake smile never left Noble's face. He muttered, "I think so."

The girl handed the phone back, raised her eyebrows and asked, "Good enough?"

"Great, thanks." Noble didn't even bother to look. He slung one arm over Hap Chan's shoulders and steered him toward a shop selling vinyl records and Beatles memorabilia. *"Can't Buy Me Love"* was playing on the speakers and a life size cutout of King Charles pointed to a rack of *I heart London* shirts with a sign; *buy one, get one half price*.

Chan clutched his battered briefcase to his chest and his brows pinched. "Should we go to the police."

"And tell them what? That you're a Chinese defector and I'm an American spy?"

Sweat beaded on Chan's forehead. "Tell them we need protection."

"Stay calm," Noble said. "I might be jumping at shadows."

He grabbed a pair of shirts from the sale rack, along with a pack of guitar strings, a Sex Pistols LP, and several plastic lighters with pictures of dead rock stars. A shrunken old lady with bad teeth rang the sale. Noble carried the plastic shopping bag back through the station toward the storage lockers. He dodged through a café selling open face sandwiches. The smell of seared onions and horseradish enveloped him. A quick look showed him the Bulldog cutting through the crowd.

Noble spotted a security officer and flagged her down. "Officer!" Noble said with a heavy lisp. "Officer, we need help. See that man? He's been harassing me and my boyfriend. He called us a pair of nasty boys and said he was going to hurt us."

"Wait here." Her face stacked up in a mean frown. She pressed the transmit button on her radio, called for backup and shouldered through the throng. She caught the Bulldog by the elbow. Noble was too far away to hear what she said, but she looked like she was reading him the riot act.

Noble and Hap Chan turned and jogged past a Starbucks, through another souvenir shop, and into the maze of lockers. Noble steered Chan into a corner and said, "Give me the research and stay put."

Chan clutched his briefcase to his chest like a mother protecting her baby. His eyes narrowed to suspicious slits. "This is my only leverage. Without this, I have nothing. America won't let me..."

Noble held up both hands for peace. He could feel a vein throbbing in his temple. It was an effort to keep his voice calm. "Hap, listen to me. You've done your part. You proved your bonafides and produced the research. You're golden. Tomorrow we'll both be on a plane bound for D.C. But for right now, we have to protect the information in that case."

The muscles at the corner of Chan's jaw bunched into tight fists. "I told you this would never work. China has a very long reach. They had people here waiting for us. They must know all of our plans."

"You don't know that," Noble said. "Hell, we don't even know those were Chinese agents."

"They were agents," Hap said in a tone that left no room for argument.

"Then the best thing we can do is stash the take," Noble told him. "If they capture us, we'll have a bargaining chip."

"*Eiiya*," Hap said. It was a typical Chinese expression without any real translation other than *man, oh man, what a day*.

"We're wasting time," Noble said. "And we're exposed."

Hap let out a shuddering breath, popped the latches on the battered briefcase and brought out a USB drive with a cartoon kitty on it.

Noble opened locker 314 and stashed the thumb-drive all the way at the back. First he wedged the LP into the locker, bending it in the process, then took apart one of the lighters and doused the t-shirts in fluid. The sharp odor quickly filled the aisle. The soaked t-shirts went into the locker next and Noble rigged the guitar wire and flint from the lighter to the inside of the door.

"What are you doing?" Chan asked.

"Rigging a bomb," Noble explained. "Anyone who tries to open this locker is going to lose their eyebrows."

"What about the research?" Chan looked ready to push Noble aside and dive in the locker for the flashdrive.

"Relax," Noble told him. "It will be a bright flash and a lot of smoke but not enough to do any real damage. The record will provide a barrier between the USB drive and the incendiary." After a beat he added, "I hope."

Noble committed the locker number to memory and pocketed the key. He wanted to get out of the station as fast as possible, but didn't want to move too fast. One of the unbreakable commandments of clandestine work is; never let the enemy force you to move faster than you can think. He checked that the coast was clear, then took a winding path toward the exit. They passed through the double doors into a bitterly cold English February. Neon light reflected in small icy puddles and quiet snowflakes drifted down from a steel gray sky but it wasn't enough to accumulate. Londoners had their collars turned up against the cold. The wail of a distant siren rose above the orchestra of a bustling city.

Noble and Hap Chan mixed with the crowd queueing up at an intersection. The light changed and the crowd spilled out into the street. They were headed for the heart of London. Noble used alleyways between buildings when possible and threaded through crowded shopping centers, occasionally doubling back. Cold was turning his toes to little chips of ice and his breath made silver clouds before being ripped apart. He kept one hand on Hap Chan's elbow the whole time.

Chan clutched his briefcase and shook like a dog with worms. His teeth were tapping out Morse Code.

Noble said, "Cold or scared?"

"Both."

"Keep it together," Noble said.

Noble considered abandoning the safehouse and taking beds at a hostel but Langley would lose their cool if he went off script. Instead, he took his time, ignoring the cold and Hap Chan's complaints, and cut through Regent's Park to the West Kilburn neighborhood where he circled the block around Sevington Street twice looking for anything out of the ordinary.

# Chapter Six

Gwendolyn Witwicky had a headset clamped on her ears and mousey brown curls pulled back in a ponytail. She was dressed in an oversized sweater with a videogame logo emblazoned on the front. Coke-bottle glasses slipped down her nose. She'd tried to make the switch to contacts but they irritated her eyes. Instead she pushed her glasses back into place every few minutes.

She was in a situation room at CIA headquarters in Langley, Virginia. The small space smelled like coffee and body odor. The carpet had been paced through in spots, showing bare concrete underneath. Computer fans gave off a continuous hum, making the room uncomfortably warm. An old note hastily scrawled on a desk read; *Jackknife actual – 1026 – confirm.*

Xander McHale, the new Director of CIA, paced the tiny situation room. His cherub face was a tight frown. He'd been running the Company just two weeks and already he'd replaced several long-standing department heads. Under his leadership, Station Chiefs were being recalled en mass and replaced by *yes men*. He stopped at Witwicky's elbow and pinched his bottom lip between thumb and forefingers. "Anything?"

"Still nothing, sir." Gwen hitched her shoulders. The security detail across the street from the safehouse were not answering their comms and the surveillance team had gone radio silent. "They're not responding."

"Try again," McHale ordered.

"I just tried, sir," said Gwen. "They aren't answering."

"I said try again."

Ezra Cook flashed her a warning look and Gwen turned back to her computer. She dialed a number from memory and waited but no one picked up. "No answer."

"Comms problem?" Wizard suggested in his sandpaper drawl. The Director of Operations was a gaunt vulture in a thin black suit with gray hair swept straight back from a high forehead. His face was a map of deep set lines and his fingertips were stained yellow by nicotine. He patted his pockets in search of a cigarette, but didn't pull one out. Witwicky knew the old buzzard was dying for a smoke but didn't dare blaze up in front of McHale.

"Negative." Ezra rapped at his keyboard and he shook his head. He was a small Jewish guy with a scrawny neck, too much nose, and jet black hair that stood up in places. A ragged scar, a souvenir from his last field assignment, made a jagged lightning bolt on his left cheek. He said, "The line is working."

"Unacceptable," McHale said. This was his first legitimate clandestine field operation since taking over the office and his inexperience was starting to show. He didn't like being in the dark, not know what was happening. He tortured his bottom lip some more and asked, "Have we got cameras on the house?"

Gwen shook her head. "No, sir."

"Why not?"

Ezra said, "The whole place is an electronic dead zone to prevent anyone hacking our network."

"It prevents us from knowing what's going on," McHale said. "Anyone ever think of that?"

Gwen shrank down in her seat like a scolded child. Over the last two hours McHale had become increasingly abusive. Gwen kept expecting Wizard to come to her aid, but the director of operations propped up the wall and watched in silence. He had one hand in his coat pocket, fingering a pack of Chesterfields, and he wore an expressionless mask. Gwen had a feeling he knew more than he was letting on. She tried to read him, but Wizard's eyes were cold blue lakes layered in ice.

"We have to proceed as if the intel is legitimate." McHale stuffed his hands in his coat pockets while sweat beaded on his forehead up high where his hair was starting to recede. He said, "Play the audio again."

Gwen brought up a file on her computer. It was an audio recording captured from Noble's phone just after he boarded the train in London. She pressed play and nudged the volume up.

An unmistakably Asian voice came through the speakers; *"Are you in possession?"*

*Noble: "I've got your man and he's got the research. We're on the train now. We'll be in London a little after six."*

*Asian Male: "Have you thought about our offer?"*

*"Half a million isn't enough. I'm not flushing my career with the Company for five-hundred Gs. I'm going to need two million or the intel goes to the CIA."*

*"You drive a hard bargain, Mr. Noble."*

*"I can afford to be pushy. I've got what you want. Two million or you can flush ten years of R and D down the toilet."*

*"Very well. The money will be in your account by the time you debark the train."*

*"Make sure it is."*

*"One more thing, Mr. Noble. The traitor Hap Chan cannot be allowed to live. He knows too much."*

*"I'll take care of Chan. You just make sure the money goes into the right account."*

Ten minutes after that phone call, two million dollars had landed in Noble's personal bank account and five minutes later the entire sum was rerouted to a numbered account in Switzerland.

McHale had her play the audio twice more and then asked, "Who is he talking to and how long has he been in contact with them? It must be someone inside Chinese intelligence. How did this happen? How did we miss this?"

"Everyone has a price," Wizard said from his place by the door. He had a cigarette out of the pack, but didn't light it. He just clutched it between nicotine-stained fingertips.

"There must be some mistake," Ezra said.

Gwen nodded. "Noble would never turn traitor."

"You're staring at the evidence, Mr. Cook." McHale jabbed a finger at the audio waves on Ezra's computer screen. "Get the local station chief on the phone. I want to know what's happening."

"That might not be such a good idea," Wizard said.

"Why not?"

"The Chief of Station and Noble have history."

"Unpleasant?"

"Downright ugly."

"Doesn't matter. We need boots on the ground. Call him."

# Chapter Seven

Noble spotted the all clear signal on a bus stop advertisement for Lasik and the tight ball of anxiety in his belly relaxed. Beneath the plexiglass case, one corner of the poster had been folded down. If there was danger and Noble needed to abort, the bottom corner would have been folded up.

The all clear meant a CIA team was in the neighborhood, probably watching him right now and reporting back to Langley. He breathed a sigh of relief and shrugged to loosen his shoulders.

Hap Chan noticed the change. "We are safe?"

Noble nodded. "We're going to be alright."

They made their way along the sidewalk to a three-story building on the east side of the street. The neighborhood was a stone's throw from a busy shopping district, close enough to get anything they might need but far enough that the crowds were lighter here, easier to monitor. Anyone approaching the building would be noticed. And Noble had no doubt he was watched as he mounted the short flight of steps to the front door.

He punched the code into the security panel. His hands were shaking from the cold. The light turned green and the door released with an electronic click. He hurried Hap Chan inside and they climbed a creaking staircase to the top floor.

A rubber ficus under the window frame on the landing told Noble the safehouse was secure. The air smelled like an attic in desperate need of sunshine and fresh air, but at least it was warm. The advance team had turned the heat on for their guest and a glass sconce over the door provided plenty of light. There was no key for security reasons and Noble was forced to pick the lock.

"Who has the key?" Hap Chan wanted to know.

"Nobody," Noble told him. "Keys can be stolen or duplicated. Only way through this door is skill and a good set of lockpicks."

He took his time feeling for each tumbler and had the door open in less than two minutes. The safehouse was a two-bedroom flat with track lighting on the ceiling and a soft beige rug underfoot. There was a small kitchen with an electric range and a living room furnished with boardgames, magazines, puzzles, and a flatscreen TV connected to a console. Life in a safehouse can be incredibly boring. Especially if the person being protected had to be there days or even weeks. Books and videogames helped break up the monotony.

Noble said, "We'll be safe here for the evening."

Hap Chan had a look around. "I wish we could go to the airport now. My country will be looking everywhere for us. The sooner we are out of Great Britain the better."

"Take a breath, Hap. This place is secret and heavily guarded. They aren't going to find us here." Noble rummaged through the kitchen cabinets in search of food. Other than an ancient pack of Ramen noodles and a few old katsup packages, the cupboards were bare.

"What about the research?" Hap perched on the edge of the sofa with his briefcase balanced on his knees.

"Soon as we're on the ground in D.C. I'll give my people directions and they'll recover it for us."

Hap's brow bunched and his mouth puckered. "Will I be alright?"

Noble closed the cabinet he was searching, turned to the little guy and said, "You're going to be just fine, Hap. I promise. Now take it easy and read a magazine or something. I'm going to get us some chow."

"You're leaving?" Hap was on his feet again, his eyes wide.

Noble held both hands up and patted the air. "I'm just going down the street for food. I'll be back in thirty minutes."

"Maybe I should go with you."

Noble shook his head. "You stay put.

"But..."

"Hap," Noble said, "you're perfectly safe."

Noble steered him toward the window and pointed to a dark building across the street. "There are two guys over there armed to the teeth. If anyone other than me tries coming in this building, they'll be across the street in a flash."

Hap narrowed his eyes like he might be able to spot the security detail through the darkened windows, but the glass was mirrored to prevent anyone seeing in and the apartment, like the safehouse, was soundproof.

"They're watching us right now," Noble said.

Hap breathed a little sigh of relief and his shoulders sagged. He turned away from the window, inspected the small living room and said, "Thank you, Mr. Jake. I'm just nervous."

Noble had not given Hap Chan his last name, in case anything went bad. He clapped a hand on Hap's shoulder and gave it a squeeze. "I know you are. Tomorrow we'll be in America and a few days after that you'll start your new life. Given any thought to what you'll do?"

A smile lit up Hap's face for the first time. He hurried to the sofa, popped the latches on his briefcase and pulled out a thick document on 3D printing. "The emerging technology of 3D printing is fascinating. I think it's really going to revolutionize the world and I have several ideas about how to reduce wasted material and solve the overheating problems of the 3D printing processes."

Noble took the big book and scanned the title. It was a scientific treatise on the process and application of 3D printing. Noble knew 3D printing existed but didn't know much about it. He grinned, laid the hefty document on the sofa and said, "Whatever gets your motor running."

Hap frowned at the unfamiliar idiom.

Noble chucked him on the shoulder. "I'm going for food. We'll use the same security phrases. Got it?"

Hap swallowed and nodded.

"And try to relax," Noble said.

Another nod.

Noble let himself out, made sure the door latched behind him, and took the steps two at a time to the ground floor. On the street, cold sucker punched him in the nose. He huddled deeper into his navy peacoat, tipped a salute to the unseen watchers in the house across the street, made an eating motion with one hand to let them know what he was doing, then started down the block toward the lights and the smell of food.

# Chapter Eight

Gregory Hunt had a champagne flute in one hand and a beautiful redhead on his arm. He limped around the room, shaking hands and smiling, dressed in a thousand dollar dinner jacket and gold cufflinks. His shoes were polished to mirrored perfection. Lady Kensington smiled and waved him over.

"Ion, this is the American diplomat I was telling you about," the heiress said in a cultured British accent. Kensington was in her late fifties and starting to show her age. She was draped in a blue silk gown. A purple shawl hid her neck. "Mr. Hunt, I'd like you to meet His Grace, the Duke of Wellington."

Gregory Hunt gave a slight bow and then clasped the man's hand. "A pleasure to make your acquaintance, your Grace."

"Please, call me Ion." He had straight white teeth and a weak chin but he made up for it with piercing grey eyes. "Only the help calls me 'Your Grace'."

The group chuckled.

"And may I introduce my companion." Hunt motioned to the redhead. "Ms. Tiffany Saville."

The Duke took Tiffany's hand in both of his own and placed a kiss on her knuckles. His eyes drank her in. She smiled and said all the right things, using her c-cups and slender waist to full advantage. In the three months Hunt had been stationed in London, he had found Tiffany to be a fantastic companion. She opened doors that had no keys and was worth every penny. Especially since he was paying for her with American tax dollars. She was beautiful and cultured. She knew when to take the attention from Hunt, and when to give it back. She blushed at the Duke's kiss and soon the two were deep in conversation, leaving Lady Kensington to Hunt. He held out his arm to her and lowered his voice to a conspiratorial whisper. "What a wonderful party. Thank you so much for the invite. I hate to be forward, but I have to ask, is there any truth to the rumor parliament will accept China's trade deal?"

She made a pouting face. "You Americans. It's always work, work, work with you."

Hunt grinned and looked her over. "It's not always work. Perhaps you could take me on a tour of this amazing home and we could find other ways to entertain ourselves."

Kensington flushed. "How positively improper. If I didn't know better I'd think you were trying to start a scandal."

"What's life without a few scandals?"

She arched an eyebrow. "Whatever am I going to do with you, Mr. Hunt?"

"Whatever you'd like."

A flush crept into her cheeks. She clutched at his arm and said, "Let me show you the upstairs."

She was taking him on the grand tour when Hunt felt his phone buzzing. At the risk of impropriety, he snuck a hand into his pocket and glanced at the number. It was Langley. The timing couldn't be worse.

He brought the phone out of his pocket and said, "I do apologize, my dear, but I must take this."

"Oh poo." She pouted and then smiled. "Go on then, have your conversation, but you owe me."

Hunt smiled. "A debt I'll gladly repay."

Lady Kensington found a knot of party goers and slipped effortlessly into the circle. Hunt hit the talk button and leaned on the balcony railing, and put the phone to his ear. "Rotten timing. I'm at a dinner party with the Crown Prince."

"That can wait," McHale said. "We have an operation going sideways. I need someone to get over to our safehouse in West Kilburn and check on the situation."

"I'm at a party with Lady Kensington and the Duke of Wellington," Hunt said. "I can't just leave."

"This is priority one critical," McHale said.

"I'm not a field agent," Hunt protested.

"Be that as it may, Mr. Hunt, we have a situation. You're the chief of station in London. That makes it your responsibility. You can either go to the safehouse and report back to me, or turn in your resignation."

"I'm on my way."

# Chapter Nine

Noble made his way along the sidewalk with a sack of Chinese takeaway swinging from one hand. The aroma was a tempting mix of ginger and pork. Noble's belly growled. He had deliberated long and hard before getting Chinese. Chances are Hap would not appreciate the British version of Chinese take-out, but the other options were fish and chips or dicey Thai cuisine from a place called Bangkok 7. There had been a flashing purple neon face next to the sign advertising authentic Thai dinning that might have been a smiling Svengali or a Leprechaun. Noble couldn't quite decide which and figured if their signage was that poor, the food must be worse. In the end he opted for Chinese and if Hap didn't like it, that was too bad.

Noble took a twisting route back to the safehouse, using narrow side streets, cutting between buildings whenever possible, in order to flush out any surveillance. He stuck mostly to the shadows. The moon was a yellow half coin in the eastern sky, skimming between dark clouds. The light threw deep shadows on the eastern side of the street, allowing Noble to move through pockets of black.

A gust of bitter cold whistled down the block, turning his breath to crystal ice. He shrugged and turned up the collar of his coat. A Florida boy born and raised, Noble had never quite gotten used to winter, even during his days with the Green Berets in the mountains of Afghanistan. He circled the block once to be certain he was alone before punching in the door code. The lock released and a minute later Noble took the creaking steps two at a time, grateful to be out of the cold and the wind. He was thinking about dinner—the food would probably be stone cold but his stomach wouldn't care—when he reached the top of steps and stopped in his tracks.

Someone had kicked the door open. The frame was splintered and the knob hung at a drunken angle.

A cold weight settled into his belly. The muscles in his back turned rigid. He put the sack of takeaway on the top step, eased onto the landing and shouldered up to the open door, straining to hear.

His heart hammered against his chest and made a dull wet *thum-thrush* in his ears. His fingers tingled with the rush of adrenaline flooding his system. The cold was forgotten; in its place was an electric charge that made the small hairs on Noble's arm stand up straight.

He put his back to the wall, unbuckled his belt, and slipped it off. A leather belt with a good solid buckle makes a great melee weapon in a pinch. Noble wrapped one end around his fist, allowing him to swing the buckle like a poor man's mace. He edged around the doorframe, eyes peeled for any sign of trouble.

Hap Chan was lying face up on the carpet in a pool of his own blood. He'd been beaten and stabbed half a dozen times. His eyes were rolled up in his head and his arms were flung out wide. His mouth was pulled back in a pain-filled grimace. The smell of hot copper filled the safehouse.

Noble hung in the door frame a moment, eyes locked on the body, then he forced himself to move. He did a fast sweep of the apartment, making sure the rooms were clear, before checking on Chan.

His heart was still hammering like a race horse kicking at the stall. He knelt and pressed two fingers against Hap's throat. He wasn't really looking for a pulse. The man had been bludgeoned and stabbed.

Someone had hit the poor little guy so hard one side of his head was mishappen and blood congealed into black puddles.

Noble gave a start when Hap made a small gasping noise. His eyelids fluttered and his lips moved. A pink bubble formed at the corner of his mouth and Hap gave a weak cough.

"It's me," Noble told him. He still had two fingers pressed against Hap's throat but he couldn't find a pulse. The little guy was hanging on by a thread. Noble said, "Look at me, Hap. Did you talk? Did you tell them the locker number?"

It took a heroic effort. Hap's neck muscles bulged and his body shook but he managed to shake his head and make a gasping, strangled, "No."

"Who did this to you?" Noble asked. He ripped Hap's shirt sleeves and used them to stuff the gaping stab wounds in an effort to stop the bleeding. The killer had rammed the knife home with surgical precision. Whoever did this knew how to kill. Hap didn't have long and Noble knew his efforts were in vain, but he went on trying. "Who was it, Hap? Was it the guys from the train station?"

Hap gave another small shake of his head and then strained to lift his arm. Noble thought Hap was trying to hold his hand in his dying moments, looking for comfort. Noble stopped stuffing the wounds and took Hap's hand, but Hap shook free and covered his left eye. His other eye swiveled to look at Noble, nearly bulging from the socket. His lips moved and a tortured note escaped. He was struggling to convey something but Noble was at a loss.

"What are you trying to tell me, Hap?"

Sirens wailed in the distance, getting louder.

Hap Chan pressed hard against his left eye and garbled sounds came from his throat. Then it was over. His hand fell away, his eyes rolled up, and he let out one final breath.

# Chapter Ten

Noble's heart crowded up into his throat. His hands were painted with Hap's blood. His shirt and pants were spotted as well. If British police found him standing over a dead man covered in blood, he'd be on trial for murder. There was nothing more he could do for Hap, and he couldn't allow himself to be arrested.

He rolled Hap up on his side, dug his wallet from his back pocket, and snatched the dead man's briefcase. The wallet along with the ID were meticulously crafted fakes forged by the CIA's Office of Technical Services. The people in the OTS are the best in the world at what they do but even the best forgery won't stand up to prolonged scrutiny. The British didn't know the U.S. had been running a clandestine op in their backyard and Noble wanted to keep it that way. It would not be good for foreign relations. Best to give the local cops a body with no ID.

He placed the wallet and briefcase by the door then hurried to the sink where he used his elbow to turn the faucet. Cold water burst from the pipe. Noble washed the blood off his hands, dried them on a dishtowel, then hurried around the apartment wiping down anything he had touched. The animal side of his brain screamed at him to get out, but he had to sterilize the site first. He wiped the kitchen cabinets, the fridge handle, and the doors to the bedrooms before racing back to the living room where he grabbed Hap's briefcase.

Tires screamed on the hardtop. The sirens reached a fevered pitch. They were on the block closing in on the safehouse. Noble hurried down the steps, stuffing Hap's wallet into the briefcase as he went. He had the dish rag clamped between his teeth and his nostrils flared with every breath. He was halfway down when cops started hammering on the exterior door. Even without the code it wouldn't take them long to get in.

Noble turned and started back up the steps. Every CIA safehouse has multiple exits in case of an emergency and Noble had memorized the routes ahead of time. Quick getaways are a part of the job. He carried a razor blade under the lining of his shoe and had a handcuff key hidden in the zipper pull on his jacket, along with lockpicks in his wallet.

He took the steps, reached the access door to the roof and shouldered it open, careful not to leave fingerprints. His DNA was all over the apartment but there wasn't much he could do about that. He exploded onto the roof and glanced once in the direction of the security detail across the street. All he saw was a dark window, like a lidless eye. There were no lights. No warning signals.

*What the hell were those guys doing? How had someone gotten into the building and killed Hap Chan without them knowing?*

All questions Noble could answer later. Right now his only concern was making sure the police didn't have a suspect. He raced toward the edge of the roof and vaulted a short wall over to the next building. The houses here were all shoulder to shoulder with no gap between. His stomach was a tight knot of buzzing electric. He spotted a small rooftop garden. The boxes were neatly arranged around a skylight and the bare stalks were all wrapped in thick plastic to protect them from the hard winter.

Working quickly, Noble grabbed what he thought was a tomato plant but could have been deadly nightshade for all he knew, jerked it out of the soil and wedged the briefcase in the cavity. He replaced the plant as best he could before ripping open a sack of fertilizer and dumping it around the base. When he'd finished, the briefcase was hidden but the plant leaned like a drunken sailor. Any uniform canvasing the area would probably walk right past it, but the poor gardener would get a surprise come Spring.

That done, Noble turned and fled along the rooftops, pausing just long enough to stuff the dishrag down a vent. He reached the last house on the block and found the access door locked.

"You gotta be kidding me," he muttered.

The door was supposed to be unlocked. It swung out which meant Noble couldn't kick it open. He'd have to work the tumblers. He knelt and dug his picks from his wallet. The cops would be inside the safehouse by now. It wouldn't be long before they found Hap Chan dead on the floor. After that they'd quickly set up a perimeter. Noble needed to be long gone by then.

First he tried scrubbing the lock, raking the pick over the tumblers quickly in an effort to snap them in place. It was noisy but it worked on cheap locks. Unfortunately this was not a cheap lock. When that didn't work, he closed his eyes, took a slow breath, and went feeling for the tumblers. It took all his self-control. His body was telling him to run, but he forced himself to go slowly and methodically, ignoring the sirens and the buzzing electric in his belly.

The deadbolt clicked open. Noble covered his hand with his shirtsleeve to turn the knob and then he was inside a brightly lit staircase headed down to an empty unit on the second floor. He finally had a bit of luck. This door was open, like it should be, and Noble passed through the dark apartment to a window overlooking the back alley.

The building had no fire escape, but it had a drainpipe and that was just as good.

Sliding the window frame up with a scrape of moldy wood, Noble climbed out and reached for the pipe. He had to stretch. A shorter operative would not have been able to span the gap. His fingers slipped off at first, but he tried again, leaning out dangerously far, and managed to latch onto the pipe.

With a deep breath, Noble swung out, got his feet planted against the wall, and started down. A heap of soggy cardboard boxes was piled beneath the pipe and Noble dropped the last few feet, landing with a muffled crash.

A white hot lance of pain spiraled up from his left knee. He bared his teeth in a silent grimace but told himself, "Keep moving, soldier."

He stumbled free of the cardboard pile and hurried toward the mouth of the alley.

# Chapter Eleven

A POLICE CRUISER SHRIEKED to a halt in a white cloud. The tires locked up and the back end bucked. The blue and yellow striped sedan blocked the alley. Lights strobed the surrounding buildings. The driver shifted into park and the doors popped open. A pair of British officers climbed out. "Alright you. That's far enough. Let's see some ID."

Noble turned on his heel and fled. There was a buzzing hive of electric bumblebees in his belly. His long legs ate up the broken concrete and his arms pumped for speed. His brain was telling him the police had arrived way too fast. It should have taken longer for them to cordon off the neighborhood. Something wasn't right here but Noble had no idea what. He pushed that problem aside for now and focused on making a fast getaway.

"Oi!" one of the officers yelled. "Stop right there!"

Both officers chased Noble on foot. Their boots hammered the pavement. The lead officer ran with one hand on his tool belt and the other grasping his radio. "Officer Reilly... requesting immediate backup. Suspect... fleeing north... in the alley behind... Sevington Street."

He panted between every breath, sounding like a winded buffalo. The older of the two rapidly fell behind, but Reilly stayed close.

Noble skirted a row of bins overflowing with rubbish and turned one over behind him, forcing Reilly to leap the can. The young officer was starting to run out of steam. He was slowing down but not by much. The big clunky belt weighed down with gear was taking its toll. Noble knew if he could reach the other end of the alley, he could make an escape. He poured on more speed, ignoring the twinge in his knee, willing his legs to move faster.

He'd almost made the mouth of the alley when a second pair of bulls spilled into the cramped lane. One of them was a mountain in a uniform with a heavy jaw and arms the size of Noble's thighs.

Noble pounded to a stop, gasping for breath, and started to raise his hands in surrender. He opened his mouth to tell the cops they had won when he was hit from behind.

Noble's head snapped back. He was thrown off his feet and landed on the pavement with a hard smack that caused fairy lights to caper in his vision. Reilly came down on top of him, two hundred and ten pounds of muscle and pride. Noble took an elbow to the back of his head, tasted blood, and felt the cop's gear belt digging into the small of his back.

"Fink your real funny do ya?" the kid growled in Noble's ear. Reilly caught hold of Noble's wrist and twisted it behind his back with a savage jerk that threatened to dislocate Noble's shoulder. One of the other officers put a knee in Noble's back, pinning him. Another stepped on his ankle.

"Don't move a muscle," Reilly told him.

Noble had to suck air back into his lungs before he could form words. His vision narrowed to a pinprick with the weight of three cops pressing him into the cold ground. He spit a pink wad and croaked out, "You got me. I won't resist."

"Ya better not." Reilly wrenched Noble's other hand behind his back. Noble felt the cold kiss of metal handcuffs. The bracelets closed with a metallic ratchet. Noble tried to lay still and relax his body, letting the police know he was not a threat. It didn't seem to help. The young officer closed the cuffs painfully tight and then Noble was dragged up off the ground and pushed against the alley wall so hard his head rebounded, causing his vision to double.

Reilly rammed his elbow up under Noble's chin, trapping him against the bricks and closing off his air. One of the other officers patted him down in search of weapons. Reilly said, "An' where're you off in such'n 'urry, matey?"

Noble tried to respond but couldn't get the sound past his pinched vocal chords. His knees were starting to buckle and his head felt like someone had filled it with helium.

One of the older officers came to Noble's rescue. He put a hand on Reilly's shoulder and said, "Give him some air, Reilly."

Reilly eased off and Noble was able to breathe.

The older officer's name tag read; Davies. He hooked his thumbs into his belt and narrowed his eyes. "Why'd you run, sir?"

"I want a lawyer."

"American?" Reilly said.

Davies liberated Noble's wallet from his back pocket. "ID says he's Jacob Goodfellow of Naples Florida. You're a long way from home. What brings you across the pond, Mr. Goodfellow?"

Noble refused to say anything else and when it was clear he wasn't talking, they grabbed him by the elbows and dragged him from the alley to a waiting cruiser.

# Chapter Twelve

Hunt took his time backing his sleek black Jaguar into a parallel spot. The back tire bumped the low curb. Hunt cursed under his breath, twisted the wheel, and pulled out to try again. He'd never been good at parallel parking and everything was backward in Great Britain. Driving on the left hand side of the road made everything more difficult. Gregory slung one arm over the passenger seat, eyed the gap, and tried again, relying heavily on the side and rear cameras. The warning light on the left hand mirror flashed once, but Hunt managed to angle the sportscar into the spot and breathed a sigh of relief as he thumbed the ignition button.

The Jaguar turned off with a soft purr and the interior dome blinked on, lighting the soft beige leather interior. Hunt spotted a smudge on the dashboard and wiped it with a crisp white handkerchief from his pocket. The dirt had probably been left behind by Tiffany. She was a marvelous companion at society functions, but tended to make a mess. Hunt pushed open the driver's side door and stepped out into a deep chill. His breath turned to icy crystals hanging in the air. He shivered and buttoned his coat all the way up to his throat. He'd parked two blocks from the safehouse and he cut across the neighborhood cursing McHale and Dulles every step of the way.

Dulles, the cantankerous old Deputy Director of Operations, was a fossil; a relic of the Cold War, long since past retirement age. He still relied on secret meetings, codewords, cyphers, and listening devices. Hunt got more done with a handshake and a smile at a cocktail party than Dulles and his bullyboys could accomplish in a month of snooping around dark office buildings and sifting people's trash. Collecting intelligence was easy. Show up to the opera with a knockout number like Tiffany Saville on your arm, drop a few hints about trade negotiations or reduced tariffs, and let the alcohol do the rest. Hunt didn't need a gun or high-tech gadgets. He discovered what people wanted most from life and dangled it on a string. He resented being called away from the important work of international relations for one of Wizard's childish little covert ops.

As Chief of Station, it was Hunt's job to know all the operations in his bailiwick. He'd scanned the eyes-only report a week ago; something about a Chinese defector, and then left the file on his bedside table in his London flat, amid a pile of other paperwork.

Hunt limped around the corner onto Sevington Street. Half a dozen police cars and an ambulance choked the lane. Lights were flashing, painting the buildings in alternating blue and white and a pair of uniformed officers were escorting a man toward a cruiser.

A shard of cold ice stabbed Hunt in the belly as he recognized Noble. Noble was the reason Hunt limped and the pain in his hip seemed to double at the sight of him. Hunt jerked out his cellphone and snapped a pick just before police pushed Noble into the patrol car.

There was a body in the back of the ambulance and a crime scene van had arrived, weaving through the network of cop cars.

Hunt stuffed his hands in his pockets, tucked his chin, and angled along the sidewalk to the surveillance building across the street. A uniformed officer tried to stop him, but Hunt flashed his diplomatic credentials and told the uniform he lived in the apartment block. The cop let him through.

Searching through a ring of keys, Hunt found the right one, slotted it and mounted the stairs two at a time to the fourth floor. The landing was dark and quiet. Hunt knocked. When he didn't get an answer, he tried the knob and found it unlocked.

The door swung in on well-oiled hinges. He stepped into a shadowy recess and felt around for a light switch. The overhead revealed two dead men stretched out on the floor and an overturned camera on a tripod.

Hunt hissed, checked the hall to be sure he was alone, then closed the door. He couldn't afford to be seen in an apartment with two murdered corpses. He covered his hand with his coat and turned the lock just to be sure before taking a closer look at the bodies.

Blood was slowly turning to sticky paste. Hunt had to be careful where he stepped. One man had been shot in the side of the head while he was sitting on a stool in front of the video camera. He never saw it coming. He went over on his side, dragging the camera down with him, breaking it in the process. The other man had turned toward the door and been shot right in the forehead. He'd fallen flat on his back, hands still in his pockets.

Someone had picked the lock, shot one man dead before he knew anything was wrong, and killed the other man before he had time to react.

"This is the work of a professional," Hunt told the empty room. He brought out his cellphone and dialed Langley.

# Chapter Thirteen

Witwicky felt like her world was coming unglued, like she'd slipped through a crack in the spacetime continuum into an alternate dimension where her world no longer made any sense. One look at Cook was enough to know he felt the same.

Director McHale had just gotten off the phone with Hunt. The Chief of Station had sent over a series of pictures taken from his phone. One was an image of Noble being pushed into the back of a squad car by British police. The rest showed the dead security detail stationed across the street from the safehouse. Both men had been shot through the head. The images were open on Cook's computer, enlarged so they filled the screen. Blood was everywhere.

Gwen covered her mouth with one hand. She was no stranger to violence. She'd been held captive by Islamic extremists just a few months ago, but the pictures of the security detail, heads blown open by a small caliber weapon at close range, caused her stomach to twist. Thankfully she hadn't eaten in hours.

Ezra frowned at the images, like he might find some hidden meaning in the carnage if he stared long enough. Thick black brows came together over his hooked nose. He had a pen in one hand and kept clicking it.

McHale paced the cramped situation room. "How did this happen? Who has Noble been talking to and how long has he been in contact with them? It must be someone inside Chinese intelligence. How did we miss this?"

"Everyone has a price," Wizard said from his place by the door. He had a cigarette out of the pack, but didn't light it.

"There must be some mistake," Ezra said.

Gwen nodded. "Noble would never turn traitor."

McHale jabbed a finger at the images. "How much more evidence do you need?"

"It's just..." Ezra fell silent. He turned to Gwen. She shrugged. She didn't want to believe it either, but the proof was right there in high definition. Less than three hours after they intercepted Noble's phone call, Hap Chan was dead, along with the security team, and Noble was two million richer.

McHale did another turn around the small room and said, "What happened to the research Chan was bringing over?"

Gwen turned away from the computers so she would not have to look at the images. "He must have it on him, right?"

"Unlikely," Wizard said.

"Why do you say that?" McHale asked.

"He stashed it somewhere in the train station."

"How do you know?"

"That's what I would have done," Wizard said.

McHale stopped pacing and stared hard at the images. He pinched his bottom lip between thumb and forefinger. "We need that research. We need to know where he stashed it."

Wizard started to raise the cigarette to his lips and caught himself. "That's going to be hard to do. He's in police custody."

McHale rounded on Wizard. A thick vein throbbed in the Director's sweaty forehead. "This is your mess, Dulles. One of your best field officers was bent and you didn't even know it."

"It would appear that way."

"I want this cleaned up," McHale said. "I'm not going to tell the president that my first official mission as Director of the CIA went sideways and now we've got an agent facing murder charges in Great Britain."

"At the moment, there's not much we can do," said Wizard.

"There must be some way to get him away from the British police," McHale said.

"A good lawyer."

McHale wiped sweat from his forehead. "So what do we do now?"

"Focus on the audio," Wizard said. "I want to know who the kid was talking to and where that money came from."

Cook and Witwicky nodded their heads in unison. "We're on it."

## Chapter Fourteen

Noble was in the squad car, hands cuffed behind his back, listening to the cheap Naugahyde creak. A knot had formed on the back of his head where Reilly slammed him against the wall and his fingers were numb. His neck felt like a bulldog had picked him up and shaken him. He'd be lucky if he could turn his head tomorrow. A vile throbbing sensation, the beginning of a splitting headache, was starting at the back of his skull and slowly creeping forward. Noble leaned back to ease the tension on his neck.

The doors were closed and his breath was fogging up the interior, turning the windows into frosted glass. He closed his eyes and replayed the last half hour in his head. Police had been on scene way too fast. Whoever killed Hap Chan was trying to pin the murder on Noble and doing a pretty good job of it. The cops had a body and Noble had been caught fleeing the scene with the dead man's blood on his shirt. It was a slam dunk case for a DA. *Where was the security detail*, Noble wondered? *They had let someone walk right past them. How? Why? And where were they now? Why hadn't they done anything to stop the murder of Hap Chan?*

Noble was puzzling over these questions when the front door opened and the car rocked on its springs. "You're in a spot of bother, mate."

Noble opened his eyes and found himself staring at Wexler. The big bruiser had been a part of the plot to cripple America's infrastructure in October. He had abducted Witwicky, tried to kill Noble, and his goons had nearly shot Cook's face off. Wexler had managed to get away and, despite being on America's terror watch list, no one had seen him in months. He'd picked up an eye patch since last time Noble had seen him and a puckered scar ran from his flaming red hairline down his cheek. Massive shoulders threatened to split the seams of a police uniform. He grinned at Noble through the safe-T-glass. "Surprise."

Noble straightened up. His hands curled into fists and his shoulders tensed. His face transformed into a collection of hatred and disbelief.

"Bet you never thought you'd see me again." Wexler turned on the heater and put one freckled white hand up to the vent for warmth.

"You killed Hap Chan," Noble said.

"You're quick," said Wexler. "You cost me ten million dollars and an eye, Mr. Noble. I'm here to collect."

"I'm gonna kill you."

"And how are you going to do that? You're under arrest for murder. They've got your DNA all over the crime scene. They'll find the knife you used to kill Hap Chan in the toilet tank. It's got your fingerprints on it, Jake. You're going to spend the rest of your life in jail for murder."

"You son of a..."

"Nasty temper." Wexler wagged a finger. "What would your dear old mum say?"

A cold weight dropped into Noble's belly. He swallowed. "What do you know about my mother?"

"Mary Elise?" Wexler brought out a phone and revealed a picture of Noble's mother on the deck of *The Yeoman*. "Sweet old gal, isn't she? Bit of a pistol. I must say, it's not too smart leaving an old lady all alone on that old tub of yours. Anything could happen. No worries though. I've got a mate on my way over to Saint Pete right as we speak. He's going to see that nothing bad happens to dear old mum."

"If you hurt her..."

"You'll what?" Wexler laughed. "Don't be melodramatic. She's just a bargaining chip. We had to be sure you'd take the fall for Chan's murder. So far our plan is working quite well. Wouldn't you agree?"

"You thought of everything," Noble heard himself say.

"Not everything." Wexler wagged a finger at him. "You threw a bit of a wrench into the works when you stashed the research."

"Yeah, I can be a real pain."

"What did you do with it, Jake?

"Flushed it down a toilet."

"I need that research. It's part of my retirement plan."

"Sucks to be you."

"I can make mum suffer."

"I'll kill you!" Noble cranked his legs up and slammed his feet against the shatterproof glass. There was a hollow thud but the glass held. He barely left a mark. Noble kicked the glass again, promising to wring Wexler's neck with his bare hands. The safe-T-glass started to warp under his attacks.

"We'll talk again when you've had time to cool down." Wexler stuffed a police cap on his head, pushed the door open and climbed out.

Noble went on kicking the glass, leaving scuff marks and twisting the steel brackets. Inarticulate screams ripped from his throat. The cold hard weight in his belly turned into a vortex of poison fire that consumed his thoughts, driving out reason. "Let me out," Noble shouted as he kicked. "Let me out of here!"

An inspector with her hair pulled back in a bun rapped the window with an open palm. "Cool it, mister."

Noble calmed down long enough to say, "He's going to kill my mother."

She frowned. "Who's gonna kill your mum? What are you on about then?"

"That officer with the eye patch," Noble said. "He's going to kill my mother. You have to stop him."

The inspector glanced around. A news van had just pulled up and the reporter was checking her lipstick in the van's sideview. The inspector scanned the crowd of police, paramedics, and journalists. "What officer?"

"He's got an eye patch and a scar," Noble said. "He's going after my mom. You have to let me out. Please."

"A police officer is going to hurt your mother?" She shook her head. "Stop your yelling or I'll put you in the boot. Understand?"

Noble cranked forward in an effort to peer through the fogged up windows but Wexler had vanished. Noble took a few deep breaths and said, "I want my phone call."

"You'll get your phone call," she said. "Once we've got you processed. Until then behave yourself."

# Chapter Fifteen

Wexler reached the end of the block, turned the corner, and then snatched the patrolman's cap off his head and tossed it at a trash can. It missed and landed in the gutter. Wexler cast one look back at the intersection to be sure he was out of sight before starting on the buttons to his uniform shirt. He stripped off the phony blouse, wadded it up and dropped it behind a lorry parked against the curb. Underneath he wore a simple beige undershirt which left him exposed to the chill, but Wexler didn't mind. Part one of the plan was a success. The hard part was done. Hap Chan was dead and Noble was in police custody. The Haitian would be landing in Tampa in a few hours and then Noble would be a puppet on a string. The missing research was the only kink but that was a small hurdle. Soon as Noble saw pictures of his mom tied up at gun point, he'd give up the intel. It was just a matter of getting into the station house for a talk. The Old Man's lawyers could handle that part.

Wexler took in a deep lungful of cold London air and let it out in a satisfied chuckle. It had been a long chase, but he'd finally cornered the White Whale and soon now he'd drive home the killing blow. Wexler lifted the patch to scratch at the scarred flesh around the empty socket.

After his failure in Cuba, Wexler had been *re-educated* by the Old Man. He'd spent three days in a two meter by two meter cell flooded with harsh white light, his ears constantly blasted by German death metal. He ate moldy scraps of bread and vomited in the corner. The door would open and Wexler would be beaten with leather saps or jolted with naked electrical wires. He thought he was going to die; he'd wanted to die. Just when he couldn't take any more, he'd been pulled from the cell and strapped naked to a chair. Keiser had explained to him, like a father disciplining a wayward son, that Wexler had to be punished. There were rewards for success and punishments for failure. The Old Man then dug Wexler's left eye out of the socket with a rusty spoon. The last thing Wexler remembered was his own screams reverberating around the room, and splashes of blood.

He had woken up sometime later in a private hospital bed. A taciturn Swiss doctor had nursed Wexler back to health and taught him how to cope with the loss of the eye. It had taken him two whole weeks to reach for a glass without knocking it over. It had been a month before he was able to drive a car. And the whole time he was recuperating, Wexler had been studying the man who'd destroyed his life. Keiser helped of course. The Old Man put together an extensive file on Jacob Noble and Wexler filled in the gaps through surveillance and wiretaps.

The underground deposited Wexler at King's Road in Chelsea. The building was an eight story art deco construction of cut stone with ivy climbing white walls. The lobby was green marble with a crystal chandelier hanging from the ceiling. A doorman in black and gold livery nodded to Wexler as he waited for the lift. He rode the car all the way to the top. The doors rolled open on a short hall guarded by two of Keiser's personal security detail. They had their hands in their coats, waiting to see who would step off the lift. When they recognized Wexler, their hands went back to their sides.

"He's got company," Schneider said.

"Very hot number," Müller agreed.

"He's expecting me."

Schneider shrugged and reached for the door.

The apartment was opulence personified. The floor was pink marble with Persian rugs. Works by famous painters hung on the walls and the soft strains of classical violin drifted from a state of the art sound system hidden in the ceiling. Wexler passed through the sitting room to the main bedroom and knocked. The door was open a crack. The Old Man was on the bed, naked with his back to the headboard, sipping from a glass of wine. Next to him was a dead call girl.

"Wexler," Keiser said. "Impeccable timing. I'll need you to clean this up."

Wexler stopped in the open doorframe. The girl was lovely, at least she had been, with long red hair and slender legs. Now her face was a swollen purple mass of bruises and her eyes bulged in silent horror.

"Why do you do this?" Wexler asked.

"She's of no consequence." Keiser sipped from his wineglass. "No one will miss her. Besides, we have far more important matters to discuss. Is Noble in custody?"

Wexler nodded. "It's not easy disposing of bodies."

Keiser clicked his tongue, placed his wine on the bedside table and lifted first one leg, then the other, out of the bed using both hands to do so. He grunted at the effort. "Come help me," he said, motioning to his wheelchair.

Wexler crossed the room like a man going to the gallows. He shuddered at the thought of touching that naked white flesh. He choked back his revulsion as he helped the Old Man transfer from the bed to the wheelchair. Folds of fat dripped and rolled. A musty smell, like rotting fish, seeped from the creases.

Keiser sank into the chair with a deep sigh, like he'd just crossed the finish line at a marathon. He scratched the inside of one thigh and asked, "Were you able to speak with him?"

"He knows we hold his mother's life in our hands," Wexler said.

"Excellent." Keiser rubbed his hands together. "I want him to know it was I who destroyed his life."

*It was me,* Wexler, thought to himself. *I was the one who hatched the plan. You only funded it.* But he said, "There was a small hiccup."

"You know I don't like complications."

"Noble stashed the intel."

"Where?"

"That's what I'm working to find out."

Keiser's face warped into an ugly frown. "This is a serious complication. The Chinese won't like this one bit."

"No reason for them to know," Wexler said. "Noble will tell us what he did with the intel as soon as he sees his mum trussed up a like a turkey."

"I have a meeting with Kwang Luo first thing tomorrow. He's going to want those files. It was part of the deal."

"He'll have them," Wexler insisted. "He'll just have to give us a little time."

"Kwang Luo is not a patient man." Keiser gripped his wheels and turned to face Wexler. "We need those files."

Wexler perched himself on the corner of the bed. "It's not a problem. Once we have pictures of Noble's mum tied up, we'll send a lawyer into the police station to pose as his legal counsel. He'll show Noble the pictures and Noble will tell us where he stashed the take. We'll have the intel by the end of tomorrow."

Keiser nodded his head as Wexler spoke. "I've trained you well, my boy. You are learning to think on your feet. Soon as this is over, you'll be rewarded."

"Thank you, sir."

Keiser thrust his chin at the body. "Now dispose of that, please."

Wexler turned to the dead woman with a heavy sigh. Sooner or later the police would start to get suspicious at all the missing call girls. Even hookers have friends and pimps, someone who would notice they were gone. He said, "Easier said than done."

"Have Schneider and Müller help," Keiser said. "After all, many hands make light loads."

## Chapter Sixteen

THE STATION HOUSE WAS in the north of London, just six blocks from the safehouse. It was an old red-brick building, raised at the turn of the century with narrow arched windows and faulty wiring which caused overhead lights to occasionally flicker. Noble had been placed in an interview room on the second floor and, because of the nature of the crime, handcuffed to a stainless steel table bolted to the sagging hardwood floor.

A single thought kept playing through his head on a loop, *save mom, save mom, save mom.*

During the drive to the precinct, he'd had time to think through his position. Wexler was involved and that meant Keiser was pulling the strings. The two were attached at the hip. They wanted him to take the fall for Hap Chan's murder. They'd use mom as leverage and once Noble had admitted to the crime, mom would die.

*Save mom, save mom, save mom.*

That's all that really mattered. He could worry about the murder charges later. First he had to make sure mom was safe. That meant a phone call.

While he waited, he stood and used his feet to turn the chair. The legs screed against the timeworn wood. The sound was sure to attract attention. There was no two-way mirror in the interview room, just a camera in one corner. When Noble had the chair turned around, he straddled it. His forearms hung over the back of the seat and the cuffs dangled from his wrists. He was pressed forward, fingers worrying at the hidden key in his zipper pull, when the lock rattled and the door swung open.

"You're in a fair bit of trouble, Mr. Goodfellow."

The detective had dirty-blonde hair gathered in a no-nonsense bun at the back of her head and a crooked nose that spoiled an otherwise pretty face. A charcoal gray suit jacket covered a flat chest and narrow hips. She had startlingly blue eyes that made up for the busted nose and spoke in an Irish brogue. "I'm Detective Inspector Stokely. Want to tell me why you killed the poor man? What was his name?"

She was trying to catch him off guard, hoping he'd slip up and admit he knew Hap Chan. She was also looking for a quick ID on the body. Noble shrugged. "I don't know what you're talking about. I didn't kill anybody and I want my phone call."

She sat across from him and dropped a thick file folder on the table. An inch and a half of paper was stuffed between the covers. It was supposed to make Noble think they had mountains of evidence. The detective opened the folder and surveyed the top page, probably an inter-office memo, before looking up. She explored a molar with her tongue and said, "Why did you run?"

"I was out for a jog."

"In the middle of the night?"

"Gotta get your cardio in when you can."

"With blood on your shirt?"

"Cut myself shaving," Noble told her. "I want my phone call."

"Alright, Mr. Goodfellow. You'll get your phone call but first you're going to answer some questions."

"You're wasting your time, Stokely."

"It's my time to waste."

"You're wasting my time."

"The way I see it, you've got nothing but time, Mr. Goodfellow. In fact, I think you're looking at twenty to life."

"For what?" Noble said. "I didn't do anything."

Stokely leaned forward and placed one hand flat on the table, looking Noble directly in the eye. "We know you were in the apartment, Goodfellow. We caught you fleeing the scene. You've got the victim's blood all over you. It's only a matter of time before we get the DNA back. Why don't you come clean? Tell us what happened. If you play straight maybe I can get you a deal with the magistrate."

Stokely was good. She knew how to leverage the facts against her subject. Under different circumstances, Noble would have been impressed. She probably had a brilliant close rate, but Noble was losing patience. He wanted his phone call. He leaned forward, invading her personal space. His voice was a cold knife. "Have you informed the U.S. consulate you've arrested an American citizen?"

"We're in the process," Stokely said, but Noble could tell by the tight lines around her mouth that they were in the contemplative part of the process. Soon as the embassy found out an American had been arrested on charges of murder, they'd swoop in and muddy the waters. Stokely wanted to have her case airtight before that happened.

Noble said, "I'm not saying another word until I've spoken to the embassy and I've got a lawyer."

Stokely leaned back and took stock. Some of the wind had gone out of her sails. She thought this was going to be open and shut. She toyed with one corner of the fake folder full of dummy paper and said, "Okay, Goodfellow. We're not here to trample your rites, but the embassy is closed for the night. We'll contact them first thing in the morning."

"And my lawyer?"

She nodded. "We'll arrange for a barrister. Mind if I ask you a few questions while we wait?"

She was trying to stop him from lawyering up. She had tried coming at him hard and that hadn't worked. Now she was changing gears, trying to be officer friendly in the hopes Noble would let his guard down.

It was clear Stokely wasn't letting him out of this room and he wasn't getting his phone call until the barrister arrived. That might take all night. Mom might not have that much time. Noble needed to make a play. He let out a breath and said, "Yeah, sure, fine. But can you take off these handcuffs? They're making my fingers numb."

His hands were blue. The lack of circulation had turned his digits into thick dumb sausages full of pins and needles.

Stokely looked down at his hands and said, "I can loosen them."

She took a set of handcuff keys from her pocket and circled the table. When she bent down, Noble caught a whiff of her shampoo. It smelled like cinnamon. She adjusted the metal bracelets and said, "Better?"

Noble flexed his fingers, trying to get some blood back into them. "Much. Thank you."

"Let's talk about what you're doing in London, Mr. Goodfellow. Business or pleasure? And how long have you been here?"

"I arrived in town a few days ago on business," Noble lied. Before she could ask any more questions he said, "Can I get a cup of coffee? It's late and I'm tired."

Stokely blinked a few times and her tongue explored that back molar again. "Alright, Goodfellow. I could use a spot of tea myself. Cream and sugar for your coffee?"

"Black."

"I'll be right back." Stokely told him and got up from the table.

Soon as the door closed behind her, Noble cranked forward, hiding his movements from the camera, and freed the handcuff key from his zipper pull with tingling fingers.

# Chapter Seventeen

Detective Inspector Stokely returned with a Styrofoam cup in each hand, a pair of stale Danishes balanced on top, and a notepad clamped under one arm. Noble was still straddling the chair, his hands down below the table. Stokely turned to ease the door shut, preventing it from slamming, and Noble was on her.

He leapt up from the chair so fast he sent it flying. Stokely heard movement and started to turn but wasn't fast enough. Before the chair had even hit the ground, Noble swatted both cups from her grasp—the Styrofoam exploded against the wall—and he snaked an arm around her neck, closing off her air supply, stopping her scream before it started.

The chair landed with a muffled bang. Stokely bucked and tried to twist around. Her face turned red. Veins stood out on her forehead. She was strong, but not strong enough. Noble was taller and had sixty pounds on her. He locked her up in a choke hold and used his knee to clamp down on the service pistol strapped to her hip. Her fingers scrambled at his elbow and, when she realized she'd never manage to pry his arm away, she went for the gun. Her hand pushed at his knee in an effort to get her weapon free but the blood flow to her brain was interrupted. She was already losing consciousness.

Her body started to relax. Noble knew she was going under and said, "Really sorry about this Stokely, but my mother is in danger and I have to help her."

Seconds later the detective was a dead weight. Noble released his choke hold and dragged her to the corner where he put her back against the wall and ratcheted the handcuffs onto her wrists, taking care to make sure they weren't too tight. Soon as the pressure was off her neck, the blood started pumping back into her brain. She gave a soft moan and her head lulled. One hand fluttered like she was trying to brush away a bothersome fly.

Noble scooped the model 19 Glock from her hip just as she was clawing back up to consciousness. He ejected the magazine from the gun and slipped it into Stokely's pocket, then yanked back on the slide. A round leapt from the chamber, tumbled over the linoleum and came to a stop in the corner. Stokely's eyelids fluttered and her chin came up. Her brow worked through a series of emotions. Then she snapped awake and her eyes locked on the weapon.

"Someone's trying to kill my mother," Noble told her.

Without taking her eyes from the gun, Stokely said, "You're insane."

"I'm walking out of this police station," Noble said, "or I'm shooting my way out. It's up to you. Scream and I'll have to use the gun. Understand?"

She nodded.

"I really am sorry about this, Stokely, but I haven't got time to go through the proper channels." He took the badge from her belt, clipped it onto his coat lapel, then took a bobby pin from her hair and pocketed it before scooping up one of the fallen Danishes and reaching for the door.

The bullpen was a silent hive of cops with tired eyes working mostly in subdued quiet. Telephones jangled and a flatscreen in one corner was tuned to BBC news. A Middle Eastern man in a heavy-duty van had barreled through a busy shopping center last week, killing seven and injuring a dozen more. According to the talking heads, it was still too early to speculate on the driver's motivation. The news broadcast was the loudest thing in the office. A coffee pot percolated on a cheap folding table next to a dirt-stained microwave and a box of day-old doughnuts. Fluorescents cast everything in a lifeless anemic glow.

During the day time, this bullpen was probably a buzzing madhouse, but this late at night, the chaos was just an undercurrent. Noble's shoes made soft peeling noises on the floor as he cut his way across the bullpen. He strode toward a stairwell at the far side of the room, not too fast, so as not to attract attention. He was praying none of the other officers glanced up from their paperwork. If any of them happened to take a closer look, the jig would be up and Noble would have to make a run for it. He wouldn't make it very far. He stuffed the pastry in his mouth and chewed. His stomach shivered in anticipation. Sugar hit his system like a dose of methamphetamine.

A uniformed officer with a clipboard in one hand and an energy drink in the other passed Noble going the opposite direction. Without glancing up from the clipboard he muttered, "How's the wife, Palmer?"

It was a second before Noble realized the young officer was talking to him. On a gamble, Noble said, "Better."

"That's good," the officer said over his shoulder. "Tell her I say hello."

Noble didn't bother to respond. Anything more and the distracted cop might notice Noble's accent. He kept moving. His feet wanted to run. There was a race horse in his chest snorting and stamping, but

Noble forced himself to walk. He was almost to the stairwell when he spotted a desk with the name plate *Stokely*. On it was a framed photograph of a young Stokely with her arms around an older man in uniform. Dad was a cop. Maybe he still was. A dozen case files were stacked on the desk. Noble paused long enough to pull open the top drawer and deposit her service pistol. He'd probably set her career back a decade. Letting a suspect escape from an interrogation room would humiliate her and might earn her a suspension. Losing her service weapon would only make things worse, and Noble didn't want the poor girl fired. He left the drawer open a crack, so that the butt of the pistol peeked out.

On the other side of the divider, a fat detective in a heavy tweed jacket was slumped in his chair, snoring, one chubby hand still on his keyboard.

Walking softly, Noble reached the door to the stairwell, eased down on the push bar and slipped through. He took pains to close the door without making a loud bang and then bounded down the steps. He leapt the last few and hit the landing with both feet. The sound echoed up through the stairwell. He dropped the half-eaten pastry and hurried down, past the ground floor, to the basement parking garage.

The smell of rubber and exhaust hung in the frosty air. Overhead lights winked on polished hoods. The exit was guarded by an attendant in a pillbox. Noble gave one of the patrol cars a solid kick.

# Chapter Eighteen

The alarm sounded, bright and shrill in the enclosed expanse of the underground garage. Lights flashed in time with the bleating horn and the two vehicles on either side lit up as well, adding their voices to the mix. Soon the whole row of cruisers screamed out a discordant symphony.

Noble sprinted across the lane and ducked behind a row of unmarked cars, hurried toward the concrete barrier and made his way forward in a crouch. He kept below the line of sight, shoulder brushing the wall and shoes crunching in decades of grit.

A large black woman emerged from the guardhouse and peered along the line of cars with a curious twist to her brow, then started down the ramp at a waddle. She had a collection of fobs attached to her belt and she sifted through, looking for the corresponding unit. She silenced the alarms one by one, restoring order to the garage.

Meanwhile, Noble hurried up the ramp at a sprint. He hung a right at the top and raced to the end of the block before slowing to a jog, then a walk. He needed to get off the street. Stokely would be out of the interrogation room soon, if she wasn't already, and the bobbies would throw up a dragnet around the station.

He spotted a sign for the underground. A small crowd queued at the turnstiles. Most were kids going home after a night of partying, or maybe they were on their way out. A few were tourists. The rest were exhausted workers.

Bright overheads reflected off sloped tile walls. Sound echoed and a scent of grease hung in the air.

Without any money, and no ID, Noble had to pick a target and bump them. He chose one of the party goers. The guy was so drunk he was barely on his feet. Unfocused eyes were rimmed in red as he shuffled forward with the crowd. Noble tangled with the drunk and mumbled an apology.

The guy sloshed out something but it was so broken and mumbled, it was impossible to make heads or tails of it. Noble waved a hand in front of his face to clear the air. The fumes alone were enough to give him a contact high. He offered up one more apology before cutting through the crowd to the turnstiles while searching the drunk's wallet. He found an underground card behind a driver's license and swiped himself through.

An electronic voice told him to mind the gap. Behind him, the drunk was asking in a loud watery voice if anyone had seen his wallet.

A push of warm air from the open mouth of the tunnel announced the train. The crowd edged forward. The train burst from the dark with a loud rush and a long sigh of air brakes. Cars eased to a stop at the platform and Noble stepped aboard, along with the rest of the Londoners, not really caring where he was going as long as it was away from the precinct.

The doors closed and the train picked up speed. Noble breathed a sigh of relief. He rode three stops and got off when he spotted an electronics kiosk. The vendor was half asleep, his feet propped on the counter top and a paperback novel open on his belly. Noble woke the man up and bought a pay-as-you-go phone with the stolen credit card from the drunk's wallet before crossing over to the other side of the platform and taking a train headed in the opposite direction.

# Chapter Nineteen

The international flight from Heathrow to Tampa touched down just after nine in the morning. The lumbering 747 dropped through heavy cloud cover, shuddered briefly on a pocket of turbulence and, moments later, the wheels kissed the runway with a ghostly shriek. The engines reversed, bleeding off the momentum and bringing the gleaming white aircraft to an eventual stop. The pilot taxied to the gate and twenty minutes later the Haitian debarked the plane with a single carryon clutched in one hand. He passed through customs on a fake passport without incident and then he took an escalator to the parking level.

The sunshine state lives up to its name even in February. The mercury rarely drops below fifty degrees and at those temperatures, locals dress like they are caught in the grip of a nuclear winter. To the Haitian, the balmy tropical air, redolent with the salty ocean breeze, reminded him of home. He stripped out of his leather overcoat and draped it over one arm as he made his way through the garage, inspecting the merchandise.

He almost opted for a shiny red Mustang with a black racing stripe. It was a hot car and the Haitian wanted to hear that powerful engine roar when he put his foot down on the accelerator, but cops are twice as likely to stop a red hotrod. Instead, he chose a gleaming black Mercedes E-Class with a ragtop.

From his carryon, he took an iPad, opened a scanner app, and within minutes had singled out the alarm codes. He disabled the security and unlocked the doors remotely before climbing inside and putting his carryon, along with the iPad, in the passenger seat. A multi-tool made short work of the steering column and a moment later the engine came to life.

The Haitian closed the driver's side door with a soft thump, cranked the seat all the way back to make room for his long legs, and shifted into drive. He followed the signs onto the highway headed west toward Saint Petersburg. As he crossed the Howard Franklin Bridge, he put the ragtop down and slung one arm over the seat back, letting warm air blow his dreads out behind him.

He left the bridge, turned onto 4th Street headed toward downtown Saint Petersburg, and passed a speed trap doing 55 miles an hour.

Two police officers were sitting in a patrol car parked up behind a large elm at the corner of 119th Avenue. The man behind the wheel was a ten year veteran with numerous citations for valor named Jimmy Holt. The other officer was a trainee, fresh out of the academy. Holt let the trainee hold the radar gun. Holt never liked the things. He feared the radiation would cause testicular cancer. Holt watched the Mercedes E-Class glide by, nudged Cooper and pointed. "Drug dealer."

Cooper sat up a little straighter. "How do you know?"

"Black guy with dreads driving a hundred thousand dollar car," Holt said. "Almost always a drug dealer."

"Aren't we going to stop him?"

"For what?" Holt asked. "We got no probable cause. He's not even speeding."

Holt had known too many good cops who pulled a character over only to lose their job and pension to the lawyers who were constantly trying to make the cops look like devils and the criminals into angels.

A moment later a fire engine red coupe blazed past doing twenty over. A teenage girl with a blonde ponytail was behind the wheel, music blasting.

Hunt said, "Winner, winner, chicken dinner. Light her up."

Cooper reached for the sirens and Holt shifted the patrol car into drive.

The Haitian continued on down the road.

# Chapter Twenty

Matthew Burke was fast asleep when the phone buzzed on the bedside table. Matt was on his back, one thick black arm tucked behind the pillow and his mouth slightly open. He didn't snore per se, but gave a heavy sonorous note with every exhale. Madeline's head lay on his barrel chest, an arm draped over his round belly and her hair spilling over his shoulder. She woke first, nudged Matt, and mumbled through a mouth sticky with sleep. "Tell 'em 'syour day off."

Matt dragged his eyelids open with a heavy groan and groped in the dark for the phone. In his twenties he'd been a member of the United States Army's 1st Special Forces Operational Detachment, Delta for short. In those days he'd been able to snap awake on command, ready to fight at a moment's notice. Now the grey in his temples was spreading to the rest of his hair and it took longer a lot longer to wake up. Most mornings he needed a cup of strong black coffee before he was any good, but running his own private intelligence firm meant he had to be available twenty-four hours a day.

*Small price to pay*, Matt told himself as his fingers found the phone.

It had taken the better part of a year to really get his business up off the ground, but once he had the right network in place, the contracts started rolling in, along with the greenbacks, and Burke found he really enjoyed being his own boss. It meant he could pick and choose his clients and because he was *THE BOSS* he never had to do the grunt work. Gone were the days of long overnight stakeouts or sifting through trash. He had people for that.

More importantly, he'd been able to repair his relationship to the most wonderful gal on the planet. After Special Operations, Matt had gone to work for the Central Intelligence Agency and it nearly cost his marriage. Matt had a large part to play in his busted marriage. He'd come to terms with that. They were even stronger now than before, but Matt would give just about anything to go back in time and fix his mistakes.

What was the old saying? You can never go home again? That might be true, but you can pay for your mistakes and rebuild, so long as both parties are willing.

He peered through bleary eyes at the vibrating phone. The call was an unknown number which probably meant a new client. Companies tend to have emergencies and call at odd hours looking for rescue. Matt was tempted to take Maddie's advice and tell whoever was on the other end to call back tomorrow, but a B.B. King lyric popped into his head.

*Paying the cost to be the boss.*

He thumbed the talk button and cleared the sleep from his throat with a loud noise like a diesel motor warming up on a cold morning. "Atlas Security."

His company wasn't listed as an intelligence firm, but then, his company wasn't listed. It was a private intelligence agency and, like most private intel firms, its most frequent customer was the United States government.

The voice on the other end rammed the last of the sleep from Matt's mind like a defensive lineman smashing a quarterback.

"I need a favor," Noble said without preamble.

Matt was awake and shifted up onto an elbow. Maddie rolled her head off him and onto her pillow with a pout but kept one hand on his chest, fingernails lightly scraping through a carpet of small black ringlets. The bedroom was a collection of dark outlines. The sky beyond the window was a black curtain shot through with stars. He knew right away Jake was calling from the other side of the planet. He said, "Where are you?"

"London, but that's not important. I need you to get to Saint Pete right away. Someone is after my mother."

Burke had recruited Jake Noble into the CIA, he'd trained him in the black arts of covert intelligence, and turned him into one of the finest team leaders in the CIA's Special Operations Group. In many ways, he thought of Jake like a son. So Burke knew he was bound for Saint Pete Florida even before he'd bothered to ask for an explanation.

Maddie mumbled, "Who's it?"

He covered the phone with one hand. "It's Jake."

"Tell him I said hello."

"Maddie says hello."

"Give her my love," Noble said. "And then get your butt on a plane. Mom is at my boat, taking care of the dog. You'll find her there."

"I'm on the next flight out," Burke said. "You want to tell me what's going on?"

"Sure," Noble said. "But I have to give you the short version. The cops are after me."

Burke was already out of bed and getting dressed. He trapped the phone between one massive shoulder and his ear, while he dragged on a pair of trousers.

# Chapter Twenty-One

The mobile phone was ringing. It shrilled an electronic version of *Little Drummer Boy*, one of Mary's favorite Songs. She'd left it next to the sink after washing the dishes and heading to bed.

Mary Elise Noble struggled to sit up and climb from the bunk, going slow, making extra sure she didn't lose her footing. She was dressed in a floral print night gown. A brass accented clock attached to the bulkhead told her it was just after one in the morning. Her heart gave out a silent warning. Phone calls in the middle of the night were never good. Her first thought was that one of her friends from the Wyndham Arms had passed in the night. A deeper, darker voice insisted that it would be Jake, and that he was in trouble.

The Beast came to his feet with a lolling tongue and curious brows. His ears were cocked forward and his nostrils flared briefly. He padded alongside Mary as she carefully navigated the narrow hall to the galley.

"Saints preserve us," she told the empty boat.

She squinted at the screen in the dark. The number was unknown. She picked up and said, "This is Mary Noble. Who's calling?"

"Mom," Noble's voice came over the line, sounding tired and frayed. "Thank God. I've called three times. Where have you been? Is everything alright?"

A cold weight dropped into Mary's belly. She didn't like the note of panic in his voice. Jake was a cool customer. He had been ever since he was boy. He rarely let his emotions slip through. Mary crossed to the galley table and sat down. "I was asleep," she told him. "What's going on Jake? What's happened?"

"I can't tell you," he said. "Not now. Not over the phone. I've sent a friend to see you. He's going to be staying with you for a few days. Just until I get back."

The cold weight turned into an anchor, rooting her to the cheap leather. Jake had never sent anyone to protect her before. She said, "Now you've got me really worried."

"Don't be worried," he told her. "You're going to be just fine."

"It's not me I'm worried about."

Gadsden's ears pricked up and his brow furrowed. He knew, in the way of all dogs, that something was amiss. He sat back on his haunches and laid one massive paw on Mary's thigh, gazing up at her with questioning eyes.

She absently scratched behind his ears.

"Don't worry about me either," Noble said. "I'll be fine."

She could hear the lie in his voice and said, "I don't believe you."

"Would I lie to my own mother?"

"Who do you work for?"

"State Department."

She said, "Busted."

It was a regular exchange between the two of them and usually got a laugh. This time neither laughed. Mary said, "I'm scared, Jake."

"Don't be scared. Everything is going to be just fine. My friend is going to come stay with you for a day or two at most and then I'll be home and we'll go to that God-awful Greek place you like so much."

Hawser lines creaked and a horn blared across Straub Park. His promise to accompany her to Tripoli, a restaurant Jake openly loathed, did little to comfort her. Mary said, "How will I recognize this friend of yours?"

"He's a big black bear of a man with a gap between his front teeth and he's graying at the temples," Noble said. "Can't miss him. His name is Matthew Burke. He'll give the security code."

Mary had to cast back in her memory for the code.

"You remember the code?" he asked.

"Of course I remember," she said with all the indignation she could muster. "You think I'm a forgetful old goat?"

"Good," he said. "Stay put until Matt arrives. Don't let anybody on board and don't leave. Not even to walk Gadsden. Understand?"

"Jake, how much trouble are you in?"

"Isn't there a verse in the Bible that says God will never give you more than you can handle?"

Mary's free hand went to the galley table and gripped hard. Her knuckles turned bone white and the beds of her fingernails flattened out. She said, "That's not in the Bible and I'm afraid that's not the way it works, kiddo. Just the opposite in fact. Sometimes God gives us more than we can handle so that we stop relying on ourselves and learn to rely totally on Him."

There was a silence on the other end while Jake digested that information. She could practically hear the circuits clicking in his head. At last he said, "How do I do that? How do I rely totally on Him?"

"Start with prayer."

"What do I say?"

"Talk to Him, Jake. Talk to Him just the way you're talking to me right now. Tell Him what you're thinking and feeling and ask Him for what you need."

"Doesn't He already know what I need?"

"Of course He does," she said, "but don't let that stop you."

He took a breath and let it out slow. "Give me some encouragement, will ya, Ma?"

Mary cleared a roadblock from her throat with a sound like stones scraping together in winter. "Though I walk through the shadow of the valley of death, I will fear no evil, because God is with me. His rod and his staff comfort me. He prepares a table for me in the midst of my enemies. He anoints my head with oil and my cup runs over. Surely goodness and mercy will follow me all the days of my life; and I will dwell in the house of the Lord forever."

"Thanks Ma."

She asked, "How bad is it?"

"Bad as it gets," he admitted and then before she could ask any more questions, he said, "Keep this line open."

He hung up and Mary Elise Noble was left to cry quietly in the shadowy galley of *the Yeoman* while the Beast lay with his muzzle between his paws, wondering what was wrong.

# Chapter Twenty-Two

Ezra Cook had two brown paper sacks in his hands as he limped along the hall toward the situation room on the fourth floor. The sacks were stuffed with paninis and garlic bread from the new sandwich shop installed next to the Starbucks in the CIA cafeteria. The mouthwatering aroma of warm bread, tomato, pesto, and mozzarella wafted along behind him. Ezra had waited in line twenty minutes. The sandwiches were the hot new item in the cafeteria. To be fair, any new offering was popular. When you ate the same thing day in and day out, new food carried a certain appeal, but the paninis, with their melted cheese and pepperoni, were better than anything the cafeteria had to offer and better than most of the sandwich shops in Foggy Bottom. They came rolled up in paper with the words; top-secret/tummy only. The shop was run by a heavyset Greek with white hair, thick black brows, and a ready scowl. Rumor around the office was that Linus the Greek hadn't been required to undergo any security protocols before opening his shop in the cafeteria and everyone agreed the paninis were worth the security breech. Others said Linus was a former field officer during the Cold War. Still others insisted the grumpy sandwich maker was a field officer during the Cold War, just not for *our* side. Inevitable comparisons were made to the soup Nazi, but everyone agreed the paninis were the best thing on offer in the cafeteria and when Cook and Witwicky had a moment to themselves, they'd drawn straws to see who fetched lunch.

Ezra lost.

Not that he minded. For Ezra Cook, life was coming up aces. He'd had half his face blown off by a bullet fragment (he'd wear the scar for the rest of his life), shattered his ankle bone (he was just now walking without the use of a cane) and, more importantly, he was dating the girl of his dreams.

One evening after work in their favorite haunt, the Town Tavern, a smarmy jock with a popped collar had been making unwanted passes at Gwen. Ezra was still wearing stitches and walking on a cane. He'd placed himself between Gwen and the jock, stared the big man down and said, "She asked you to leave her alone."

That was all it took.

The jock took in the locomotive track of stitches crisscrossing Ezra's cheek, turned and walked away. Ezra had taken Gwen in his arms and kissed her deeply. It was the first time they'd kissed in public, in front of other CIA employees. Since then she'd practically moved into his place. She had mostly taken over his bathroom, something Ezra didn't mind at all. She even had her own drawer in his dresser.

But all that was on the mental back burner as Ezra limped along the hall. His mind was occupied by questions for which he had no answers. First and foremost; was it possible Noble was bent? Had he been bought out?

Ezra didn't even want to consider it.

Ben Jameson lumbered past going the other direction and said, "Paninis! Are there any more?"

"Yeah but you'd better hurry," Ezra told him. "They were running low by the time I got to the front of the line."

Jameson hustled his bulk along the hall, thick thighs rubbing together.

Ezra stopped in front of the door to the secure situation room. He clutched one of the sacks between his teeth and searched his pockets for his swipe card. He had a wallet and car keys, but no card. He growled in frustration and knocked.

"Password," Gwen called out in a playful voice.

"No soup for you."

The door unlocked with a soft electronic beep.

She caught him the moment he walked through the door, planting a kiss right on his lips. Ezra felt his heart swell and his pants shrink. Her lips pressed tight to his and she made a soft noise. The kiss greetings had started not long after Ezra had stared down the Jock at the Town Tavern. They'd been curled up on Ezra's sofa watching the Star Wars Christmas special, bathed in the light from a Christmas tree and a menorah, and Gwen had whispered those three big words in his ear between passionate pawings. Ezra had said it right back, had been wanting to say it, but unwilling to say it first. From then on Gwen greeted him with a kiss anytime they were apart more than a few hours. Ezra didn't think he'd ever grow tired of that hello kiss. That simple gesture was, perhaps, the best part of being in a relationship. It let Ezra know that there was someone in this big old world who loved him and missed him when he was gone, and was glad when he came back. It was a simple thing, but a simple thing that Ezra's life had been sorely lacking.

And it was nice to know that Gwen felt the same. They'd even discussed meeting each other's parents, but that would be tricky. Gwen's parents were strict Roman Catholic and Ezra's mother was, well, a Jewish mother. Enough said.

They came apart—sweet sorrow—and Ezra passed her a sack.

"Extra mustard?" Gwen asked.

"Of course, your highness."

"Thank you, sir knight."

Wizard and McHale had left the computer jockeys in charge while they deliberated in private how to handle the situation. With Noble in police custody, and a Chinese defector dead, the situation was primed to blow up into an international incident. Eventually British Intelligence would figure out Noble's real identity and it would be an embarrassment to the CIA at the very least. If the British learned that Noble had sold out to the Chinese...

Gwen was about to take a bite of her sandwich and paused. "You think it's true?"

They had spread their feast on the small bit of empty desk space in the claustrophobic situation room. Ezra had peeled up the bread on his panini and ripped open a packet of salt. He shook his head. "I don't know what to believe."

"It's Jake," Gwen said, as if that should settle it. "Our Jake."

Ezra knew just what she meant. He didn't want to believe Jake was capable of treason any more than Gwen. It didn't seem possible. The three of them had been through blood and fire together. Ezra and Gwen had been on the other end of Jake's mission into Iran when he'd overcome incredible odds to free an Iranian girl from the repressive regime, and they'd been with Noble in the thick of the action when terrorists tried to destroy America's power grid. They'd all spent a week aboard Noble's boat in Saint Pete soaking up sun and recouping from their injuries after their last mission. He'd taken them to his favorite jazz club, a place called Ruby's Elixirs, and they'd convinced him to sit through a marathon viewing of Lord of the Rings. They had eaten gross amounts of pizza and been surprised to learn Noble possessed an almost encyclopedic knowledge of the original Star Trek. Apparently, his father had been a fan of the show. The age-old question of who made the best captain had been hotly debated. Which Jake more or less settled when he pointed out the fact that Shatner was the only captain who had actually been to space.

In all they'd spent a very pleasant week with Jake, getting to know him on a human level. And when the Director of Operations had tapped Noble for the mission to bring a defector out of China, Noble had specifically asked for Cook and Witwicky. In Noble's own words, there was nobody he'd rather have backing his play.

Now he was in custody for murder.

Ezra chomped a bite from the corner of his sandwich and chewed. He was trying to square up everything he knew about Jake Noble with everything that had happened in the last few hours.

As if she were reading his mind, Gwen said, "None of it adds up."

"Agreed." Ezra spoke around a mouthful of food. "But how do you explain the phone call?"

Gwen propped her elbows on the desk, panini held in both hands, and stared into the distance. "There has to be something else going on here. Something we're missing."

"If you've got theories, I'd love to hear them."

She put the panini down without taking a bite and dusted crumbs from her fingers. "He had to know we'd be monitoring his phone? Maybe he's trying to send a message?"

"And the money?"

Her brow twisted.

"What if he is bent?" Ezra said. The words nearly choked coming from his throat.

She breathed out a sigh. "I don't even want to think about that."

"Me neither but..."

Before he could say any more, the phone next to Gwen's computer rang. She nearly leapt out of her seat. Her mouth opened in a comical little O. She jammed her glasses into place with an impatient stab and squinted at the incoming call log on her screen. The only people who had this number were directly involved in the operation, and Gwen could count them on one hand. She knew before she picked up that it was going to be Jake. He was probably calling from lock up. She took the phone off the hook, put the call on speaker and answered; "Westmore Holdings and Associates. How may I direct your call?"

"I'd like to check on my portfolio," Noble said. "But I'm on a business trip and I don't have my passcode with me. Can you put me in touch with my rep? I think her name is Hornsecker."

It was Noble's voice. The code phrase confirmed his identity but signaled immediate danger. Gwen covered the mouthpiece, turned to Ezra and mouthed the word, *Wizard*.

# Chapter Twenty-Three

Dulles swiped through the door to the situation room five minutes later, a cigarette clamped between his thin lips. One arthritic claw cradled a lighter. He made sure the door closed and the lock engaged with an electric *beep* before asking, "What have you got?"

Gwen swiveled in her chair. Her eyes were wide behind the coke-bottle glasses and her cheeks were flush. "Noble's on the line."

Wizard's scraggly grey brows scaled his forehead. "Now?"

"Speaker," Ezra said.

"How much have you said to him?" Dulles asked in a low tone.

Witwicky only shook her head.

Dulles put flame to his cigarette, took in a lungful of sweet tobacco, and breathed out a silver cloud. "Jake, can you hear me?"

"I hear you, sir. I'm on a pay as you go phone. It's not secure." Noble's voice was thin and hollow. They could hear the reverberation of hurtling subway cars echoing in a cavernous space and the quiet din of passengers. "I'm priority one. Say again, priority one."

Witwicky was on the edge of her chair, back ramrod straight and her mouth frozen in a silent O. Cook turned an ink pen over and over in his grasp, clicking the end methodically.

Dulles took a moment to collect his thoughts. He needed a heart pill but that would have to wait. He propped his boney hips against one of the desks and said, "Have you got the take?"

"I stashed it," Noble said and his tone made it clear he wasn't saying any more on the subject.

Cook and Witwicky shared a look.

Dulles raised the cigarette to his lips and smoked in silence for several seconds, considering all his options. In the world of intelligence, what you don't know throws a mission into chaos. And chaos was the only word to describe this operation. At last, Dulles said, "What happened at the safehouse?"

"Not over an open connection," Noble said.

Dulles's eyes narrowed. "How did you escape police custody?"

There was a long pause and then, "You know about that?"

"We know about a lot of things, Jake. What happened at the safehouse?"

"Hap Chan is dead, okay. Is that what you want to hear?" His voice was a knife edge. In the background, a loudspeaker announced the stop. Dulles snapped his fingers and pointed at Cook, but the net ninja was already jotting the information down and Witwicky was running a trace on the phone. Noble was saying, "Police like me for the murder."

"I read you, Jake. Let's get you off the street. Proceed to emergency rendezvous Charlie."

"I can't do that."

"Why not?"

"I'm not sure who to trust," Noble said.

The kid was clearly coming unraveled. It was plain in his voice. Dulles decided to roll the dice. "I can't help you if I don't know what the problem is."

"Hap Chan is dead and I'm wanted for murder. That's the problem."

Dulles absently knocked ash from his cigarette and let it flutter to the shabby carpet. "We need you to come in," Dulles said. "That's the only way we're going to figure this thing out."

"Charlie is out of the question," Noble said.

"Fine. You pick the meeting place. The station chief will be there within the hour."

Cook and Witwicky had their heads together, whispering in secret. Then she turned and gave Dulles a thumbs up. Cook pointed to his computer screen where he had a map of London and Noble's location marked with a blinking red dot.

"Saint Martin in the Fields in Trafalgar Square," Noble said. "One hour."

The line went dead.

"Got a fix on his position?" Dulles asked.

"He's at Tottenham Court Road underground station," Cook provided. "Just a few blocks from Trafalgar Square."

"Get a security team over there on the double," Dulles said. "And get Hunt on the line."

# Chapter Twenty-Four

Detective Inspector Stokely stood at attention, letting DCI Conagher's tirade wash over her in cold waves. She was in Conagher's office, under the harsh glare of soulless fluorescents, listening to his verbal abuse. He'd arrived just after midnight, unshaven and bleary eyed. His thinning hair stood up in places and his oxford was buttoned wrong. He paced back and forth. A vein throbbed in the center of his forehead. Stokely listened without really hearing. Each icy breaker came roaring in to crash against the seawall of her carefully constructed façade. Her lips pressed together and her brow pinched as a fresh wave assaulted her defenses.

"Had him in custody," Conagher was saying. He could chew you out without ever raising his voice. "Had him handcuffed in an interview room and you somehow let him escape. Just what kind of copper are you?"

Stokely didn't bother to respond. Her face was a broken mask held in place by glue made from pride.

Conagher stopped pacing and planted both fists on his desktop. "I've given you a lot of slack, Stokely. Mainly because of your father, but you've really stepped in it this time, old girl."

That last wave put a crack in her seawall. She could feel tears building behind her eyes and promised herself she wasn't going to cry, not in front of Conagher. He shook his head and peeled back his lips in a grimace, showing white teeth that should have had braces in his adolescence but never did. His eyes were thunderclouds building to a great whacking deluge. Stokely braced for impact.

Conagher pointed at the door to his office. "If you want to save your career, get out there and find this Jake Goodfellow and put him in custody. If you can't manage that, you'll spend the rest of your days as a traffic warden. Understood?"

She reached for the door. "Perfectly clear, sir."

"I'm going home and going back to bed." Conagher snatched his muffler from the back of his office chair and rummaged through the stacks of cases on his desk for his gloves. "When I get back here in the morning, I expect good news."

"You'll have it," Stokely said and fled before he could say any more.

She wanted to lock herself in the bathroom and have a good cry, but the whole bullpen was watching. Conagher's blinds were open and every cop on the second floor had witnessed her getting dressed down. Some had been good enough to turn away and pretend they weren't seeing it. Others watched with savage glee. Instead of the bathroom, she went to the tea pot and poured herself a cup.

The scent of the cruddy black swill was familiar and helped calm her nerves. It was an effort to hide the tremors. Her hands shook like loose gravel in a train yard. She filled half the mug—emblazoned with the precinct house number—with tea and the rest with creamer.

Conagher stormed from his office, slamming the door behind him with enough force to rattle the glass, and disappeared down the stairs without a backward glance.

Stokely watched him go and her thoughts turned to Goodfellow. He'd breezed right out of the office like he owned the place. He'd even slipped Stokely's magazine into her pocket without her knowing, and left her service weapon in her desk drawer. *Cheeky bastard.*

Stokely had reviewed the footage from the interview room but still didn't know how Goodfellow managed to unlock his cuffs. In the black and white image, he hunched over and a minute later he had the cuffs off. It was like something from a magic show. *Change-o-presto!* A minute later Stokely had walked into the scene and she got to watch all over again as Goodfellow easily overpowered her, proving everything male cops already believed about women in uniform.

She sipped her tea and turned to the bullpen. She wanted to dress down the general assembly. Excrement, after all, rolls down hill and these morons had let Goodfellow walk right past them. Officer Braddock had even spoken to him. Said he thought Goodfellow was Detective Inspector Keene. To be fair, Goodfellow did bear a passing resemblance to Keene. But Stokely wasn't going to scream or yell. She wasn't going to curse and chew them out. That would only make her look weak. Instead she said, "Where are we on Goodfellow?"

"Got an APB out with all patrol and transit officers," Braddock said.

"And we're sending out his pictures to all the local stations," said Graham.

DI Singh was on the phone. He held up a hand for attention, nodded once like the person on the other end of the phone could hear a nod, and then slapped the receiver down on the cradle. "Someone matching Goodfellow's description was just spotted leaving Tottenham Court Road station five minutes ago."

"I want every available patrol unit to converge on that location," Stokely said. "And let's pull footage from every traffic and surveillance cam in the area. I want this cheeky bastard back in custody within the hour."

# Chapter Twenty-Five

Jake had a tail. He felt it the way native Floridians feel rain before the first thunderheads gather on the distant horizon. It was instinctual, something born from years living and moving through the world of covert intelligence. And like a gathering storm cloud, it was a static charge in the air that made the small hairs on his arms stand at attention.

He passed Foyles, a coffee shop pretending to be a book store. He was making his way south along Charing Cross Road, hands stuffed deep in his peacoat and his collar turned up against the chill. A patina of worry was etched upon his brow. His mouth was a strict line. His eyes cut one way and then the other, looking for any sign of trouble. People prowled the sidewalks and cars hissed along the wet pavement. A 24-hour convenience store with neon signage advertised; *beer, wine, cigarettes*. Light from the big picture window made a glowing rectangle on cracked asphalt. A Pakistani man in a red turban was ringing up a pack of smokes and a bottle for a wino in a dirt-stained overcoat. The wino watched Noble through the glass. His eyes were sharp, drinking in details, not the sudsy eyes of an alcoholic.

Noble hunched deeper into his coat and picked up the pace. He took the first left, cutting across traffic and jogging down a twisting lane that ran in back of the convenience store, then over another block, dodging between cars, and into a little Chinese laundry. He hurried past the front desk, ignoring the indignant protests of the small woman behind the counter, and ducked a rack of clothes on a large automated belt, through thick clouds of billowing steam, and past surprised workers to the rear door. A sign over the door said the alarm would sound. That turned out to be a lie. Noble exploded into a lane littered with trash and an old galvanized tin washtub that had been repurposed as a vegetable garden. Barren sticks poked up from frozen soil. Noble turned right and sprinted for the far end. His body was a mass of aches and pains from officer Reilly's tackle. He could already feel bruises forming on his back and someone had replaced the collagen in both knees with broken glass.

*The years are starting to catch up*, Noble told himself. And then corrected himself. As Dr. Jones had so famously stated; *it's not the years, it's the milage*. Whichever it was, it was slowing him down, taking away his edge. It didn't help that he was tired and hungry.

He ran to the end of the alley and slowed to a walk as he turned onto a wider boulevard dotted with several busy pubs. He cut a wandering path through an outdoor beer garden, then back onto the sidewalk, trying to flush his tail.

At the corner, a couple stumbled from an open door, carrying with them a draft of warm air and smoky jazz. A sign over the door advised people to check out the rooftop bar. The man staggered and might have gone down but Noble reached out a hand and caught him. "Steady as she goes."

"Thanks, mate." He found his footing and offered Noble a two-finger salute.

"How's the beer tonight?" Noble asked.

"Wet."

"Just the way I like it." Noble let himself into the club, made his way past a long mahogany bar to a narrow stair and climbed to the top where an open seating area looked out across the rooftops. A chill wind turned his hair into a cloud around his head. Several propane heaters kept the worst of the cold at bay. Warmth radiated from the tall chromium sentinels in pleasant waves that helped thaw Noble's toes.

The Londoners didn't seem to mind the cold. The tables were full of cheery men with rosy cheeks and tall lagers. Well-dressed women sipped from wine glasses. The mood was jolly despite the recent economic downturn crippling the British economy and decimating Europe. There was a small dance floor and tables arranged around the outside. A low wall of frosted glass ringed the rooftop. Noble wound between tables in a drunken stumble, bumped a corner hard enough to turn glasses over and, while everyone was jumping up to avoid the spill of beer, he snagged a man's overcoat off the back of a chair. He carried it to a small shack that served as a restroom.

The men's room smelled like vomit and Noble's feet stuck to the floor. He choked down a mouthful of bile that tried to climb his throat, made sure the place was clear, then draped the stolen coat over an empty stall door before slipping into the next cubicle. He eased the door shut, but didn't latch it, and he waited. His pulse was a steady sloshing rhythm in his ears.

Wind rattled the walls of the bathroom. Someone came in long enough to whizz, belch, and shuffled out again. Noble gripped his stall door and focused on ignoring the cold. The next time the door opened, the man who entered stopped just inside for a look around and Noble knew he had his shadow. He put his face to the gap for a peek. It was the hobo from the convenience store, only he had shed the bulky coat covered in bird poop and now he wore a smart black bomber jacket. His eyes swept the bathroom and spotted the stolen coat draped over the door. He crossed the room in two long strides, reached for the door, and yanked.

At the same time, Noble exploded from his stall, using the door like a battering ram. He swung the composite plastic door wide, catching the man off guard. The door smacked his shoulder and sent him tumbling. Noble smashed the man against the wall of the bathroom, shaking the small building on its foundations. He followed up with an elbow that caught the man in the cheek, rocking his head back. Noble grabbed him by the collar, gave him a shake and said, "Let's have a talk."

The man responded with a flat hand strike to the side of Noble's neck that sent him reeling.

# Chapter Twenty-Six

Noble ducked a fist aimed at his head, felt knuckles glance off the side of his skull, and responded with an uppercut that caught his enemy off guard. The man rocked back on his heels and would have gone down but fell against the row of sinks, twisting a tap in the process. Cold water burst from the faucet, filling the basin.

The man pushed off the sink, blocked Noble's follow up with his forearms, and delivered a punishing series of rabbit punches to the gut that threatened to double Noble up in pain. It felt like someone was beating him with a baseball bat. White-hot knives rocketed up his spine and into his brain. Fireworks popped in his vision.

Noble turtled up in a boxer's stance, using his elbows and forearms to protect his body. The man waded forward, fighting like a cornered polecat, fists flying. This guy was no amateur. He had training and experience. Some of his moves were a mixture of Shaolin Kungfu and Wing Chun, along with good old fashioned American boxing. He tried to slam a knee into Noble's groin.

Twisting at the last possible second, Noble took the blow on the meat of his thigh, high up near the hip. It was a crushing impact that deadened nerve endings and turned his foot into a lifeless stump dangling at the end of his leg. He hobbled backward, warding off a series of attacks, looking for an opening. He managed to duck a haymaker and drove his fist up into the man's throat. He pulled the punch at the last possible second. He was trying to question the guy, not kill him. Noble's knuckles sank into soft flesh with enough force to make the man's eyes bulge from their sockets. His mouth gaped open like a fish and he made a gagging noise. Noble drove a fist into the low ribs, heard a pop, and stamped down on the man's left foot with enough force to flatten a tin can.

The impact rattled the bathroom shed again. People outside had to be hearing the commotion. The music was loud, but not that loud. Noble knew he had a very narrow window to find out who was following him, and why, before making an escape. He grabbed a fist full of lapel, brough his knee up twice like a steam powered piston and the man let out an agonized *oyahhhh!*

Before he could recover, Noble had him pinned, face first, against the stall door with an arm twisted behind his back. He gave the appendage a sharp jerk, heard tendons in the shoulder twang like piano wires, and said, "Try anything and I'll break it."

In reply, the man spat. He tried to spit on Noble, but with his chest pressed against the wall, the best he could accomplish was spitting over his shoulder onto the bathroom floor.

Noble increased the pressure on the arm. "Who do you work for?"

"You go to hell." His voice, laced with pain, rang with Asian tones.

Noble grabbed a fist full of the man's bottle-blond hair and twisted his head for a better look at his features. There were tell-tale indicators of plastic surgery around the eyes, and a doctor had worked on the nose. Reconstructive surgery and a bleach job allowed him to pass for a westerner at a distance, but close inspection made it obvious he was Asian.

"Chinese?" Noble asked.

He got no response.

Noble said, "How did you get onto us?"

The Chinese agent sagged forward, like all the fight had gone out of him, then arched back, catching Noble with a headbutt to the chin. It wasn't enough to do any real damage, but it broke Noble's hold. The man whipped around like a snake and the fight was on. Noble had to shuffle backward to avoid being pummeled.

There was a knock at the door. Someone called out, "Hey, what's going on in there?"

Then the knob was turning.

Noble backed up until he impacted the door. Then the Chinese agent was on him, one hundred and sixty-five pounds of muscle, ramming Noble backward.

The flimsy door split with the high crack of balsa and the hinges ripped clear of the frame. The patrons gave a collective gasp. Noble and the Chinese agent went stumbling through the opening, trampling the door in the process along with the guy who'd been on the other side. One woman screamed and several partiers took out their phones to record the whole thing.

Pain radiated out from Noble's side and fairy lights capered in his vision. The man had caught him with another short rabbit punch. He had fists like knotty tree trunks. He was smaller and weighed twenty pounds less, but he was fast as a cobra and backed his punches with everything he had. He was also a decade younger. Noble had to end this quick, without killing the man, and make an escape, but the Chinese agent forced Noble's hand when he reached for a bottle.

# Chapter Twenty-Seven

The Chinese agent snatched a lager by the neck, smashed it on the table corner, and lunged. The crowd gasped. Music still piped through the speakers but the rest of the noise died away. The only sound was the hum of traffic from the street below and the hiss of the propane heaters.

Noble leapt aside in time to avoid the broken bottle. Jagged edges whistled past his stomach, slicing his peacoat. He ducked as the Chinese agent swung around, trying to catch him with the razor shards. Noble sank his head in time to feel the bottle whisper through his hair, inches from his scalp. A woman in a red dress and heels screamed. A few burly soccer hooligans worked up their courage and started forward, meaning to restrain the bottle wielding ruffian.

Noble warned them back with a wave of his hand. The Chinese intelligence agent was cornered in a foreign country and the low melody of police sirens floated on the breeze. He was desperate to escape. That made him a very dangerous man.

Noble lunged backward, forcing his opponent to close the distance, and met the Chinese agent with a kick. Noble put all his weight behind it, stamping his foot into the man's chest.

The kick caught the Chinese by surprise, knocking all the air from his lungs and driving him backwards. The bottle slipped from his fingers, hit the floor, and went rolling. The agent stumbled, wheeling his arms for balance. Noble realized his mistake a second too late. The Chinese agent hit the low frosted glass wall ringing the edge of the roof. The glass cracked and the agent went over.

"No!" Noble sprang forward, both hands out in an effort to grab on, but he wasn't fast enough. The Chinese agent disappeared with a shriek that ended in an awful thud.

Noble went to the broken railing.

The man lay in a sprawl. His head was bent at a stomach-turning angle and his hips were twisted the wrong way round. His eyes were open and staring.

Noble shook his head. One hand closed in a fist and went to his mouth. He was now on the hook for a double homicide.

Sirens were closing in. It was time to go.

Noble turned and headed for the door, but the soccer bros in their West Ham jerseys blocked his path.

One propped a fists on his hips. "Can't let you just walk away, am I right?"

His buddy nodded.

Noble stamped the man's knee without breaking stride. It made a sound like an oak knot popping in a fire. His leg bent the wrong way and the big bruiser doubled over with a groan.

Most men are courageous only in groups. Soon as they're alone they lose their moxie. The second guy took one look at his buddy's broken knee and decided Noble wasn't worth the effort. He stepped aside and allowed Noble to pass.

A police cruiser howled to a stop on the street below. Lights bathed the surrounding buildings in alternating flashes of red and white. Noble heard a second cruiser pull up behind the first as he made the stairs and started down.

He reached the second floor landing where a window looked out the back of the bar into a private courtyard for delivery drivers. Noble tried the latch but it had been painted shut years ago. He spotted a tarnished brass trumpet hanging on the wall as a decoration and used that to break the glass. He took a second to knock the loose shards from the frame before dropping the trumpet and scrambling through.

It was a short drop to the pavement. Noble gripped the frame and lowered himself down before letting go. He had a momentary feeling of weightlessness before landing with a bone rattling bang on the pavers. He took the impact with his knees bent and went into a combat roll, trying to spread the hurt out evenly over the rest of his body. He was convinced the paratrooper landing only worked for eighteen year old kids fresh out of Army basic training because the older Noble got, the more it hurt.

He came back to his feet, with far less finesse than he'd managed it fifteen years ago, and sprinted toward the exit. The door was set in a brick arch. He hit the wooden slat gate at a run and bounced off, his shoulder throbbing. Chain-link rattled. Noble groped in the shadows and felt a padlock. There was no way over. He cursed and turned back to the little courtyard.

# Chapter Twenty-Eight

DI Stokely was in her unmarked, both hands wrapped tight around the steering wheel, headed west on A40. A determined frown creased her brow. Tires hummed on the blacktop, thumping through potholes and splashing puddles.

She braked, slowing the cruiser enough to take a turn without slipping all over the road, and then she was back on the gas. A pair of patrol cars were tight on her bumper and more units were closing in on Goodfellow's last known location from the opposite direction. Stokely entertained visions of slamming the arrogant jerk against the door of her cruiser as she cuffed him. This time she was going to cuff him hand and foot and dare him to pull another Houdini.

The radio crackled and a call came over the net. Dispatch reported a fistfight at a rooftop bar just three blocks away. The description matched Goodfellow.

Stokely reached for her mic, thumbed the talk button and spat, "This is Detective Inspector Stokely, all units in connection with the Goodfellow case, converge on that location. I say again, all units converge on that location."

She dropped the mic in the passenger seat, cut the wheel hard, and sent her unmarked car into a slide that nearly put her into the side of an oncoming lorry. Horns blared and Stokely yanked the cruiser back into the left lane with a hiss of rubber on wet tarmac. She switched on her sirens and swerved around the back of a slow-moving Volkswagen. She stamped the gas, taking another curve at speed, and spotted flashing lights up ahead. Traffic was at a standstill. She was forced to stop a block away.

The brakes locked and the tires let out a soft shriek. Stokely shifted into park, snatched the keys from the ignition and didn't bother to close the door. She was out and running between cars, one hand clamped over the pistol on her hip to keep it from bouncing. Air burst from her lungs in silver ghosts that lingered a moment and then faded. She was almost clotheslined by a car door when a motorist decided he was going to get out and see about the hold up.

Stokely juked around his open door, catching her hip on the metal, and said, "Stay inside your vehicle, sir."

An ambulance was working its way through the traffic from the other end of the street, siren blasting. Drivers tried to move their cars and ended up making more of a mess, slowing the progress.

The address was a jazz club that served overpriced drinks. Stokely had been here a few months ago on a blind date set up by well-meaning friends. The guy had been a complete buffoon who spent most of the night telling Stokely how much he could squat and kept making jokes about creative uses for her handcuffs. By the end of the night, Stokely felt like cuffing him to the bar and flushing the key down a toilet.

There was a body on the pavement and the glass wall that ran around the rooftop had a break in it. Someone had taken a plunge. Stokely couldn't make out the victim through the forest of people. A team of paramedics weaved between cars on foot while the ambulance continued its slow push through traffic. A pair of uniformed officers were already there, speaking with the crowd.

Stokely arrived, breathing heavy, and flashed her shield. "Stokely. What's happened here?"

"We just arrived on scene," one of the unis informed her. "Seems there was a fight on the roof and one drunk pushed another off."

The stiff on the sidewalk was not Goodfellow. Blood and broken glass lay everywhere, shining like diamonds in black liquor. The paramedics finally cleared the traffic jam and ordered everyone out of the way. First thing they did was check for a pulse. One of them jammed his finger tips into the man's neck, waited, and then shook his head.

Stokely pushed past the uniformed officers to a waitress. Her chin was bunched and tears pearled up on her lashes. Her eyes kept going to the broken body and all the blood.

Stokely took her by the arm to get her attention. "Is the other fellow still upstairs?"

She nodded. "I think so, yeah. I didn't see him come out."

Stokely signaled the officers to follow and started inside. "You two on me."

# Chapter Twenty-Nine

Noble scanned the small courtyard for any other means of escape. Air burst from his lungs in harsh gasps. He needed to get away and fast. He hurried around the perimeter of the courtyard, yanking on door handles. The ground floor doors were solid metal and locked from the inside. With the right tools, Noble could get one open, but it would take time.

He cursed and turned his attention to the small collection of automobiles parked in the lot. There was a black Porsche 911 that probably belonged to the club owner, a shiny new Nissan, and an ageing Renault with one mismatched door. A crack ran along the front windshield. The front bumper was held in place by an old metal clothes hangar and the tires needed air.

He needed something he could hotwire quickly without making too much noise. The Porsche and the Nissan would both be equipped with alarm systems. That left the Renault which had rolled off the production line during the Margaret Thatcher administration.

Police were already on scene. Uniformed officers wouldn't waste much time in their search. They'd find the busted window and move to block the tradesman's entrance.

Noble braced his back against the Porsche and kicked the passenger window of the Renault. It took two tries. The window spiderwebbed and sagged with the first impact. It fell in on the second. Noble reached inside, unlocked the doors and climbed through. Broken shards needled his knees and thighs. The inside smelled like stale cigarette smoke. Noble ignored the stinging glass insects and shifted around in the seat so he could use his boot on the steering column. It took three more kicks to smash open the key housing and then Noble went to work sorting the wires.

Without a knife, he had no way to cut the connections. He popped the glove box, found a half-empty pack of smokes, along with a license, registration, and crumpled petrol receipts. In the center console he found a stub of pencil and a pink Bic lighter. Working quickly, he wrapped the wires around the pencil, flicked the lighter, and starting burning through the rubber insulation.

***

Stokely scanned the stunned faces in the ground floor. None of them belonged to Goodfellow. She started up the steps and felt the draft from the broken window before she saw it. She stopped at the landing and stuck her head out. It was a short drop to the flagstones. A guy in Goodfellow's physical condition could easily make that jump. Stokely wheeled around and started back down. She reached the bottom, navigated a small corridor with a bathroom, and located the backdoor. It was locked from the inside. Stokely tried the push bar but it refused to budge.

She told the officer, "Find the manager. I want this door unlocked. Now."

He hurried off and Stokely cut back through the club, intent on circling the block.

\*\*\*

Noble twisted the wires together and the beat up Renault stuttered to life. A black cloud of oily smoke farted from the tailpipe. The fumes backfilled into the cab. Noble coughed and waved a hand in front of his face. The engine wheezed and chugged, threatening to stall every few seconds. Noble shifted into reverse and put his foot down.

The little Renault let out a bubbling scream as it hurtled backward toward the slatboard fence. Noble threw one arm over the passenger seat and twisted around, driving with one hand. The junker flounced over a sewer grate and threatened to go slipping over the flagstones, but Noble gripped the wheel hard and kept it on track. The rear bumper hit the timber construction at thirty miles an hour. The impact slammed Noble against the driver's seat, wrenching his neck painfully hard. There was a shriek of buckling wood and twisting metal. The doors parted enough that Noble was able to scrape the Renault through. The car launched from the tradesman's entrance like a cork from a bottle and clipped the front end of a minivan. Bumpers crunched with a twist of plastic and a jingle of glass.

# Chapter Thirty

Stokely leapt back in time to avoid being swatted by the wood slat door as it crashed open. A Renault shot through the opening, expelling clouds of noxious petrol. The rusted out wreck careened from the tradesman's entrance with a shriek of metal. Balding tires slipped over the pavers and the Renault cracked up against a blue minivan. The minivan came to a stop with a sudden jerk that slammed the driver into the steering wheel.

The Renault hitched and stalled.

The back bumper had missed Stokely by less than a foot. If she'd been just a little faster, she'd be road paste right now. One hand went to the gun on her hip while her heart migrated back down to her chest.

Goodfellow was behind the wheel and he locked eyes with Stokely. His brow warped into a frown. He turned his attention to the broken steering column, fumbling with the exposed wires.

Stokely dragged the department-issue Glock from her hip and took a two-handed grip, pushing it straight out with both hands, the way they'd taught in the Police College. "Out of the car, Goodfellow!"

He ignored her and sparked the wires under the dash. There was a loud rattle from under the bonnet. The Renault belched out a black cloud that smelled like burning oil.

"Goodfellow," Stokely shouted. She advanced on the Renault, aiming through the busted passenger side window. "Turn the car off and step out with your hands in the air. *Now!*"

He had one hand on the steering wheel. The other was on the gear shift. He shook his head. "I can't do that, Stokely. I'm sorry for jamming you up, but my mom is in danger."

"Let me guess," said Stokely. "The mysterious man with the eyepatch."

"That's right."

"Don't make me shoot you, Goodfellow." She advanced another step. She was close enough to reach out and grab the door handle. She might have done it, but feared Goodfellow would gas it and drag her along the cobblestones.

He studied her a moment and then said, "You're not gonna shoot me, Stokely."

He was right, of course. He was an unarmed man and shooting him would only land Stokely in front of a review board for unlawful use of deadly force. The case would be splashed across every headline by journalists eager to prove coppers were bloodthirsty sadists looking for any excuse to use their guns on innocent people. Never mind the fact that letting Goodfellow go meant more potential victims. She growled and reached for the door.

Goodfellow mashed the accelerator to the floor. The Renault leapt forward. The rear bumper came off in a scree of metal and snapping plastic, clattering across the pavers. Stokely snatched her hand back at the last second, unwilling to risk being dragged, and cursing herself for her cowardice. Goodfellow slalomed up the road, leaving a choking cloud of burning oil in his wake.

The driver of the minivan was out of his vehicle and shouting after Goodfellow, then demanding to know why Stokely hadn't done something to stop him. A bib of dark blood soaked his shirt front. Stokely ordered him to remain in his vehicle and wait for emergency services, an order he ignored.

Uniformed officers rounded the corner seconds later. Stokely gave them a description of the car and told them to put out an APB. She also ordered a point by point search of the surrounding neighborhoods. Goodfellow wasn't going far in that old death trap. The thing sounded like a diesel tractor with a broken head gasket.

She shook her head and holstered her weapon. That was twice she'd had Goodfellow dead to rights, and twice he'd gotten away. Conagher was going to have her guts for garters.

# Chapter Thirty-One

A FOG HORN SOUNDED in the mist-shrouded night. The sonorous voice echoed across the waters of the Thames. Wexler stood on the stern of the *Fair Fields*, an eighteen foot fishing trawler, one boot propped on the gunwale and his eyes scanning the lights of the distant shoreline. A cold wind blew across the river from the west, carrying a hint of brine and frost. Wexler's fingers felt like frozen stumps. Waves lapped silently at the hull and a buoy dinged occasionally.

Schneider appeared at Wexler's elbow. He was wrapped in a heavy coat with his collar turned up. He too eyed the shoreline, then the river, looking for other vessels. He said, "Think we're good?"

Wexler went on surveying the river for several seconds in silence then said, "Bring her up."

Schneider turned and snapped his fingers.

Müller came up the hatch dragging the dead girl's body wrapped in a tarp. "One of you give me a hand," he panted. "She's not light, you know?"

They had weighted the body and wrapped it in a heavy canvas tarp. The whole bundle probably weighed two hundred pounds. That was no guarantee the corpse would stay down. Wexler had disposed of his share of bodies in the past and sometimes they came bobbing back up even with all that weight. You never can tell. But dumping the body in the drink was better than dropping her in a dumpster or an alley. Salt water helps destroy evidence.

Schneider took hold of the other end. He and Müller hefted the dead girl up and over the side. The bundle hit the water with a smack, bobbed for a moment or two and then slowly sank. The three men stood on the deck of the boat and watched the evidence until it was swallowed by the depths.

Müller spat over the side. "Let's hope we don't have to do any more of those."

Schneider agreed, then climbed into the pilot house and fired up the engines. The trawler gave out a throaty snarl. Black water churned into white foam and the boat started for the shoreline.

Wexler watched the spot where the body had gone under, wondering what to do about his boss's new hobby. She was number four. The first had seemed like an accident. The Old Man liked things a little rough and it got out of hand, or so he said. Wexler could understand that. He liked a bit of rough play himself. Sometimes a lass needs a strong hand on the tiller. But the bodies were starting to pile up, so to speak.

Keiser's new fetish jeopardized the whole operation. They were so close to exacting revenge on Noble, the last thing they needed were a bunch of coppers snooping around.

Wexler felt his phone vibrate and put it to his ear without bothering to look at the number. "It's done."

"I thought you said Noble was going to cooperate," Keiser said.

Wexler frowned at the phone. "He knows we have his mother in our sights. He should behave himself."

"Think again," said Keiser. "He's escaped police custody and he's on the run."

"How do you know that?"

"It's all over the television," Keiser said. "What do you plan to do about it?"

Wexler's mouth was bone dry. He licked his lips. "The plan is still intact. The Haitian is on his way to Tampa and there's nothing Noble can do to stop him."

Keiser's voice was a deadly whisper. "Noble is dangerous as long as he's free. The plan hinges on his arrest and imprisonment."

"He can't get far," Wexler said. "All of London will be on the lookout. The police will pick him up before morning."

"And if they kill him?"

"Isn't dead just as good?"

"If I wanted him dead," Keiser shouted, "he'd be dead."

Wexler took the phone away from his ear and swallowed a hard knot of acid fear forming in his throat. For a moment he could feel the heat and searing pain. One hand went to the eyepatch. He said, "I'll find Noble. I'll put him back in police custody."

"See that you do."

The line went dead.

# Chapter Thirty-Two

Detective Inspector Stokely stood over the body on the sidewalk with her hands in her pockets and her shoulders drawn up. The man had fallen head first. Half his skull was sunken in and one side of his face bulged grotesquely. A police photographer snapped pictures from every angle, getting closeups, while a crime scene tech put down evidence markers. The bar had been closed for the night and the drunks were giving statements to a team of uniformed officers. Television crews had arrived. Three trucks were parked a block away and reporters at the yellow crime scene bunting clamored for a statement, but Stokely had sealed off the area to allow her people time to work. She ignored the reporters, gathered the ends of her coat, and hunkered down for a closer look. "Is his hair dyed?"

The medical examiner, a doctor named Sharma who had immigrated to the UK from India, nodded. He was kneeling next to the corpse, a clipboard in one hand and an ink pen tucked behind one oversized ear. "That's not all."

"What do you mean?"

"This man's had work done."

"As in plastic surgery?" Stokely asked.

Sharma used his ballpoint to indicate a small white line nearly hidden in the dead man's hairline. "It's good work and hard to tell, because the head is now deformed, but this man had surgery to alter the shape of his eyes."

"His eyes?"

Sharma bobbed his head up and down, then used his fingertips to pull the skin of his own forehead up, causing his eyes to open wider. "It was done to give him a more European appearance. If you ask me, this fellow is probably of Asian descent. I'll know more once I've had time to make a thorough investigation."

"Two Asian men," Stokely said to herself.

"What's that?" Sharma asked.

"Nothing." Stokely shook her head and stood up. She explored a molar with her tongue. Goodfellow had iced two men, both Asian, and one of them had undergone plastic surgery to change his appearance. This was looking less like a random murder and more like a conspiracy. How did Goodfellow, an American, connect to the Asians? Her first thought was drugs. Perhaps Goodfellow was part of an international smuggling ring and he'd had a falling out with his partners? That didn't explain Goodfellow's claim that he was innocent and that his mother was in danger. Goodfellow might just be a lunatic, but that didn't jibe with Stokely's read on the man. He seemed to be in control of his mental faculties, coldly calculating even. He could have killed Stokely in the interrogation room and he'd let her live. That part of the puzzle didn't fit with two dead bodies.

She was just about to go upstairs for a look about when she spotted DCI Conagher duck the crime scene tape. He'd dressed in a hurry. His tie was skewed and his collar stuck up in the back. His face was a mask of cold fury. He stamped up to Stokely and read her the riot act while reporters snapped pictures. Tomorrow's papers would feature black and white images with a body in the foreground and a Detective Chief Inspector chewing out a subordinate in the background.

"A fine mess you've made," Conagher was saying. "Bodies on the sidewalk. The press is going to have a field day."

"Something odd is going on here," Stokely told him. "This new victim is likely Asian as well. He's had plastic surgery to change his appearance."

"Lots of people do that nowadays," said Conagher. "I've got a niece not more than thirteen years old who wants a double mastectomy 'cause she's decided she's a he. And the hell of it is, if my sister doesn't allow it, the government says she can be put in jail. It's a funny old world. What does it matter?"

"I think we might be dealing with something more complicated than a simple killing spree. Goodfellow is mixed up in something and we need to figure out what. He insists he's innocent and that his mother is in danger."

"He's a criminal," Conagher said. "Did it ever occur to you he might be lying?"

"The thought crossed my mind."

"Don't get cheeky with me, Inspector."

"No, sir," Stokely muttered.

Conagher held up two fingers. "Twice now you've let this tosspot slip through your grasp."

"It won't happen a third time."

Conagher blew out his cheeks. "I'm beginning to think you aren't up to the job, Stokely. Maybe it's time I put someone else in charge of this investigation."

"This is my case. I can get Goodfellow. I just need a little more time."

Conagher considered it a moment, scratched absently behind one ear and said, "Stokely, I don't think you're cut out for this job. You want to prove me wrong? Put Goodfellow in bracelets."

"I'll bring him to you with a bow on top," Stokely promised. She had no clue how she was going to fulfill that promise, but she wasn't going to let Goodfellow scuttle her career. She didn't care what he was wrapped up in. She was going to find him and bring him to justice.

Conagher studied her another minute before turning on his heel and stalking away. Stokely watched him go, ignoring the cold hard fist closing around her heart. She waited until he ducked the crime scene tape and then went upstairs to see what she could learn about the fight and, hopefully, figure out just what in the hell Goodfellow was up to.

# Chapter Thirty-Three

Noble sheltered in the shadowy alcove of a recessed doorway. The hands on his Citizen were pointing to 3 in the morning and, at this hour, even London was getting sleepy. The streets were starting to empty out and the bars were closing. A social media whore—that's how Noble thought of them—plodded through Trafalgar Square with his phone attached to a stick, talking about hauntings in the area. Noble didn't know about hauntings, but there were certainly spooks about. He scanned the thinning crowd for familiar faces, at the same time he was searching for cops. He was just four blocks from the club and police would canvas the area. The stolen car was parked in a garage three blocks away. It wouldn't take Scotland Yard long to locate it. Noble needed to find the local station chief and get off the street before that happened.

He took a deep breath, blew out his cheeks, and stepped from the alcove. A bitterly cold breeze blew his hair back. Soft white flakes were coming down and melting before they reached the ground. The pavers were slick. Noble made his way across to Saint Martin in the Fields, stuffed his hands in his coat pockets and pretended to stare up at the architecture. He was watching the open square from the corner of his eye. No one took any notice of him but Noble felt exposed. He waited there as long as he dared, minutes stretched long, and he was just about to walk when a familiar voice said, "We meet again."

Noble rolled his eyes. "You gotta be kidding me. They made you Station Chief?"

"I've moved up in the world." Gregory Hunt cast a cautious look about the square and said, "Unlike some people."

Hunt was two years younger with blond hair and boyish good looks. He and Noble had found themselves on opposite sides of an operation in Mexico City not too long ago where Hunt had taken a bullet in the butt and now walked with a limp. He was dressed in a smart wool overcoat that cost as much as Noble's entire wardrobe and handmade Italian shoes. Hunt always did have an eye for the finer things.

They faced each other in front of the church, hands in their pockets and wind snatching at their coats.

"NOC work isn't for everybody," Noble said. "Some people are better off behind a desk in a nice cushy embassy job."

Hunt closed the distance. "Hell with you Noble. I was a first rate field officer until you got me shot."

"Keep dreaming Hunt. Money and fancy firearms don't make a good field officer. You were Foster's errand boy, nothing more. Now you've managed to land an embassy job because the new Director is more interested in yes-men than national intelligence."

The muscles in Hunt's jaw knotted into fists. "Keep your voice down."

Noble turned for an exaggerated look at the empty square. He said, "Someone would need a parabolic mic to hear us, and if they've got that kind of technology then it doesn't matter how loud we talk."

"You've got all the answers." Hunt took another step forward and now they were practically nose to nose. "If you're so smart, how'd you end up in such a mess?"

Noble wanted to sock him in the mouth. He clamped his teeth together and stared daggers.

Hunt grinned. "Not so smart after all. Where's the take?"

"I stashed it."

"That's awfully convenient," Hunt said. "You managed to stash the take before the defector got turned into a voodoo doll. How very convenient, for you."

"Believe me," Noble said. "Nothing about tonight has been convenient. My defector is dead, my op is blown, and the police are looking for me. I need to get off the street."

"Now you want my help?" Hunt showed mock surprise. "A minute ago you seemed to be implying that I wasn't in the same league."

"Cut the school yard crap, Hunt. You're the Station Chief," Noble reminded him. "It's your job to help non-official cover operatives in crisis. Now are you going to help, or not?"

Hunt cocked a thumb over his shoulder. "My car is this way."

They started across Trafalgar Square, Hunt limping on his bum leg and Noble walking beside him. Both men had their heads on a swivel. Noble should have felt better, but his sense of impending dread had only increased. Maybe it was the surprise appearance of Hunt, his hated nemesis, into an already stressful situation or all the questions surrounding Hap Chan's death, but Noble felt like he was getting closer to danger rather than further away. And that sense of foreboding built with every step.

"So where's the take?" Hunt asked again as they left the square for the ring of roads surrounding Trafalgar. He was stumping towards a grey Jaguar with dark tint idling at the curb. Silver exhaust clouds breathed from the tailpipe.

"Told you," Noble said. "I stashed it."

"Care to tell me where?"

"Nope."

"You always have to be a hardcase, don't you, Noble?" He opened the back door of the Jaguar and motioned Noble inside. "Okay tough guy, we're going to see just how tough you really are."

Noble stopped next to the open door and chewed the inside of one cheek. He asked, "Where are we going?"

"Someplace safe."

Noble's eyes narrowed. "I'm not getting in that car until I know where we're going."

"Don't make this hard on yourself, Noble. Get in the car."

Noble shook his head and started to back away. A gun barrel jammed into his ribs. A massive man, built like a dump truck in a dark suit with a military haircut, crowded close. He was half a foot taller and two feet wider. And he seemed to be smuggling bowling balls under his sleeves. He rumbled, "Get in the car, Noble."

# Chapter Thirty-Four

Detective Inspector Stokely was at her desk in the bullpen. A cup of Darjeeling was slowly turning to ice water at her elbow and the clock on her computer said 6:42 am. Her ponytail was falling out, leaving a few wild strands dancing on the air. She had a team of investigators scrubbing traffic cam footage around the club. Goodfellow had driven the busted old Renault three blocks before turning down an alley with no coverage and vanishing like smoke. So far they'd found no trace of him.

Stokely combed the national immigration database, searching through all the Asian immigrants into the country over the last few weeks. So far none of them matched the two dead men but it was like looking for a needle in a field of haystacks. It would help if she could narrow it down by ethnicity, but Stokely didn't even know if they were Chinese, Japanese, Korean, Filipino, or … At this early hour Stokely couldn't think of any other Asian countries.

The dead man from the club had a British driver's license with the name Terrance Graham. It was a forgery and a good one. The address on the driver's license was bogus. There were over a hundred Terry Grahams in the London phone book, more if you included the surrounding areas. Still, Stokely had a team calling every name on the list. Someone had his identity stolen and didn't even know it. Bit of a nasty surprise to be rang by the London police first thing in the morning and discover you're dead on a slab in the morgue.

Stokely opened another file, this one from Singapore, and scanned the face. No match. She closed the file and opened the next. Hopefully the ME would have an ID on the two victims soon. Knowing who had been murdered would go a long way in helping to figure out why they'd been killed.

Sleep crowded her brain and Stokely reached for the cold cup of Darjeeling. *Sleep when you're dead,* she told herself. She had a case to solve. She wanted Goodfellow in cuffs before the sun went down again and she had a suspicion that the two dead men would not be found in a database of legal immigrants. She gulped tea, put the cup aside, nearly missing the saucer, and closed out of the immigration database.

On a hunch, she navigated to the website of the Thai consulate in London—Thailand is synonymous with drugs—and she checked the staff page. None of the faces matched. Next she tried Vietnam, then Cambodia. It was a wild shot in the dark, but dead men with flawless fake IDs had Stokely thinking this was more than street thugs killing each other over territory or a drug deal gone wrong. Maybe Goodfellow was involved in international espionage. Nobody on the list of employees of the Cambodian embassy matched her corpses either. Stokely was just about to check China when her phone rang.

She put the receiver to her ear with one hand, operating the mouse with the other. "Stokely."

"Detective. It's sergeant Riley. You're not going to believe this."

"Try me."

"Remember the house where we found the dead Asian and apprehended Goodfellow? We found two more bodies."

"You're joking?" Stokely asked.

"They're in a flat across the street," said Riley. "Both shot in the head and, get this, the place is full of surveillance equipment."

Stokely felt like someone had just caught her an open hand blow to the face. She sat up straight in her chair. "Lock that scene down. No one goes in or out before I get there, not even forensics. Understand?"

"I'll make it happen," Riley said. "Think this has something to do with Goodfellow and the corpse we found next door?"

"It would be a wild coincidence if it wasn't," Stokely told him.

"My thoughts exactly."

She checked her watch. "I'll be there in ten minutes. I don't want anything touched."

"It's as you say, inspector."

Stokely hung up, snatched her coat from the back of her chair, and started for the elevator. She was halfway there when the door to Conagher's office opened and he stuck his head out. "Stokely. A word."

"I'm on my way to a crime scene right now, sir." She thumbed the button for the lift. "Uniforms just found two more dead bodies in a house right across the street from the first."

Conagher said, "My office. Now."

The lift dinged and the door rolled open but Stokely ignored it and went to Conagher's office on wooden legs with a belly full of acid fear, wondering what she had done now. She pushed past Conagher, smelling his cheap cologne, and he closed the door behind her. Then he stopped to pull the shades and Stokely's fear doubled.

"Should I sit down?" She asked.

"You're off the case," Conagher said.

"Please, sir. I can do this. We've got two more bodies and a room full of surveillance equipment. This is looking more and more like some kind of international spy ring. I think we've stumbled onto some kind of Oriental intelligence operation gone wrong."

"I know," Conagher told her. "I just got off the phone with a bloke from MI6. You're off the case. We've been ordered to stand down."

# Chapter Thirty-Five

She was crying again. Ezra was at his computer, working to isolate all the sounds in the audio recording. That's not as easy as they make it look on television. The call had been captured on a single audio channel, which meant Ezra had to load the file into Adobe Audition—the CIA was a multi-million dollar government funded program that still had to license private software from big tech companies—and painstakingly separate the voices from the background noise, then isolate the noises. It was long, tiring work that required all of his flagging concentration. He hoped to find something, anything, that might prove Noble's innocence. He was hard at it when he heard a gentle sniffle.

His fingers paused on the keys.

Gwen had pushed her glasses up on her head and was dabbing red rimmed eyes with a tissue. She sniffed, trying hard to keep quiet, and wiped her nose. She'd been crying off and on ever since they'd learned Noble had been picked up by Gregory Hunt and was being held for enhanced debrief—industry slang for interrogation. Neither analyst had any illusions about what that meant.

Torture.

And Greg Hunt had beef with Noble that went all the way back to Mexico City. Noble had hooked Hunt up to a car battery. Ezra could only imagine what inventive tortures Hunt had in store for Noble.

Turnabout is, after all, fair play. The thought sent a shiver up Cook's spine.

He wheeled across, his chair making a small scree on one bad caster, and put an arm around Gwen, pulling her into a sideways hug. She stuck her face against his chest and let out a choked sob. Ezra whispered, "Don't let McHale catch you crying."

"McHale can stuff it," Gwen said in a desultory voice heavy with tears. "He's a big dummy."

Ezra cracked a grin despite himself. "I'll see your dummy and raise you a poopy-head."

Gwen curled a fist and popped it against Ezra's arm, but there was no malice in it, only exhausted defeat. She said, "The Noble I know isn't capable of treason."

"I don't want to believe it either," Ezra said.

"So what are we going to do about it?"

"We're going to do what we do best," Ezra said. "The only thing we can do. We're going to take this audio recording apart piece by piece, we're going to dig through the financials, we're going to look at everybody involved, and we'll keep at it until we've got something, anything, that blows this phone call up."

She took a deep, shuddering breath, pushed gently away from him and mopped tears from her eyes. Pushing her glasses back into place, she said, "Sorry I'm such an emotional wreck."

"Don't apologize."

She tried a smile and it came off an embarrassed lopsided grin. "Guess you're having second thoughts about letting me move in now that you know what a big cry baby I can be?"

Ezra leaned forward and fixed her with a serious stare. "Goonies never say die."

It was a line from one of their favorite movies.

Gwen took his face in both hands, kissed him and asked, "How did you get so sweet?"

"I come from a long line of sweet," Ezra told her. "My family has been sweet for several generations. Just wait till you meet Grandma Cook."

Gwen turned serious. "I'm meeting the family now?"

Once upon a time, Ezra might have retreated from this topic. Things with Gwen, current situation notwithstanding, were going great and he didn't want to screw it up. But that was the old Ezra. Having half his face blown off by a ricochet had realigned his perceptions. Life was short. Laying in the hospital, rehabbing his busted ankle, Ezra had decided to go after what he wanted, and he wanted Gwen. He said, "I'd like that."

She smiled. "Me too."

"It's a date," Ezra said, "but first we have to untangle this snafu in London."

Gwen snapped off a salute and turned back to her computer. "How's it coming with the audio?"

"Found something that I think warrants looking into."

"Oh?"

"Something about this word bothers me." Ezra had been listening to the audio on headphones. He unplugged them so Gwen could hear and played the bit of recording.

Noble's voice came through the speakers; "*...not flushing my career with the Company for five-hundred Gs.*"

"Did you hear it?" Ezra asked.

Gwen shrugged and shook her head.

"Listen again," he said. "Pay close attention to the hard G consonant at the end."

He played it again.

Gwen listened intently and asked, "What are you thinking?"

"Something about that consonant is off," Ezra said. "I don't like it."

"I don't like anything about this," Gwen said.

He was about to play it again when his line buzzed. The call was coming from the third floor basement where Ben Jameson was working to ID the voice of the Asian male on the audio recording. Ezra put it on speaker. "What did you find out, Ben?"

"Got a preliminary on that voice sample," Ben told them, "but it's not a hard match."

"Who is it?" Gwen asked.

"Comp analysis says it's a Chinese intelligence officer for the People's Republic named Kwang Luo. I pulled his file. He's a high-ranking officer in the CCP. He got his start in the field and, rumor has it, did wet work for the Chinese before rival intel outfits made book on him. After that he got moved up to operations. Our info on him is spotty at best, but we think he's in charge of China's Macau desk."

Ezra closed his eyes and breathed through his nose. A deal for millions with a high-ranking CCP intel officer would put the final nail in Noble's coffin so far as McHale was concerned.

Gwen had a look of utter defeat on her face. "You said it wasn't a hard match. How close?"

"Eighty-seven percent."

"Good enough for government work," Ezra muttered.

"More than enough for McHale," Gwen said.

Ezra nodded slowly. A seventy-five percent match was close enough to positive for operational standards. Eighty percent was enough to act on. Eighty-seven? It was practically a signed confession. There was very little chance the computer had made a mistake at that point.

"What do you want me to do?" Ben asked.

"I don't want you to do anything until you hear back from us," Ezra said and hung up the phone.

# Chapter Thirty-Six

Hunt and a pair of bully boys from the CIA's Office of Security took Noble to a safehouse less than a block from the River Thames. Hunt took a winding route in an effort to throw off Noble's sense of direction. It almost worked. London is a confusing warren of twisting lanes, but Noble glimpsed the wide expanse of the Thames out the passenger side window as they turned down a narrow side street. Hunt backed into a private garage on the ground floor and Noble was herded from the car.

They marched him through the silent residence, into a back room with shuttered windows, and searched him before putting him in a hardback chair and securing his wrists together behind the backrest with zip ties. They took his wallet, his shoes, and his belt, but missed Stokely's hairpin attached to his coat sleeve.

Soundproof tile lined the walls. The floor was bare concrete with a drain in the center. The smooth slab against the bottoms of his bare feet felt like ice on a frozen lake. An overhead vent blew cold air on the back of his neck. The whole experience was designed to scare and demoralize him. Noble had been the one doing the questioning plenty of times. He knew how the game was played. He was supposed to see that drainage hole—which was not a drain at all, but a simple hole dug in the floor—and wonder what sort of nightmarish tortures they had in store.

The door, a stout oak portal lined with riveted steel, groaned open and Hunt came in carrying a car battery with leads attached.

Noble took one look at the battery and snorted. He'd used a similar method to get info out of Hunt a few years back. But Noble hadn't been working for the CIA back then, at least not in any official capacity, and didn't have to worry about an after action report. "Piss off, Hunt. You don't scare me."

"No?" Hunt asked with a friendly smile.

"No." Noble shook his head. "We both know you aren't going to use that on me."

Hunt, boyish grin firmly fixed on his handsome features, laid the battery at Noble's feet, took the leads, and touched them to Noble's thigh.

The veins in his neck bulged. Shockwaves of exquisite pain raced up Noble's frame. Every muscle in his body contracted agonizingly hard. Sweat sprang out on his skin and his jaw clamped tight.

It was only a moment—Hunt pulled the leads away after one quick tickle—but for Noble the brief second stretched out like a lifetime of anguish. His muscles went on contracting painfully for several seconds afterward and one of his wisdom teeth had shattered. A loud buzzing filled his ears. He let out a string of curses, turned his head to the side and spit out the broken remains of his tooth.

Hunt said, "Hurts, doesn't it."

With the electricity gone, cold set in, weaving icy fingers through his skin and into his bones, making his whole frame shake painfully hard. Noble tried to control the trembling but it was a wasted effort. He said, "Screw you, Hunt."

"I guess the shoe is on the other foot." Hunt put the leads down, laying them on the bare concrete teasingly close to Noble's bare toes, and then went and fetched a folding chair from the corner. He sat down, took a moment to adjust his trouser legs so that he didn't ruin the crease and said, "A little role reversal if you will."

"You sick bastard," Noble said, breathing through the pain. "This will never fly. You think you'll get away with this? Think you can torture a field officer and no one's going to question it? Wizard's going to nail you for this."

Confusion passed over Hunt's features. "What game are you playing, Noble?"

"I could ask you the same thing," Noble spat. "My mission went off the wire. My defector is dead, murdered, and there's a contract out on my mother. The police like me for murder. I need to get out of London and fast. Instead you're using this as an opportunity for a little payback."

Hunt watched Noble as he spoke, studying him, and then said, "Where's the take?"

"Didn't you hear me?" Noble said. "Someone is going to kill my mother. I need to get out of here."

"Sure." Hunt nodded. "Where's the take?"

"Hell with you," Noble said.

Hunt bent down, grasped the leads and brushed Noble's bare foot. Pain rocked his body again. He arched back in the chair, heard the wood start to creak under the strain, and a long stuttering scream jerked from his throat.

When it was over and the wave of pain was washing back down his mental shoreline, Hunt asked, "Where's the take, Noble? What did you do with the Chinese research?"

"I told you." Noble spoke between gasping breaths. The ache in his muscles was cold fire and his brain felt too big for his head. "I stashed it."

"Where?"

Noble shook his head.

Hunt held up the leads. "Want a little more?"

"Get Wizard on the phone," Noble said. "I'll talk to Wizard. I'm not talking to you."

"Dulles can't help you now, Noble. You're in a world of trouble. We know all about your little deal with the Chinese."

"What're you talking about?"

"Did you really think you could get away with it?" Hunt set the leads aside and took out his phone. He queued up an audio file and pressed play.

Noble heard his own voice coming from the speaker and the bottom dropped out of his world.

# Chapter Thirty-Seven

"That's not me." Noble listened to the recording and his pulse was a wild drumbeat in his ears. It sounded like him, but he had never said those things. He'd never made that phone call. His mind raced to make sense of it. How could he be having a conversation he didn't remember, with a man he didn't know? None of it made any sense. He shook his head. "That's not me. I never said those things. This is some kind of trick."

Hunt rolled his eyes. He sat across from Noble in the flimsy folding chair, holding the phone out so Noble could hear. "You really expect me to believe that?"

"Hunt, listen to me, I never made that phone call." Noble was leaning forward, straining his arms against the back of the chair. His feet were numb and his mouth kept filling with blood from his shattered tooth. He turned his head to the side and spat the hot copper taste of pennies. "I'm being set up."

"Someone forced you to make that call?"

Noble opened his mouth to deny the accusation, but it was no good. Hunt had an axe to grind and no amount of logic or reason was going to bring him around to the truth. He wanted Noble to be guilty and the audio was incredibly convincing. If the shoe were on the other foot, and Noble were in Hunt's place, he'd be convinced too. Noble closed his eyes a moment and said, "This was all set up by Otto Keiser."

"An investment banker is framing you for murder?" Hunt put the phone back in his pocket. Noble was afraid he'd reach for the leads again, but he folded his arms across his chest and shook his head, a school teacher dealing with a particularly petulant child who has become exhaustive.

"Get Wizard on the phone," Noble said. "He knows about Keiser. He'll back me."

"You don't get it. Do you?" Hunt grinned, and it was a nasty, vindictive grin. "Dulles isn't running this op anymore. McHale is in charge now and he's authorized me to use whatever means necessary."

Noble felt an iron band closing around his chest. "I'm innocent. I'm being set up."

"Then why did we find the two million in a Swiss account belonging to you?"

"You really think I'd be stupid enough to wire money to an account with my name on it?"

"It's a numbered account, but we traced it back to you," Hunt said. "It's all over Noble. You're bent. You tried to make a play and you got caught. Now man up. Tell us who your contact is and what you did with the Chinese research."

Noble pressed his lips together and worked to silently pry Stokely's hairpin from the sleeve of his coat with his fingertips.

"There's no sense playing tough," Hunt said. "You're going to break eventually. Everyone does. Why don't you tell me where you stashed the take and make this easy on yourself?"

Noble had the hairpin wedged into the locking mechanism on the plastic zip ties and he was leveraging it back and forth, trying to separate the teeth. It was difficult to know if he was making any progress without being able to see, but he kept at it. There was no sense trying to reason with Hunt. He was beyond reasoning. Noble slowly wedged the hairpin deeper into the plastic teeth, flexing his forearms in an effort to quietly loosen the zip ties.

Hunt said, "Last chance, Noble. I want the name of your contact and the location of the stash."

"Sorry, Hunt. That's classified. I could tell you, but then I'd have to kill you."

"Funny guy," Hunt said without a trace of humor. He nodded, reached for the leads and said, "Okay, funny guy. Let's see how tough you Special Operations people really are."

The hairpin separated the last of the teeth and the plastic restraint went slack. Noble lashed out with his bare foot, kicking Hunt's shin, then exploded from the chair.

His fists pumped like mad pistons. A wild melee ensued as Noble pressed Hunt into the corner with a flurry of desperate attacks. He had just seconds before the Office of Security people came crashing through the door. Noble used his forearm to block a haymaker aimed at his ear, slammed an open palm into Hunt's mouth, rocking his head back on his shoulders and mashing his lips flat. Hunt rebounded off the wall with a hollow boom. Blood rimmed his mouth and his eyes were swimming, unfocused. Noble used the opportunity to swipe Hunt's legs out from under him with a swift kick, then wrapped Hunt in a choke hold.

The door burst open and the two Office of Security men spilled through.

Noble yanked Hunt around, using him as a shield, one hand pressed savagely against his head and the other cranking his chin around until his neck was at the extreme limit of its flexibility.

"That's far enough," Noble told them. "Drop those guns or I'll snap his neck like a chicken."

# Chapter Thirty-Eight

Stokely arrived at the medical examiner's office just after nine in the morning. She was running on caffeine and curiosity. She didn't like losing her case, especially to shadowy government entities. She'd come up against the Ministry of Intelligence twice before and both times there had been a reason for the stand down order. This was the first time she had been told to back off a case without being told why. It didn't sit well.

She flashed her badge at the desk clerk, signed her name into the log book, and then pushed through a pair of swinging doors into the *bodyshop*, as the cops jokingly called it. The room was long, low, and cavernous, if caverns could be brightly lit. A dozen examination tables were lined up along the length of the room and one whole wall was covered in freezers. The smell of disinfectant stung Stokely's nostrils. Sharma was at the far end, leaning over the body of a young blonde girl.

Stokely took a seafoam green smock from the bin, grabbed a pair of safety goggles and made her way along the line of tables, searching for her most recent murder victims. None of the bodies matched.

"Hey Sharma," she said as she pulled on the smock just to be in compliance with city ordinances. She wasn't observing a cut, and didn't really need the protective gear, but if anyone spotted her without regulation safety precautions in here, she'd be in a jam.

Sharma glanced up at her and then pointed to the blonde girl. "See this? Seventeen and she dropped dead of cardiac failure. She's not the first either. There's a pandemic of otherwise young healthy people dying suddenly. I'm at a loss to explain it."

"That's a real shame," Stokely said and changed the subject. "Two new cuts came in." She gave him the address and said, "I think they're somehow related to the Asian man who was stabbed to death, along with the guy we scraped up off the sidewalk early this morning."

He nodded. "I know the ones you're talking about."

"Where are they? I'd like to get a look at them."

He reached for a crisp white linen and used it to polish the scalpel he was holding. "I'd love to help you, but they're gone."

Stokely's brows went up. "Gone? Where did they go?"

"Several men from the Home Office swooped in and loaded up all four of your victims." He finished cleaning his tools and then draped the blood spotted linen over his shoulder. "You just missed them. They gave me the usual lines about national security and top secret."

Stokely put her hips against one of the tables and crossed her arms. "MI6 wants to make sure no one gets a look at those bodies. Wonder why?" She was speaking more to herself than Sharma.

He shrugged. "I can't say, but I did get a preliminary on the two new bodies before they were carted off, and I can tell you with almost one hundred percent certainty they were both American."

"What makes you say that?"

An embarrassed smile reworked the lines of Sharma's face.

"Out with it," Stokely said with a laugh.

"Dentistry mostly," Sharma said in an apologetic tone. "They'd both had braces."

Stokely nodded. She had a slightly misaligned tooth right in the front but it had never really bothered her. The British certainly didn't share the American obsession for precision dentistry, though that attitude had been changing in recent years. Stokely blamed Hollywood. Suddenly the whole world felt they needed straight white teeth and washboard abs. "You said it was *mostly* dentistry. What else did you find?"

He held up a finger, like a professor pointing out a particularly interesting fact to a room full of students. "Their pocket litter was distinctly American."

Medical examiners and homicide detectives are good at decoding bits of information from seemingly inconsequential detritus found in the pockets of murder victims. You can learn a lot about a person from the random collection of junk in their pockets.

Stokely said, "I'm listening."

"One man had Marlboro cigarettes," Sharma said. "Not damning by itself but he also had a breath mint tin from a shop in Washington DC."

"Bit of a dead giveaway," Stokely commented.

Sharma nodded. "The other was carrying a pocket knife. I'd never heard of the brand so I looked it up online. It's a very expensive folding knife made by a company in Colorado. Retails for about three hundred U.S. dollars."

Her brows went up. "People pay that much for a folding knife?"

"Americans do apparently."

"Yes well, gun culture and all that," Stokely muttered. "What about the bloke with the bad dye job? Did you find out anything about him?"

Sharma shook his head. "He's a bit of a mystery I'm afraid. He'd had plastic surgery to make himself less Asian, but that's about all I can tell you. However, I'm one hundred percent certain your first victim was Chinese, from Shanghai."

Stokely gaped. "How do you know that?"

Sharma looked proud of himself. "As you know, I'm from the mysterious sub-continent of India." He placed his palms together and gave a slight bow. "We have our ways."

Stokely grinned. "Give."

"He had a Chinese identification card hidden in the sole of his shoe."

"Mysterious sub-continent my arse," Stokely said.

They shared a laugh.

Stokely thanked him for the info, asked him to keep her visit quiet, and left wondering what sort of drama the Americans and Chinese were up to. And how much did MI6 know? More importantly, was it worth pursuing?

# Chapter Thirty-Nine

Noble pressed hard against Hunt's jaw, twisting his head round until he heard vertebrae creak like rusty screen door hinges. Hunt let out a plaintive wheeze and his face turned the color of ripe tomatoes. Noble used Hunt's body as a shield and said, "One more step and I'll break his neck."

"Really think you can win?" Simms asked.

Dunlop and Simms had blocked the door and their guns were drawn. Both men would be good shots, not good enough to squeeze a bullet past Hunt's head and into Noble's face, but they'd pull the trigger the first time they found an opening. Noble adjusted his grip on Hunt and said, "I think if I can't win, I can at least do some damage on my way out. Which one of you boys wants to explain how a Station Chief got his neck broke on your watch? What do you think that will do for your careers?"

Their confidence slipped.

Noble said, "Put those guns on the floor unless you want to call Langley and tell McHale the Station Chief is dead."

When they didn't move fast enough, Noble gave Hunt's jaw a hard jerk. Hunt let out a piercing scream.

The security men hesitated a fraction of a second longer, then lowered their weapons. They bent and placed them on the ground at their feet, stood back up, and stared balefully at Noble.

"Now kick them behind you."

After a brief, bitter glance between them, they did as Noble instructed and sent the handguns sliding across the bare concrete.

Noble said, "You know the rest. Come on."

Simms laced his fingers together behind his head and got down on his knees. Dunlop took a little longer but he got there in the end.

Hunt said, "I'm gonna make sure you pay for this, Noble."

His words came out strained and thin.

"Temper," Noble said. "It's unbecoming of a Station Chief."

"You're finished," Hunt choked out.

Noble said, "Let's have it, Hunt."

"Have what?"

"I know you've got a ridiculously expensive piece on you," Noble said. "I want it. Now."

Hunt reached in his jacket and slipped a nickel-plated Kimber with mother of pearl grips from a shoulder holster.

"By the barrel," Noble ordered.

Hunt passed it over his shoulder.

Locking his left arm tight around Hunt's neck, Noble let go with his right hand just long enough to snag the weapon. He ripped it from Hunt's grasp and smacked the muzzle hard into Hunt's temple. Stainless steel met flesh with a solid crack. Hunt winced.

"How many other people in this safehouse?" Noble asked.

"It's just us," Hunt said.

"You sure about that?" Noble asked. "I see anyone else and I'll kill them on sight."

"It's just us three," Hunt insisted.

"Good." Noble adjusted his grip and started edging toward the door. "We're all going to the car. You two stay on your knees and keep those fingers locked tight."

"What do you want us to do?" Dunlop asked. "Crawl on our knees?"

"That or I could ice you both right now," Noble told him.

Hunt said, "You've lost it, Noble. You're completely off the deep end. You know that?"

"What was it the cat said to Alice?" Noble asked. "We're all a little mad here?"

"Psychopath," Hunt muttered.

"Careful," Noble told him. "This psychopath has a gun to your head. And I'm desperate, Hunt. Plenty desperate. Don't push me."

"Fine," Hunt said. "What's your play, Noble?"

"Let's move," Noble instructed. He dragged Hunt backward through the door into the short hall that led to the garage and the two security men shuffled forward on their knees.

# Chapter Forty

Fifteen minutes later, Hunt had an icepack pressed against the back of his neck. His blond hair was in disarray. His face pinched in pain and a fire raged in his gut. His neck wasn't quite as bad as he was making out, but he was on a video call with Langley, waiting for McHale. He wanted to look convincing. He adjusted the icepack and let out a long theatrical sigh.

He worked out of a small room on the third floor of the US Embassy. The office was just a desk with a lamp, a computer, and a wall-mounted safe hidden behind a famous reprint of a John Everett Millais. Hunt thought the title of the piece was *Ophelia*, but it might have been *The Lady in the Lake*. Fine art was not his area of expertise. Late morning sunlight flooded the single window. The computer was on a secure, encrypted connection to Langley and the office was soundproof, swept twice a week for listening devices.

Gwendolyn Witwicky's face filled the laptop screen. Her eyes were huge and worried behind thick lenses. She said, "Noble did that?"

Hunt started to nod, winced, and said, "Nearly twisted my head right off. He would have killed me but Dunlop and Simms stopped him before he could manage it."

Cook raked a hand through his hair. "None of this makes any sense. We know Jake. He wouldn't do something like this."

Hunt gave the nerd a flat look. "Remember Mexico?"

Cook rocked his head side to side. "Okay, point taken, but we really think something else might be going on."

"Noble's finally flipped his lid," Hunt said. "Happens all the time. Field agents watch drug dealers and rogues getting rich and Noble decided it was his turn to make a pile of money."

A look passed between Cook and Witwicky. Noble had clearly done a number on them. Before they could offer up any more excuses, the door in the situation room clicked open and McHale swept in, closely followed by the Deputy Director of Operations.

Hunt fixed his face, making sure the pain was evident, and moved the ice pack around to the side of his neck, so that it would be clearly visible.

McHale pushed between the pair of computer cowboys. He said, "Do I understand correctly, Mr. Hunt? Noble has managed to escape your custody?"

Hunt launched into his story, making it seem as if Noble had done his level best to kill Hunt and the security men. He finished with, "We'd all be dead right now if not for our training."

Wizard said, "Training my foot."

"What's that?" McHale asked.

"Nothing," Wizard grunted.

McHale turned back to the camera. His peevish face twisted in a frown. "Any idea where Noble is now?"

Hunt started to shake his head and a very real bolt of pain raced up his neck into his brain. He grimaced. "None. He stole my car and that's the last we've seen of him."

"Any tracer on the car?" Wizard asked.

Hunt hesitated a moment. "It's my personal car."

"That's no excuse," Wizard said. "You're the station chief Mr. Hunt. What if something happened to you? Ever heard of a guy named William Buckley?"

Hunt let that go. He hadn't bothered to put a tracer on his personal vehicle, because he didn't want the CIA monitoring his every move. He said, "It wouldn't matter. Noble's a field agent. He knows what we know. He'd either find the tracer and remove it, or ditch the car."

"At least we'd have some idea where to start looking," Wizard said.

"Done is done," McHale said, putting an end to the debate. "Noble is a serious threat to this agency, Mr. Hunt. Use every tool at your disposal to find him and bring him in, do you understand me?"

"Yes, sir." Hunt nodded and this time forgot to play up his injuries. "I'll take Noble down."

"That might not be so easy," Wizard said.

McHale turned to him for an explanation.

Wizard thumbed the unlit cigarette like he was thumbing a rope of ash. "The police have an APB out on Noble. Every bobby in London will be looking for him."

"We're the CIA," McHale said. "I should hope we can manage to find him before a bunch of untrained Brits."

"Many hands make light loads," Wizard rasped. "Lot of police in Great Britain."

McHale looked like he wanted to curse but he turned back to the camera. "Hunt, I want you to co-ordinate with Cook and Whitaker..."

"Witwicky," she corrected him in a small voice that McHale ignored.

"... and find Noble before the British authorities. If you can't manage that, your next posting will be Chief of Station in Antarctica."

"Consider it done," Hunt said, silently seething with newfound hatred for Noble.

McHale turned back to Wizard. "Jacob Noble is *not* going to make an international incident and embarrass me my first month in the director's seat."

# Chapter Forty-One

Noble had both hands cramped on the wheel of the Jaguar and his knuckles were white moons. Hunt's expensive Kimber semi-auto .45 caliber lay in the passenger seat. Noble was headed west, along Grosvenor Road, careful to stay below the speed limit, but his mind was working at warp speed.

He badly wanted to get his hands on a phone. He wanted to call Burke. His old mentor should be at the marina by now. Noble needed to know mom was okay.

He stopped at a red. Icy droplets peppered the windshield of Hunt's car, triggering the auto wipers.

Hunt's car!

How long had he been driving it? He'd escaped just after nine in the morning. The digital display on the dash said it was almost ten. The numbers blazed at him in soft neon green. He'd been driving random loops around London for nearly an hour. It felt like minutes.

Noble scanned the street. He was on a commercial boulevard with shops lining both side. A corner café was busy with patrons filling up on java before they started the work day.

A horn sounded behind him. Noble glanced up. The light had turned green. He eased on the gas and glided through the intersection, searching for a place to park.

As Station Chief Hunt would have top of the line security and that meant his vehicle likely had a tracker, in case he was ever rolled up by a foreign intelligence service. Hunt and his bullyboys were probably tracking the car right now.

He wedged into a spot a little too tight for the Jaguar, knocking the back bumper against a Mini Cooper, switched off the engine, stuffed Hunt's pistol in his waistband, buzzed all the windows down, climbed out and put the keys on the roof.

He was counting on an enterprising thief to come along and steal it.

His bare feet touched the cobbled stones and an electric chill went up his legs. He resisted the urge to hop around hooting like an owl. His flesh felt like it would stick to the pavers and his core temperature plummeted despite his overcoat. He crossed his arms over his chest and shivered. Even a winter parka won't help a guy with frozen feet. The cold was sapping Noble's ability to think.

*Get some shoes and get off the street,* he told himself.

He hurried along the sidewalk, trying not to run, but he didn't want his bare feet touching the freezing pavers any longer than absolutely necessary and that forced him to do a comical jog. His breath steamed out in silver bursts. He hurried past a breakfast nook with a big picture window where people gave him funny looks. One man nudged his wife and pointed.

Noble's internal chant had changed to; *find shoes save mom find shoes save mom*

He had already determined to walk in the first clothing store he found, pick up the first pair of shoes that fit, and run. The employees would call the cops and the theft would be reported. They'd give a description and then Stokely and the cops would be prowling the area, but Noble's toes would have frost bite if he went much longer without shoes. He couldn't save mom if he had to go to the hospital and have his toes amputated.

Before he could put that plan into action, Noble spotted a small knot of people in front of a clinic handing out leaflets. They were modestly dressed, none of them had blue hair dye, and they weren't wearing sandwich boards that said the end is near. In short, they looked like regular folks.

He hurried up to them on bare feet, arms clasped around his chest, shivering. He had pink roses in both cheeks, his hair was a mess, and Hunt had split his bottom lip in the fist fight. A bit of blood had frozen into a black clot in the corner of his mouth.

The building was an abortion clinic and the group was handing out tracts about the sanctity of human life. A middle-aged man in a heavy parka and a pub cap saw Noble and said, "Looks like you've had a hard go of it, mate. Need the police?"

Noble shook his head. It was a shuddering jerky movement. "Couple of punks mugged me. Took my shoes and wallet."

"We should have the police around," one of the women said. The others agreed. One already had her phone out.

"No sense bothering the police," Noble said. "The muggers will be long gone by now. I just really need a pair of shoes. My feet are freezing. Can you spare a little cash."

The heavyset man with the parka looked Noble over and asked, "What size are you then?" He stepped over and put his own foot down next to Noble's.

Noble had to do the conversion in his head. UK sizes tended to be a half step down. "Ten."

"I'm eleven." The man bent and unlaced his boots.

"I can't take your shoes," Noble said.

"Not to worry," he said. "My car is parked right over there and I've got a pair of trainers in the boot. Promised the wife I'd start running more."

"A promise he hasn't kept," one of the women piped up.

The man slipped off his boots and passed them over.

"Thank you," Noble said as he pulled the boots onto his bare feet. The insides were warm and slightly damp, and he'd probably end up with athlete's foot. Small price to pay. He thanked the man profusely as he laced them up.

The group took up a small collection, each of them donating a few pounds, and they put the money into a tract about God and salvation. One of the women pushed it into Noble's hands. "Hope your day gets better, luv."

He took the tract and thanked her. "This means a hell of a lot."

He was about to say more when sirens screamed.

Adrenaline flooded his arms and legs. He turned in time to see two blue and yellow police cruisers brake at the curb. Flashing lights strobed the front of the clinic. Noble was backing away, ready to run, when a uniformed officer stepped from the lead car and said, "Going to have to ask you folks to disperse. It's illegal to protest in front of a medical office."

"We're not protestors," the heavy-set man, now in his socks, told the officer. "We're just handing out literature."

The cops weren't interested in excuses and ordered them to move along. An argument broke out about the right to peaceably assemble. People on the street stopped to watch. Some of them told the police to leave off, others wanted the Christians in handcuffs. The latter group got their wish. When the heavyset man and his friends refused to leave the police started rounding them up and shoving them in the back of the squad cars. By that time Noble was halfway to the corner, the Bible tract with the money clutched tight in one fist.

# Chapter Forty-Two

The sun was a fat red fruit hanging low when Noble joined a line of tourists for the Tower Bridge. There was a short movie on the history of the iconic structure and then the crowd pressed into a lift that carried them to the top. Noble stepped out into a long glass corridor that spanned the Thames, one hand still clutching the Bible tract.

His thoughts turned to mom. Burke had promised he was on the first flight to Tampa. It was the best Noble could do. There was no way he could get there in person, not in time to save mom. And Burke was a former Delta Operator. He might be past his prime, but still plenty capable of violence when the situation called for it.

*If he makes it to Saint Pete in time*, Noble's brain insisted. *God, please let him make it in time.*

He wasn't even aware it was a prayer. Ever since Iran, he'd been doing that a lot, talking to God without realizing he was doing it. He leaned on the railing and looked at the Bible tract without really seeing. His fingers worried at the edges while he waited.

After picking up a new burner phone, Noble had placed a call to an old acquaintance and cashed in a chip. It was a huge ask and had taken the better part of an hour, cajoling and threatening, but he'd finally convinced his friend to meet. Now he stood in the center of the span, gazing across the wide and winding expanse of the Thames.

He waited the better part of an hour and had just turned to leave when he felt a gun poke him in the ribs.

Sasha Duval was a small man with thinning white hair and a rodent face. He had haunted eyes and a weak chin. Noble was reminded of a frightened mouse. Duval was bundled in a thick parka and pressed close to Noble so that no one could see the little .22 caliber semiautomatic in one trembling hand.

Noble said, "Is that a gun in your pocket or are you happy to see me?"

"You said never break protocol." His accent was laced with French. "This is not how it's supposed to work. We were never to meet in person."

A few years ago, Duval stole classified information about illicit government dealings and published the information on the internet. His website made him famous, but also put him in the crosshairs. He was wanted by the United States and Great Britain, along with a dozen other countries, for espionage. Noble had rescued him from a rogue CIA agent and stashed him, much to the chagrin of the CIA.

"We can't talk here," Noble said. "We're exposed."

Duval dug the pistol into Noble's ribs. "What's so important that you break protocol and ask to meet in person?"

"Someone is trying to kill my mother."

"Your mother? How's she wrapped up in it?"

"I'll explain later."

"I'm not going anywhere until I know what's going on," said Duval. "How do I know you aren't going to turn me over to the CIA?"

"I'm the guy who helped you escape them."

Duval shrugged. "That was a long time ago."

"Not that long ago." For Noble, it felt like yesterday. He still had nightmares where he watched Sam Gunn die over and over. He heard the gunshots in his sleep and saw the stricken terror in her eyes as she pitched over the railing into the icy waters of the Seine. He heard the awful splash and woke in cold sweats.

"In our world, alliances change with the weather," Duval said.

"I'll give you the short version; an investment banker framed me for murder and sent a hit man to kill my mother."

"How do I know this isn't a trick?" Duval asked. "How do I know you aren't here to kill me?"

Noble reached the end of his tether. He didn't have the time or the patience to handle Duval with kid gloves. His arms moved with the muscular grace of a hunting panther, trapped the pistol, locking up Duval's wrist, and gave a savage twist. Duval let go of the weapon with an effeminate shriek.

Noble turned the pistol around and stuffed it against Duval's ribcage. The barrel sunk into soft rolls of flesh. "If I wanted you dead, you'd be dead," Noble said. "Walk with me."

Duval swallowed and walked on wooden legs. "Where are we going?"

"Your safehouse," Noble said. "Every cop in London is looking for me. I need someplace to lay low."

They joined the flow of tourists headed for the far side of the bridge. Noble hunched his shoulders against the cold and discreetly inspected the gun. It was a Walther; a fine brand, but the slide was sticky and the oil smelled gummy. "How long has it been since you cleaned this thing?"

"I don't know," Duval admitted with a shrug. "A year. Maybe longer."

Noble ejected the magazine and cycled the action. There was no round in the chamber. Noble gave Duval a look.

"I'm a lover not a fighter."

Noble shook his head, slotted the magazine back into place, and hauled back on the slide. He did a press check to make sure it had chambered a round.

Duval said, "Careful, eh? Those things make me nervous."

"Not having one makes me nervous," Noble told him.

"Americans and their guns," Duval said.

"Without this American you'd be floating face down in the Seine."

"Fair point." They reached the far side and crowded into the elevator. "Want to tell me what's going on?"

Noble pocketed the pistol and told Duval everything that had happened so far, starting with the defection of Hap Chan from China by way of Macau. By the time he finished they had reached an old theater in the heart of London called The Bristol, but the B was missing and the R had been broken so that now the sign seemed to read *THE PISTOL*.

One of the first theaters to adopt electric bulbs, The Bristol had been a stage theater, performing Shakespeare at the turn of the century. In the late forties, after surviving German bombs, the Bristol had been converted into a movie theater. In the eighties it was a porn theater and then, in the late nineties, had been briefly turned back into a stage during a resurgence in live theater. The most notable performance was a rendition of *Death of a Salesman* which was the venue's swan song. The owner went bankrupt, swallowed a handful of pills, and the theater went into receivership. It passed through a number of hands over the next thirty years until a small import business, based out of the south of France, had bought the dilapidated wreck for more money than it was worth.

The import business was a hastily constructed front set up by Noble and Duval after their escape in Paris. With his tech skills, Duval had created a GoFinanceMe page for a child battling leukemia. The child, who never actually existed, sadly passed away after raising a little over one hundred thousand dollars. The money would go to the aggrieved parents, of course. Two months later another unfortunate youngster came down with a crippling disease and another GoFinanceMe page was created. Duval had been able to fund his fake import business with money from crowdfunding campaigns which he used to remodel the old theater. A sign hung in the dusty ticket window; *Closed for Renovations.*

# Chapter Forty-Three

Wizard stood with his hips against the hard edge of his cluttered desk, staring at a wall covered top to bottom in faded photographs, brittle newspaper clippings, and red string. Several articles dated back to the Vietnam War and the fall of the American consulate in Iran. Various world leaders had earned a place on the wall, along with a few American presidents. Scattered among the clippings were yellow sticky notes with reference numbers to various clandestine operations by the CIA. At the center of this web was an 8x10 black and white photo of Otto Keiser.

Keiser had tried to crash the U.S. dollar by flooding the market with counterfeits and, when that didn't work, he'd tried to send America back to the Stone Age with an improvised EMP warhead.

CIA knew Keiser was behind both plots. Trouble was, they had no evidence. Keiser always worked through intermediaries. He was a fat, liver-spotted spider crouching at the center of a web of international crime and conspiracy, but there was no way to prove it.

Dulles had a Chesterfield cigarette pressed between thin lips and a kitchen match in one hand, his thumb poised to strike. His other hand cupped the match from a non-existent breeze. He'd been standing like that for the last twenty minutes. His eyes roamed the lines of red, tracing the invisible bonds between the crash of the British Pound Sterling in the nineties, the bombing of a passenger jet over South

America, and the impending crash of the petrol dollar. All roads led back to Otto Keiser.

Keiser's father had been a Nazi officer who blamed America for the fall of the Third Reich and he'd passed his hatred of America on to his son, who used his position as one of the world's most wealthy investment bankers to finance a decades-long cold war against the United States.

Could the millionaire banker be somehow wrapped up in this business with Noble?

"Grasping at straws," Dulles told the empty office.

He turned back to his desk. He had other business that needed his attention. He had covert operations running in Laos, Cambodia, Israel, Saudi Arabia, Brazil, Argentina, Ukraine, and Russia. His new boss was a political hack trying to score points with the media elites and his boss's boss was a senile old goat. Wizard forgot about his cigarette as he sifted through a pile of paperwork in search of a tearsheet about CIA operations in Poland to undermine the war in Ukraine.

Cook and his girlfriend Witwicky—they thought they were clever enough to hide their relationship from an office place full of spies—appeared in Wizard's doorframe.

Cook had a laptop tucked under one arm. Witwicky rapped her knuckles against the frame. Cook said, "We have something we think you should see."

"Is it about Noble?" Wizard dropped the file folder on his desk and grumbled, "It better not be another silly cat picture."

Cook shot a stern look at his girlfriend. "Told ya."

Witwicky muttered an apology.

Three weeks ago, she had close copied a picture of a cat who wanted a cheeseburger to Wizard, only the cat couldn't spell and possessed a faulty command of English grammar. It was supposed to be funny—Wizard wasn't too old or far gone yet to grasp that fact—but he didn't find cats or poor grammar particularly funny and had made certain his secretary blocked any further meaningless emails.

"It's not a cat meme," Cook assured him.

Wizard had no idea what a meme was, but he took the meaning. He motioned them into the office, struck the kitchen match with his thumb nail and touched flame to his cigarette. "Close the door."

Witwicky swung the door shut, making sure it latched, while Cook hurried around Wizard's desk and searched for a place to put his laptop computer. He started to move a tottering pile of reports.

"Not there. You'll wreck my whole organizational system." Wizard breathed smoke, pushed two mostly equal stacks together, and pointed. "Put it there."

Cook balanced the laptop on the piles and drew Wizard's attention to a sound wave file.

"What am I looking at?" Wizard asked.

"This is the audio recording of Noble's phone call with the Chinese intelligence officer, Kwang Luo."

"You ID'd the other speaker?"

Cook pressed his lips together and nodded. "A few hours ago, but that's not the important part."

Witwicky circled the desk and stood on Wizard's other side. Her hands were twisting together. She hurried to fill in the excuse for their delay. "There are discrepancies in the recording."

Failure to report something this important would have landed anyone else in boiling hot water, but Cook and Witwicky had earned a long leash when they saved America from an EMP attack. Wizard tapped ash into a cut glass tray with his alma mater stamped in the base. "I'm listening."

Cook hit play.

*I'm not flushing my career with the Company for five-hundred Gs.*

"Listen to the last consonant."

He played it again.

*I'm not flushing my career with the Company for five-hundred Gs.*

"Sounds like one of my best field officers selling out to China," Wizard remarked.

"That G sounded off to me and I couldn't figure out why," Cook said.

Witwicky continued, "So we snipped it and compared it to the rest of the recording. We found this..."

Cook played another snatch of dialogue.

*I've got your man and he's got the research.*

Wizard listened to it twice while he dragged on his cigarette then asked, "What are you two driving at?"

A smile lit up Cook's face, like an archeologist who's uncovered a priceless artifact. "It's the same G sound all three times."

Wizard shook his head. "I'm not sure I understand."

"The G in five-hundred Gs is the same exact sound as the G in the words 'got'."

Wizard leaned back in his seat and looked at Cook, then Witwicky. His eyes narrowed. Clouds of blue smoke rose in silent ghosts. "Is that supposed to mean something?"

"It's a statistical impossibility," Witwicky said.

"Look at the audio waves," Cook said and brought up a recording where all three G sound waves had been laid over one another. They matched perfectly. Cook said, "They are exact duplicates."

Wizard said, "They're all spoken by the same person. Isn't that what you'd expect?"

Witwicky shook her head. "Hardly."

"No two sounds are the same," Cook said. "Every sound you make is like a fingerprint. You'll never make the exact same sound twice. Each repetition of a word or phrase will be slightly different."

Witwicky said, "You could say the same phrase over and over, singing your favorite song perhaps, and to the human ear it all sounds the same, but a computer would be able to pick out slight discrepancies in each new repetition."

"Exactly," Cook continued. "Each and every time you say the word, it's going to come out slightly different depending on where you are. Are you indoors or outdoors? Sitting or standing? Are there other sounds in the background? Microscopic changes in your environment will affect the sound in ways that only a computer can detect."

Wizard said, "And all three of these G sounds are duplicates."

They nodded in unison.

"Which indicates they could have been faked."

Cook shook his head. "It doesn't indicate a fake, it proves it."

"It does?"

Witwicky smiled and jabbed at her glassed, which were slipping down her nose. "We checked this G sound against the rest of the recording and found the same sound again."

Cook played another snippet.

*You just make sure the money goes into the right account.*

"The same G sound again?" Wizard asked.

"Yes, and the J sound," Witwicky said.

"What about it?" Wizard asked.

"It's the same sound," Cook told him.

"The exact same sound?"

They nodded.

"How can that be?" Wizard asked. "It's a different letter? A different sound."

Cook said, "It's a statistical anomaly."

"I assume you've got an explanation?"

Witwicky said, "We think this is a deep fake."

Cook continued, "In recent years computer AI has learned to replicate human voice to near perfection. So far it's been mostly used to create imitations of celebrities saying funny things."

"Did you hear the one of Elon Musk on the phone with the President," Witwicky asked Cook.

"Hilarious," he laughed.

Wizard snapped his fingers. "Back to the point."

"Right," said Cook. "So computers can fake a human voice by taking a sampling of a person's speech patterns. It doesn't take much, just a few short recordings of someone speaking and the computer can put together, more or less, all the sounds in the English language. Once the person's voice has been sampled and analyzed, the computer can make them say anything."

Witwicky said, "It's amazing technology but there's one flaw."

"What's that?" Wizard had smoked his cigarette down to the filter and stabbed it out in the ashtray.

"Any sound it doesn't have a sample for, it has to borrow from the closest match," Cook said.

"In this case, the G sound," Witwicky said.

"Which is why it matches the J sound," Cook went on. "Vowel sounds are easy. There are only six, but consonants are much more difficult. With hard and soft consonants, there are hundreds of combinations in the English language. When the computer doesn't have a sample of a certain sound, it will borrow from the next closest sound, in this case the J sound. J and G are very close."

Wizard lit another cigarette, leaned back and said, "So someone is trying to frame Noble."

Cook and Witwicky nodded together. She said, "Whoever did this is very good."

"The audio is a ninety-nine percent match for Noble's voice," Cook said. "Which means they had a pretty good sample from which to work."

Wizard's gaze travelled to the wall of news clippings. "Problem is, would anybody else believe it?"

"Most people don't even believe deep fakes exist," Cook said.

Witwicky said, "People think they're a conspiracy theory."

"Today's conspiracy is usually tomorrow's fact." Wizard stood up, aging joints creaking with the effort, and went to his wall. "This isn't going to be enough for McHale. Keep digging and don't stop until you can prove Noble is innocent in a court of law."

"That might not be so easy." Witwicky said.

"This job never is," Wizard told them.

## Chapter Forty-Four

Noble came awake with a gasp, his pulse racing and his mind confused. It was a moment before his brain could make sense of his surroundings. He was stretched out on a sagging threadbare sofa in Duval's makeshift living room. A clock on the wall said it was 3:27 but was that AM or PM? Without windows, he had no way to be sure.

He groaned and stood up to get the blood flowing again. Young officer Reilly's body slam had left him covered in bruises. His back was a mass of tight knots and his neck felt like someone had filled the muscles with quick-dry cement.

A hot soak in Epsom salts would go a long way to alleviating the pain, but there was little hope of that. Instead, Noble went through a series of stretches to loosen aching muscles and reflected on the fact that he was now mentally referring to twenty-year-old men as 'young' and longingly thinking of hot baths with Epsom salts.

*Slowly turning into Wizard*, he thought has he hooked an arm over his head and winced at a lightning bolt of pain in his shoulder.

Duval's living space was a cavernous chamber in the belly of the theater with exposed pipes overhead and a collection of mismatched rugs thrown haphazardly down on a bare concrete floor. The walls were covered with fading movie posters. There was a police scanner on a table. LED lights on the front jumped in digital waves to the soft sounds coming from the small speaker. A collection of bootleg DVDs were piled on a low table in front of the sofa and the television was a state-of-the-art flatscreen with a crack in one corner. A battered violin, fitted with new strings, hung from a peg on the wall.

Through an open alcove on his left, Noble heard the steady click-clack of keys and saw the blue glow of a computer screen. As he passed through the arch, he scratched the stubble on his cheek. His fingernails made a sandpaper rasp.

Duval was hunched over a keyboard, eyes wide and bright, his fingers racing. There was a large mug of something that looked like hot coco at his elbow, but smelled like loamy soil. He noticed Noble from the corner of his eye and asked, "Sleep well?"

"My back is killing me," Noble said. "How do you sleep on that thing?"

"It folds out into a rather comfortable bed."

"Thanks for telling me now."

Duval shrugged. "You fell asleep before I had a chance."

Noble checked his watch. "Is it day or night?"

"Afternoon," Duval told him. "You slept the day away, mon ami."

"I needed it," Noble said. "Had a long night."

"So I gathered."

"Find anything?"

"Oh, I found something alright." Duval stopped pecking keys and swiveled in his chair. "I found a Swiss bank account in your name with over two million dollars in it. Are you sure you're not a traitor?"

"It's news to me." Noble looked around, found an empty milk crate, and turned it over so he could sit. "If I had access to two million bucks, I wouldn't be slumming here with you. Did you manage to find out who opened the account or where the money came from?"

"The account was opened two weeks ago, but if you want to know who opened it, you'll have to go to Switzerland and ask to see the security tapes."

"I wouldn't make it to the end of the block."

"Probably not," Duval said. "Your face is all over the television. You are wanted for murder."

"I didn't kill Hap Chan," Noble said.

"And the other man? The one who tried to imitate Peter Pan off the roof?"

"That was an accident," Noble said. "Tell me about the money. How did it get there?"

"That question is a little more difficult to answer." Duval brought up a series of screens showing registered wire transfers. "The money landed in the account roughly the same time your train arrived at King's Cross. Where it came from is hard to say. It was routed through a dozen different accounts around the globe. I lost the trail in Dubai. A company by the name of Mid-East Trading. A generic name for an obvious front company."

"It will trace back to Keiser," Noble said, scanning the list of transfers.

"You are sure this investment banker is behind the plot to frame you?"

Noble nodded. "What about the call? Any idea how someone could fake a telephone call with my voice?"

"My first thought would be a talented voice actor," said Duval. "But if you're right about Keiser, he would have the money and resources to create a deep fake."

"I've heard of that," Noble said. "They take a sample of your voice and a computer does the rest."

"Barely an inconvenience to a man like Keiser. No?"

Noble started to lean back and almost tumbled over backward before remembering that he was on a milk crate. He said, "Cook and Witwicky need to know about the deep fake."

"What is a cooked witwicky?" Duval asked.

"Not what," Noble said. "Who. Cook and Witwicky are a couple of computer nerds who work out of the basement at CIA. No offence."

"None taken." Duval shrugged. "I take it you can't just call them?"

"They're part of the team hunting me."

"This complicates things." Duval picked up his mug of fowl-smelling brew and sipped.

Noble hunched over, elbows on his knees, chin sunk in one hand, and considered the problem. Phones were out and mail would take too long. Email would be monitored. He needed a way to get in touch with them, without the Company finding out. It came to him in a flash. He snapped his fingers. "They play a game."

"Most computer people do," said Duval.

"An online game," Noble told him. "We were having pizza at Cook's place while we were prepping for this assignment, and they were trying to convince me to play this game. There's a whole online community and they are able to send messages back and forth in the game. It's called something like the Realms of Savagery, or something."

"Savage Realms," Duval said.

"You know it?" Noble asked. "Is there a way to get a copy of the game and contact them?"

Duval grinned. "Know it? I'm a level two-hundred and seven warlock."

# Chapter Forty-Five

Cook and Witwicky were also working on tracking the money in the Swiss account, though they hadn't gotten nearly so far as Duval. For them, the money trail evaporated in Brazil. They were still working on the next step when Cook's phone chimed.

The small fourth floor operation room was now littered with food wrappers and empty soda cans. The stale odor of cold French fries mixed with unwashed bodies. Gwen had excused herself twice and gone to the bathroom where she took a birdbath in the sink, using soap under her arms, but Ezra had worked straight through, unconcerned about hygiene. His black hair stuck up in places and was mashed flat in others and, combined with the scar on his cheek, people around the office had started referring to him as Harry Potter. He leaned back in his seat, pretending to stretch, while gazing at Gwen, wondering how he'd ever managed to land such an amazing girl.

Gwen stood, taking some of the strain off her back, and leaned over her terminal. Mousy brown curls were trapped back in a ponytail. Ezra took a moment to admire her bottom and the smooth lines of the corduroy before turning his attention to his phone.

He grunted.

"What is it?" Gwen asked.

"There's a raid on," he told her as he scanned the message. His mobile gave him notices any time someone sent him a message in the virtual world of the video game.

Gwen clicked her tongue. "Too bad we're going to miss it."

"Yeah," Ezra agreed and started to put the phone aside when another notice dinged.

*This job really cuts into my game time,* Ezra thought as he put the phone down.

Only the device wouldn't stop beeping. Six more messages came through in as many minutes.

"What is going on over there?" Gwen asked, slightly annoyed.

"Dunno." Ezra picked up the phone again. "The Eastern Trolls are mounting a raid on our capital."

"Tell whoever it is, they'll have to get along without us," Gwen said. "We're a little busy."

Ezra checked the sender. His brow furrowed. "That's odd."

"What's odd?"

"The message is from one of the Eastern Trolls," Ezra told her. "A warlock named Duvalord. Know him?"

She shook her head without taking her eyes off her computer screen. "Why would one of the East Kingdom Trolls tell us they're about to raid us?"

"Friendly heads up?" Ezra suggested. He read further and the spit dried up in his mouth. His eyes nearly popped right out of his head. "You're not going to believe this."

"Ez, we haven't got time for video games," Gwen said. "Jake is in real trouble."

"I know." Ezra held up the phone. "This warlock says they want to discuss our mutual friend Goodfellow."

"It's Jake," Gwen said, a smile springing onto her face. "We showed him the game, remember? Tried to get him to play it. He must be using it to contact us."

"I don't think so." Ezra shook his head. "This person is a level two-hundred and seven. There's no way Jake got to level two-oh-seven in a day."

"Still," said Gwen. "It's Jake's cover legend. It must be Jake, or someone who knows him."

"So how do we contact him?" Ezra showed his teeth as he considered the problem. His phone gave him a notice whenever someone contacted him in the game but he couldn't reply without playing. He said, "We can't download the game onto one of these computers. It's like one-hundred and sixty gigabytes. It would take all afternoon."

"Not to mention we'd have to explain to Wizard why we put an internet game on a CIA computer hardwired into the mainframe."

"He'd probably be upset about that."

"One of us will have to go home and log in," Gwen said.

"How're we going to do that?" Ezra asked. "We're in the middle of an operation. We can't just leave."

"I could say I'm having really bad period cramps," Gwen offered.

Ezra frowned and dismissed that with a wave of his hand. "That excuse will never pass muster with Wizard. He'd tell you to pop a Midol and get back to work."

"Probably right." Gwen sat down and clasped her hands together between her thighs. After a moment she perked up. "Ben Jameson has a gaming laptop he keeps in his car."

Ezra nodded. Ben was a gamer as well, and Ezra knew for a fact he played Savage Realms. He'd have a copy installed on his laptop. Ezra said, "Think he'd let us borrow it?"

"If he says no, I'll flash him," Gwen said.

"That should work," Ezra said with a laugh. "Any ideas on how we can get it into the building? Security isn't just going to let us carry in a high-end laptop."

"One problem at a time," Gwen said. "Let's go have a talk with Ben."

# Chapter Forty-Six

Burke parked a rented Ford Escort in front of an ice cream parlor on Beach Drive. An apple pie-scented air freshener hung from the rearview and a sack filled with protein bars, bottled water, and snap peas was in the passenger seat. He was dressed in a floral print Hawaiian shirt, tan slacks, and boat shoes. He was trying to blend, but it seemed the locals were sporting parkas. Some of them looked like they were wintering in Aspen, headed for the slopes, instead of strolling a beach in pleasant fifty degree weather.

The rearview mirror gave him a view across Straub Park to the marina and it was easy to pick out Jake's wooden schooner amid all the blinding white fiberglass. The sky was an angry gray overcast and the water was choppy, causing the vessels to roll and pitch, but the weather service wasn't predicting storms.

Burke switched off the engine, started to reach for a protein bar, and his eyes strayed to the ice cream parlor. He was doing good on his diet. He'd managed to whittle himself down from two-hundred and sixty pounds to two-forty and he could tell the difference in his energy level. The protein bar was the smart choice, but every once in a while you had to reward yourself.

*That's what it is,* Matt told himself as he got out and headed for the door of the ice cream parlor, *a little reward for all the hard work.*

They had the heater going inside. The place was hot enough to melt rubber. Burke didn't know how they were keeping the ice cream cold. Floridians, he decided, had lost the ability to cope with temperatures below eighty degrees. He smiled at a small white girl with a nose ring behind the counter, browsed the selection, and decided on chocolate and peanut butter in a cone. But he only got one scoop instead of two.

Sacrifices.

"Where ya from?" the girl asked as she loaded a waffle cone with ice cream.

"Pennsylvania," Burke lied. "Is it that obvious that I'm a tourist?"

"No Floridan dresses like that in winter," she said. "It's freezing out there."

Burke paid, thanked her for the cone, and went back outside where he sat in the rental and watched the boat for a while, looking for any sign of danger. No one else seemed to be watching the marina, at least not that Burke could see. He finished his ice cream and got out of the rental without realizing he had a large dollop of chocolate on his collar. After making sure the car was locked, he crossed the park beneath the shade of oaks bearded with Spanish moss to the marina.

He cut his way along floating aluminum catwalks between vessels to *The Yeoman* and was greeted by a shrill voice the moment he stepped foot on the gangplank.

"You'd best clear off, buster. I've got a gun and I know how to use it."

"You might have a gun, but I doubt very much you know how to use it, Mrs. Noble." He stopped on the gangplank and spread his hands to show he was unarmed. He couldn't see Mary. He spoke to his mirror reflection in the galley windows instead. He tried not to look intimidating which is difficult when you're a six foot black man with a linebacker's physique in a whiter than wonder bread part of town. "I'm a friend of Jake. I'm here to help."

"When did you get into town?" Mary called out the first half of the security code.

Burke said, "Doesn't matter. I'm here now."

The galley door popped open and Mary Elise Noble stuck her head out. The head of a massive Czechoslovakian wolfhound appeared as well. Lips peeled back from pointed yellow fangs. It had paws the size of paperback novels. Mary took her time studying Burke and then said, "Let's see you smile."

Jake had told her about the gap between his teeth. Burke spent the first thirty years of his life trying not to show that gap. Smiling with his lips pressed together had become habit. He was past the point of caring these days. In fact, he'd come to appreciate the gap. It gave him a unique smile, and he flashed his teeth at Mrs. Noble.

"I guess you're the real McCoy," she said. "How long have you known Jake?"

"Since he was in Special Forces," Burke said. "I'm the guy who recruited him out of Green Berets."

"Then I have you to blame?"

"I guess that's true," Burke said without taking his eyes off the dog. He motioned to the deck of *The Yeoman*. "Permission to come aboard, Captain?"

Mary hesitated a moment longer. One hand went to Gadsden's head and she scratched around his ears before saying, "Permission granted, but don't try anything funny. A single word from me and this monster will rip your leg right off."

"I believe it," Burke said as he stepped onto the deck. He knelt, held out a hand, and the dog emerged from the galley. Jake swore the beast was properly trained but that didn't stop a tight knot from forming in Burke's belly as the animal padded over.

Gadsden sniffed his open palm, sat back on his haunches, and lifted one paw to shake.

Burke grinned and shook, then rubbed around the dog's neck, ruffing his fur. "Who's a good boy? Who's a good boy? Are you a good boy?"

Gadsden seemed rather pleased at the idea that he might be, in fact, *a good boy*.

"How much do you know about what's going on?" Mary asked.

"Not much, I'm afraid." Burke shook his head. It was a lie. He knew a fair bit, in fact. But Burke knew Jake would have shielded his mother from the unpleasant details and said, "Jake asked me to come down here and check on you. Make sure you're safe. So here I am."

His answer didn't seem to satisfy Mary, but she said, "You'd best come in out of the cold."

Burke ducked into the galley. Mary had a portable space heater turned up to ten and the small kitchen felt like a blast furnace. Gadsden followed Burke, watching close. His behavior clearly said Burke was on probation. One wrong move and Gadsden would have him by the throat.

"Have you really got a gun?" Burke asked.

Mary reached inside the pocket of her floral print dressing gown and took out a small black Bersa Thunder pistol chambered in .380. Her finger was on the trigger, but thankfully the safety was on. She held it up for Burke's inspection. "Found it stuffed behind the toilet in the bathroom."

"Do me a favor and take your finger off the trigger," Burke said.

She weighed the weapon in her open palm a moment while she made up her mind, then passed the gun to Burke. "I suppose you had better hold onto it. I'm not even sure it's loaded."

"It's loaded."

"How can you tell?"

"Belongs to Jake."

# Chapter Forty-Seven

"We might have to name our firstborn after him," Gwen said when she swiped through the secure door two hours later with Ben Jameson's high-end Alienware gaming laptop tucked under one arm.

"You got it!" Cook had been slumped in his chair, staring blankly at the screens, when the door lock released. He sat up straight and asked, "How'd you get it past security?"

Every entrance to the buildings, both old and new, were heavily guarded and anything carried in or out was checked by security.

Gwen held up the laptop, showing a bright yellow sticker on the front that marked it as evidence in an ongoing operation, which made it permanent property of the Central Intelligence Agency. She said, "We owe him a new laptop."

"Why did you do that?" Ezra asked.

"It was the only way to get it past security. I had to tell them the hard drive had mission-sensitive intel."

"Great," Ezra said. Alienware PC's did not come cheap. He was already calculating the cost in his head when Gwen said, "I promised him we'd get him something with a Ryzen Threadripper CPU."

Ezra's jaw hinged open. "Are you kidding me? What's he need a Threadripper for?"

Gwen placed the laptop on the workstation and raised the lid. The Alienware sprang to life with a flashing logo. She said, "Along with an RTX 4090 graphics processor chip."

Ezra was out of his seat now and practically dancing. "That's twice what he's got in this unit."

Gwen shrugged an apology. "It was the price of admission."

"That's going to cost a small fortune."

"You want to find out what Noble has to say, right?"

Ezra sighed. "Fine, but this is Ben's birthday and Christmas all rolled into one."

"There's one other thing," Gwen said as she launched the game. "I tried to tell him no, but he wouldn't give me the laptop unless I agreed."

Ezra was already picturing Gwen on a date with Ben Jameson. "What is it? What did that pervert want?"

Gwen turned to Ezra and laid a hand on his forearm. "I promised him your Sword of Nightfire."

His brows wrinkled and his mouth dropped into a comical frown, a little boy who's just been told Santa isn't real. Suddenly the idea of Gwen on a date with Ben didn't seem so bad. "My Sword of Nightfire? You know how many hours of questing it took me to earn that?"

Gwen kissed him on the cheek. "We'll get you another, sweetie."

Ezra's face turned scarlet and his pulse pounded in his temples. "I can't believe he'd take my Sword of Nightfire."

"His character is a rogue elf."

"Rogue elves," Ezra spat. "You can't trust any of them."

"Where are we supposed to meet?" Gwen asked.

Ezra checked his phone. "The Creaking Gallows Tavern in the Thieves Quarters of Celegaurd City."

"Dodgy place," Gwen remarked.

The game had finished booting up and Gwen logged in. She played an elvish mage and she cracked her fingers before navigating the fantasy landscape, through a dangerous forest of wolves and spiders, toward the capital city.

"Hurry up, will ya?" Ezra said. "If Wizard comes in now we're going to be in real trouble."

"I'm going as fast as I can," said Gwen, who had been waylaid by a horde of foul undead zombies. She made short work of the shambling hordes with a few well-placed fire spells and finally reached the city, hurried along cobbled stone streets, and found her way to a candlelit tavern where a troll warlock was waiting in a dark corner, drinking a flagon of ale.

He was dressed in night-black armor with the blood-red insignia of the Eastern Trolls on one shoulder. He was not the type of character with which Gwen and Ezra normally associated.

Gwen sat down across from him and typed out, *Are you the one who contacted us about Goodfellow?*

*That's right*, he told her. *I'm a friend.*

*Where is Goodfellow? Is he alright?*

*He's here with me*, the warlock said. *I'm going to let him have control.*

A moment later the warlock said, *This is Jake. Am I talking to Ezra or Gwen?*

*Gwen, but we're both here.*

*Is the line secure?*

*We're safe*, she told him. *For now. What's going on Jake?*

*I'm innocent. You both know that right?*

*Of course. We never doubted you. But McHale is convinced you're bent. He's issued a capture or kill order on you.*

*It's a frame*, Noble typed. *Keiser set me up to take the fall for Hap Chan's murder.*

He started to tell her about the deep fake and Gwen interrupted him. *We already know the audio is a fake, but getting McHale to buy that is another story. He's going to need proof.*

*Duval might be able to track down the computer that made it*, Noble told her. *But we need a copy of the audio file.*

Ezra grasped Gwen's shoulder and squeezed. "Sasha Duval? He's in London? That's where Noble stashed him?"

"Guess so," said Gwen.

Sasha Duval had been in hiding since he'd escaped the embassy in Great Britain and tried to make it to a non-extradition country. American intelligence services had been trying, unsuccessfully, to track him down ever since. Noble was the only one who knew where the infamous hacker had gone to ground.

"All this time," Ezra said, "he's been in London."

"Last place anyone would think to look," Gwen said. "It's actually pretty clever when you think about it. Noble stashed him in the very place he had worked so hard to escape."

Ezra was nodding. "I'll bet CIA has been looking everywhere *except* England."

Gwen asked, "Are we going to tell anyone?"

"Not unless we have to," Ezra said. "I'm not interested in Duval. I'm only interested in clearing Noble's name. Tell him we can send over a copy of the file."

Gwen typed their response. The warlock gave them a temporary email address and told them to send the file encrypted.

*Won't you need the encryption key?* Gwen asked.

Duval must have taken control of the character again because he laughed and slapped his knee, as if that were the funniest joke he'd heard all day.

# Chapter Forty-Eight

Stokely sat on a ratty sofa in thick woolen socks, blue panties with pink paisleys, and a bulky knitted sweater that had once belonged to her father. Her flat was shabby but tidy, with a rug she had rescued from a dumpster and a coffee table gifted to her by a neighbor before he moved out of the building. In fact, everything in the apartment was secondhand. Even her laptop had been bought refurbished. Stokely had an iron-clad retirement plan and half of every paycheck went right into her SIPP. It didn't leave much left for creature comforts.

She had a bowl of microwave noodles in her lap while she combed hours of CCTV footage from the areas around the various crime scenes hoping to find something that would connect the dead men.

The laptop screen was divided into a grid, with four different video feeds scrolling at the same time. It was the only way she could get through all the footage in her spare time.

Her phone buzzed and Stokely reached for it without taking her eyes off the screen. It was an insurance salesman she'd been on a date with two weeks ago. She glanced at the caller ID and put the phone back on the table. "Boring," Stokely announced to the room.

In the last five years Stokely had been out with an accountant, a school teacher, a personal trainer, and an American airline pilot who wrote pulp mystery in his spare time. All four men had bored her to tears. The only guy she'd really been interested in was a bloke with

Scotland Yard's Critical Response Team. They'd had a pretty good thing going, at least Stokely thought they did. When she refused to put out after the third date, he went and started a rumor that Stokely batted for the other team. Now all the cops in London thought she was a lesbian and the only ones who paid her any attention were a handful of women in the department.

She stabbed her fork into her noodles and brought them to her mouth. On screen, an officer with an eyepatch climbed into the patrol car with Goodfellow. Stokely saw herself in the frame, her back to the car. The officer spoke briefly with Goodfellow, then he got out and walked away, turning briefly toward the camera. She backed the image up and watched again.

Stokely cursed. She backed the image up and watched it a third time.

Goodfellow hadn't been lying about a cop with an eyepatch, but Stokely knew most of the uniformed officers in her department and none of them wore an eyepatch. She still had noodles hanging from her lips while she backed up the video and watched it again. It was a moment before she remembered to chew. The ends of the noodles plopped back into the bowl as Stokely froze the image for a better look at the man's face. He was tall and, because the image was black and white, it was hard to tell if he was blond or ginger. Could be either.

"Eye patch," Stokely said and then remembered she had seen it before.

She went digging through her computer files until she found the footage she was looking for. It was the same guy, forty minutes earlier, only now he was dressed as a civilian as he circled round behind the building where they'd found the two dead Americans.

Stokely set her bowl of noodles aside and fiddled with the feed until she had the best stills she could manage. When she'd finished, she sent the images over to the Yard's Identification Lab to run matches. With any luck she'd have a name to go with the face in a few hours.

She'd been backward and forward through the footage. Goodfellow had never gone anywhere near the building where the Americans were murdered, but this mystery man with the eye patch had let himself in, right around the time of death, then paid a visit to Goodfellow posing as a police officer. And Goodfellow had sworn that an officer in an eyepatch was going to hurt his mother. That couldn't be coincidence.

Stokely finished her noodles while she went through the rest of the footage, just to be thorough, and her phone rang an hour later. The caller ID said Conagher.

He didn't even bother with a hello. "I heard you sent images to the lab for identification. That's odd because I didn't know you were working a murder case at the moment, Inspector Stokely. You aren't snooping into the Goodfellow case, are you?"

She spent the next twenty minutes convincing Conagher that she was just looking into a few old cold cases with her free time.

"Good," Conagher told her. "Because if I find out you're anywhere near the Goodfellow business, I'll have your badge, Stokely."

The line went dead.

Stokely tossed the phone on the sofa and then shot it a double bird while sticking her tongue out.

# Chapter Forty-Nine

"Normal vocal samples rely on twenty-four points of similarity," Duval was saying, "but deep fakes are quite advanced so I doubled the sample rate, and then doubled it again. And discrepancies begin to appear. The vowels are all accurate, because there are only six vowel sounds in English, but the computer can't fake any consonants for which it doesn't have a sample. And several consonants are off."

The pale blue light from the monitors lit the dingy room, highlighting Duval's hatchet face, and computer fans made a gentle hum in the background. Noble was perched on a rolling stool next to Duval's state of the art workstation listening to him go on about the recording.

"We already know it's a fake." Noble pinched the bridge of his nose between thumb and forefinger.

"Yes, but now we can prove it."

"I need to know who created it."

Duval's shoulders sagged. "I'm sorry, Jake. Whoever created this file is a real pro. He left no digital fingerprints behind."

"Get this information to Cook and Witwicky," Noble said.

"Already done," Duval told him. "We've set up a secure line."

"Careful," Noble said. "Remember they work for the CIA."

A half smile tugged at Duval's mouth. "It's okay. These friends of yours are my kind of people. We have an understanding. Question is, what are you going to do, my friend?"

Noble closed his eyes and chewed the inside of one cheek. He knew Keiser was behind the plot against him, but he couldn't prove it and unless he came up with some rock solid evidence, he'd spend the rest of his life in a cell.

At the very least, mom was taken care of. He didn't have to worry about that any longer. He'd texted Burke with one of several burners Duval kept on hand and gotten a response. Mom was safe. Noble opened his eyes and said, "I need to find Keiser. I want to have a talk with him."

Duval cocked an eyebrow. "Are you sure?"

Noble nodded. "If I'm going down for murder, I'm taking Keiser down with me."

"I had a feeling you'd end up taking a run at Keiser," Duval said. "I took the liberty of tracking him down. He's here, in London. He's going to be at a charity gala tonight at eight."

"So Keiser is in London," Noble thought out loud.

Duval inclined his head. "Probably wanted to be here to gloat."

"He won't be gloating long," Noble said. "Any chance you can get me through the door?"

"I can probably work up a fake invitation that will get you past security. It won't stand up to in-depth scrutiny."

"What's the dress code?"

"Black tie," Duval said. "I'm afraid I can't help you there."

"Shouldn't be too hard." Noble checked the digital time display on the computer screen. It was almost 4:30. He had three hours to find a tuxedo and prepare for his meeting with Keiser. First he needed some paper and a pen.

Duval dug out a yellow legal pad and a ballpoint. Noble carried them into the other room where he sat down on the musty smelling futon to write.

The first went to his mom. Noble took his time and wrote out all the things he could never find a way to say in person. The second had detailed instructions and went to a contact in Egypt. When he'd finished, he gave both to Duval. "Can you make sure they get where they're going."

He checked the addresses. "Florida is easy," said Duval. "But this one to Egypt doesn't even have a name. How will I know if it goes to the right person?"

"Just make sure it gets to that address," Noble said.

Duval shrugged. "I'll see that it gets there. It might have to pass through several hands."

"The more the better," Noble said.

# Chapter Fifty

The Haitian was slumped in the driver's seat of the Mercedes, watching the boat. There was a cold sun overhead and he had the ragtop down. He was parked in a parallel spot across from a tea shop with a sign in the window proclaiming the establishment a gun-free zone. The Haitian snorted.

He'd already scored a piece from a local gang contact. Getting his hands on a gun was child's play. The Tampa-Saint Pete area is part of what federal authorities collectively refer to as the Cocaine Highway. Drugs, money, and guns stream up through the Florida Keys into Miami and then spread throughout the rest of the nation.

It made him smile to think that right now, somewhere in Washington, some bureaucrat was arguing for tougher gun legislation, as if criminals went through legal channels to buy guns. America was a strange place where civilized people clung to illusions of an ordered society where they could control the evil aspects of human nature if only they passed enough laws.

The Haitian turned his attention back to the boat. It was a beautiful wooden schooner with brass accents and neatly maintained sails bobbing on a gentle swell. A lone seagull perched atop the main mast.

He'd watched the big bear of a black man go up the gangplank, watched him talk to the old lady, and then they'd both gone below. The Haitian had been hoping he was just a friend stopping in for a visit, or maybe a salesman trying to talk the old lady into more life insurance, but he'd been in there close to two hours now.

The Haitian checked the clock on the dash. If the man hadn't left in another hour, he'd die along with the old woman. Collateral damage is bad for business but sometimes it can't be helped.

A large delivery truck rumbled past, leaving the noxious smell of diesel in its wake. The Haitian took a Browning 9mm semiautomatic from the glovebox and stuffed it under his thigh. The weapon was loaded with hollow points. The sights were factory standard and not much good outside twenty feet. An old oil can was fixed to the barrel as a poor man's suppressor. The Haitian didn't plan on doing any shooting. The gun was just a precaution really.

Fifteen minutes ticked slowly past. The fat black man still hadn't come out and the Haitian ran out of patience. He glanced briefly about the boulevard to make sure no one was watching before stuffing the gun in his leather overcoat, getting out, and starting across the park.

\*\*\*

Burke relaxed in a deck chair, enjoying the sea breeze, with a bottle of water in one hand. His other hand rested on the dog's head. He absently ran his fingers through the thick fur. Every time he stopped, Gadsden would lift his snout in a manner that clearly said, "Keep going."

Mary was curled up across from him, a thick woolen blanket over her legs and the Bible open on her lap. She proved to be a pleasant companion. They'd talked about Jake and then she'd asked Burke about himself, his time in the military, and how he ended up working for what she called the Pickle Factory. Burke told her more than he should have but now that he was no longer officially employed by the federal government, he had a little more room to talk. Not much, but definitely more than he'd had when he was running operations at Langley.

Mary's husband had been a Navy man and she knew instinctively when they were moving into territory that Burke couldn't discuss without risking serious jail time, which meant she knew more than she let on.

The whole time, there was an undercurrent of fear and strain running through the polite back and forth. Both were worried about their safety and, more important, they were worried about Jake. He was their one point of contact, their mutual connection, and that seemed enough for now. The conversation would stray onto topics like baseball but would eventually come back to Jake.

"He was the best pitcher on his high school team, you know," Mary was saying. "Pitched a no hitter his junior year." She smiled at the memory and reached for a cup of tea.

"It's too bad he blew out his shoulder." Burke had heard the tale of the no hitter, more than once. Jake didn't talk much, but he would tell that story to anyone who would listen. "He might have gone pro if not for the injury."

Mary shook her head. "He was good enough but I think he was always destined for the military and spook work. Jake needs to feel he's making a difference. Throwing baseballs never would have fulfilled him."

"This mean you forgive me for getting him wrapped up in all this espionage business?"

Her eyes narrowed down to slits. "Not just yet."

Burke laughed. He finished the bottle of water and looked around for a trash can but there was none on deck.

"In the galley under the sink," Mary said.

Burke stood and the dog came to his feet as well. Gadsden padded after him into the galley, toenails click-clacking on the hardwood. Burke mashed the plastic bottle down as small as he could. Madeline was a stickler for crushing bottles and cans—we have to take care of our planet after all and those things make a lot of waste—and he dropped it into a waste basket. When he straightened up, he saw a tall thin man with long dreadlocks in a black leather coat striding along the docks.

"Mary," Burke called out.

"Yes, Matthew?"

"Get below."

The woolen blanket dropped from her legs as she stood. It slid down into a pile on the deck. She clasped the Bible in both skeletal hands. "What's wrong?"

"I think we have company." Burke's ears were tingling. A sure sign of danger. Maybe it was the leather coat, or the dreadlocks, but the guy spelled trouble. Burke reached into his waistband for the Bersa pistol.

# Chapter Fifty-One

Stokely was back at the precinct, dressed in business stripes and flats. She leaned back in her chair, an ink pen tucked behind one ear and her hair in disarray. She'd lost her hairpin somewhere and hadn't bothered to replace it. She was too busy working on the timeline. The timeline made no sense.

Stokely reached for a mug of tea, sipped, and set it down on a stack of papers covered in brown tea rings. Her laptop was open with the surveillance images of Wexler and one of Goodfellow coming out of a Chinese takeaway two blocks away. She had a print out on Wexler two inches thick.

It hadn't taken the Identification Lab long to put a name to the face. Ronald Wexler had several offences as a juvenile, and had spent six months in a correctional facility at the age of seventeen; that was back when they'd still put underage offenders in lockup for felonies. Wexler had done his bid in the juvenile correctional facility, finished out his primary education, and gone into the military where he'd been tapped for Special Air Service. His life seemed to be on the right track. He was a highly decorated soldier with a promising future. Then there was a dishonorable discharge.

British Armed Forces wouldn't say why he'd been sent packing, they never did, but it couldn't be anything good. After the military, Wexler had put his skills to use as a demolition expert for construction companies until finding work with a firm called Global Security Solutions.

It had taken Stokely two hours of research, and she'd had to call in a few favors, to find the parent company of GSS. It was owned by a billionaire investment banker by the name of Keiser. The name was familiar, but Stokely couldn't place it. A quick internet search jogged her memory. He was the man who'd broken the bank of England in the early 90s by betting against the British Pound.

Stokely had been a little girl, knee high to a gnat as her father loved to say, but she had vague recollections of the turmoil. She'd heard stories of bankers jumping from windows and families who could no longer afford to put food on the table. It was a bad time and innocent people suffered all so that Keiser could put a few extra zeros on his balance sheet.

Stokely lifted the thick file on Wexler, weighing it in her hand while she asked herself the question; how and why did a former SAS commando end up working for a hedge fund billionaire who liked to bet on currencies? What did a man like Keiser need with a private mercenary?

The answer: nothing good.

Stokely sucked her teeth as she paged through Wexler's service records. She was halfway through, thinking it was time for more tea, when patrolman Reilly arrived at her desk. He had a long roll of receipt tape in an evidence baggy.

"Checked that Chinese Takeaway like you asked." Reilly handed over the evidence. "Goodfellow picked up his dinner at five past ten pm."

"You're one hundred percent certain?" Stokely asked. "You checked that the time on the register was correct."

Reilly held up his phone. "Check the register against my smartphone. These things don't lie. The clock on the register is slow by two minutes. Why? Is the time important?"

"Changes everything," Stokely said.

"What are you on about, inspector?"

"Goodfellow is not our guy," Stokely told him.

He frowned.

She tapped a printout on her desk, the same one covered in brown tea stains. "The emergency call that sent us to the dead man's address came in at one minute past ten. You said it yourself, Goodfellow was two blocks away in a Chinese takeaway."

Reilly didn't look happy at this turn of events. "If Goodfellow didn't kill the Chinese man, who did?"

Stokely thrust her chin at the pictures of Wexler. "I'd bet my very last pence it was this bloke."

"Who's he?"

She passed the two inch thick folder to Reilly. "Everything you need to know about him is in here. Put out an APB, and be careful. He likes to pose as a cop."

Reilly clasped the file in both hands and considered it a moment before saying, "Sure you want me to do that? There's no way I can keep it from Conagher, and you're not supposed to be working this case."

"Put out the APB," Stokely said. "I'll take the heat from Conagher."

Reilly shrugged. "Better you than me."

# Chapter Fifty-Two

Burke slipped the Bersa Thunder from his waistband. He didn't need to check that the weapon was oiled and well maintained. It belonged to Jake. It would be clean and in good working order. The .380 was a small round, but in the close confines of a boat, it was more than enough. Burke gripped the weapon in one large hand and watched the black man with the dreads making his way along the docks.

"You think he's here for me?" Mary asked, her voice tight with strain. She joined Burke in the galley and gazed out the window. Her face was pale with spots of color in her cheeks and her hands were knotted together. Arthritic knuckles made large white moons in her thin skin.

Burke said, "He look like a yacht club member to you?"

Mary peered out the window, narrowing her eyes in suspicion. She had cloudy cataracts but even she could make out the leather overcoat and dreadlocks from this distance. She said, "I've never seen him around here before, but I'm not here much."

A small grin touched Burke's lips. It was the politically correct answer. Mary—a small white woman—did not want to assume the man was a criminal simply because he was black in a predominantly white part of town.

He steered Mary toward the ladder to the stateroom below decks. "Lock yourself in and don't come out until I tell you."

"But..."

"Do it now."

Mary had been about to tell him that she'd left her phone on the deck chair outside. Instead she clambered down the short ladder.

Outside, the thug stopped to inspect a sixty-five foot catamaran, then continued along the docks. He barely passed an eye over *The Yeoman* before moving on. Burke watched as he loafed along between the lines of boats, the breeze blowing his long dreadlocks out behind him until he disappeared from sight.

Some of the tension drained from Burke's back and neck. He shrugged to loosen his muscles. He'd been certain the man was a threat but as he stood at the galley window, watching, doubt started to creep in.

Had he racially profiled a black man because of a leather coat and dreadlocks? Maybe the guy had been invited out for a day on the water and was walking along the docks, looking for the right boat? Could it be that simple?

Burke remembered all the times he'd been followed around a store by employees convinced he was there to steal simply because he was a large black man. A bitter taste filled his mouth.

He went to the hatch and stepped out on deck, scanning the parking lot of boats. Seagulls lined yard arms and Gadsden was on the prow, nose to the wind. There was a party going on three boats down. A knot of bleach-blonde white girls danced to Bob Seager singing *Her Strut*. One of the men spotted Burke and lifted a can of beer in greeting. Burke waved before taking a slow tour around *The Yeoman*. He shimmied along the gunwales, searching for any signs of tampering, saw Gadsden with his tongue lolling and his ears cocked forward, and Burke stopped to ruff his fur before heading back to the stern. Nothing was out of place and there was no sign of the black man with the dreadlocks. Burke went to the open hatch. He was just about to call out to Mary, let her know it was safe, when he spotted movement from the corner of his eye.

He started to turn and felt cold metal bite his temple.

# Chapter Fifty-Three

"You'd best have a damned good explanation, Stokely." Conagher stood behind his desk, face purple with rage, and his fists planted on the desktop. His top button was open and his tie loose. One eye twitched. He leaned across and fixed her with an icy glare. "I specifically ordered you off this investigation."

He'd stormed into the office at half past six and barked Stokely into his office. She'd known she was in for it even before she closed the door. The latch had hardly clicked into place when Conagher laid into her. She stood there and let his tirade wash over her, painfully aware the blinds were open and, even if they weren't, Conagher was so loud the entire bullpen could hear every word. But Stokely had come prepared.

She held up a thick folder. "Goodfellow didn't kill the Chinese man," Stokely said. "He couldn't have. He was nowhere near the flat when it happened and I doubt he killed the two Americans either. There's a conspiracy here and I've got evidence to back up my theory."

She slapped the file down on Conagher's desk.

His mouth twisted with rage and he eyed the folder like a man watching a poisonous snake, but finally picked it up and flipped it open. He grumbled, "What am I looking at?"

"The bloke with the eyepatch is named Wexler," Stokely explained. "He's former SAS."

"One of ours?"

"Used to be," Stokely corrected. "Now he's a gun for hire. He works for a security firm controlled by a man named Otto Keiser. Have you heard of him?"

Conagher's face twisted with bitter memory. "Everyone who was old enough to bank in the nineties remembers that name. He practically wrecked the country. I lost most of my savings in one afternoon. Lot of people lost a lot more than me. You telling me this slimy git is wrapped up in all this?"

Stokely nodded, happy to hear Conagher bore a personal grudge against the hedge fund billionaire. "Flip to the traffic cam footage at the back. His man Wexler was caught on camera near both crime scenes."

"That can't be coincidence."

"My thoughts exactly," Stokely said. "And it gets even more interesting."

"I'm listening."

"When the Chinese bloke was murdered, Jacob Goodfellow was four blocks away picking up takeaway. I've got him on video coming out of the shop and the register in the business corroborates the timeline. Jacob Goodfellow did not kill the Chinese man. The emergency call came in while he was at the takeaway picking up dinner. And to make matters worse, the Chinese man was killed moments *after* the call was placed."

"So someone called emergency services first and then killed the Chinese man in the hopes of framing Goodfellow," Conagher said.

"My money is on Wexler," Stokely said.

"Anything to back that up?" Conagher asked.

"The very last image," Stokely told him.

He shuffled through the printouts. The final black and white was an image of Wexler speaking to Goodfellow in the back of the squad car. Conagher's brows tripped up his forehead and his jaw nearly hit the floor. He stared at the grainy black and white in silence for several seconds. "It's the same man, dressed in a police uniform."

"He walked right past us, dressed like one of us, and had words with Goodfellow in the radio car."

"Cheeky little bastard," said Conagher. "Isn't he?"

"Bold," Stokely agreed. "He certainly fancies himself cock of the walk. He was dishonorably discharged from the Special Air Service, he's got a criminal record, and an employer with very deep pockets."

"The kind of employer who could set him up with a patrol uniform good enough to fool cops." He held up the photo of Wexler in the patrol car speaking to Goodfellow. "So you think Keiser and his bully boy are setting Goodfellow up to take the rap?"

"Only question is why?"

"And what do the lads in MI6 have to do with it?" Conagher wondered aloud.

"Let me bring Wexler in for questioning."

"He's probably out of the country by now."

Stokely shook her head. "His boss is in town for a gala fundraiser tonight. I'm betting Wexler will be in attendance as well. Remember, he doesn't even know we're looking for him."

Conagher sat down and massaged one temple. "You want to bring in one of Keiser's employees, you'd better make it stick, Stokely."

"We've got him on camera impersonating a law officer," she said. "That's a criminal offence."

Conagher picked up the photograph and studied it some more while making a clicking sound at the back of his throat. "Okay, Stokely, I'll back you on this but you'd better make your case air tight. The boys at MI6 won't be happy to learn we're nosing in on their turf."

Stokely tried and failed to hide a smile. "Thank you, sir."

"And none of this clears Goodfellow for the fourth murder," said Conagher. "The man who got thrown off the roof. That was definitely Goodfellow."

"I've got a theory about that as well."

Conagher sighed. His facial expression said, *in for a penny, in for a pound*. "Let's hear it."

"Self-defense."

Conagher chuckled.

"Think about it, sir. Goodfellow was being set up to take the fall for the murder of the Chinese national but he escaped police custody. I think when the plan went haywire, Keiser sent out his personal army to find Goodfellow and shut him up before he could uncover the truth. One of them cornered Goodfellow in the bar and a fight ensued."

"It's a sound theory," Conagher said. "It still doesn't get Goodfellow off the hook. Even if he is being set up, he hasn't got the right to throw people off rooftops. This isn't Iran after all. Bring in Wexler, find out what he knows, and find Goodfellow while you are at it. But make sure you've got the goods, Stokely, or we'll both be writing parking tickets this time next week."

# Chapter Fifty-Four

Fireworks popped in Burke's vision. His world tipped on end and he went stumbling through the hatch into the galley, trying desperately to stay on his feet. The gun slipped from nerveless fingers and tumbled over the floor, coming to rest under the galley table. Burke grabbed at the countertop, lost the battle and went sprawling.

Pain radiated out from his temple in sickening waves that made him feel like he would throw up. Panic clawed at his brain, telling him to get back up and get in the fight, but the boat seemed to be doing slow loop-the-loops around him. He gripped the hardwood floor until everything stopped spinning. He heard rubber soles on the deck and a shadow blotted out the sunlight coming through the galley door. He expected to hear a loud pistol crack and feel a bullet punch through his back, right between the shoulder blades.

A heavy Haitian accent said, "On your knees old man."

He took a little too long to get up and the Haitian cracked the back of his neck with the butt of a pistol, driving Burke back to the floor with a loud *Oof!*

"I said on your knees." The Haitian grabbed his collar and yanked.

Burke was pulled, arms flailing, into a kneeling position. His balance was still tenuous at best and he put one hand out to steady himself against the kitchen cabinets. A bundle of slippery eels twisted in his belly. He didn't want to throw up but the crack to his skull had rung his bell. He had a concussion at the very least and if he was really unlucky, internal bleeding. The back of his neck felt like someone had taken a ballpeen hammer to his spinal column. To top it all off, he'd been called an old man. Burke had been called *mister* and *sir*, but this was the first time anybody had called him old. It added insult to injury. He'd let a young punk get the drop on him. That never would have happened even five years ago. Coming fast on the heels of that knowledge, was the realization that Burke was going to die and Noble's mother would pay the price for his failure.

"Turn around," the Haitian ordered.

Burke was forced to do an awkward turn on his knees. His attacker was tall with a shark's lifeless eyes and a gold tooth winked every time he spoke. He pointed a pistol fitted with a poorly crafted sound suppressor made from an oil filter at Burke's forehead. "Where is the old lady?"

Burke took a moment to gently probe the side of his head. He winced at the touch and another ripple of pain made his vision shiver. He said, "Don't know what you're talking about. I'm all alone."

The Haitian stepped forward and drove his foot into Burke's crotch with devastating speed. Pain doubled him over. His face stretched in a silent scream but it took several seconds for the sound to materialize. Then he was hunched over, holding his package, moaning like a dog in heat.

The Haitian pressed the make-shift suppressor against the top of Burke's head. "Not gunna ask you again. Where's the old lady?"

The pain subsided in slow waves that left Burke feeling sick and shaking. He managed to straighten up, both hands still cradling the family jewels, and growled, "You kick like a girl."

***

Mary Elise Noble was below deck in Jake's bunkroom trying to load a 12 gauge shotgun. It was a long black weapon that, in her spindly arms, seemed to weigh more than a full size refrigerator. She'd found the shotgun under the bed, along with a box of shells that advertised 12 gauge slug. She had no idea what that meant but felt reasonably certain the ammo was intended for self-defense, after all there aren't any elk in Saint Pete Florida.

Pearly tears stood in her eyes as she worked to figure the shotgun out. Her heart was a shuddering bird inside her chest, crouched and cowering. She had heard Burke's bulk land with an ominous thud on the ceiling and for a moment thought he'd been killed, then she heard muffled words. Mary knew she had to act quickly. The mean-looking customer up top meant business. He was here for one purpose and that was to kill. Mary, never a violent person, knew she had to fight or die and this gun was her only hope of winning against a grown man.

With trembling fingers and straining biceps, she turned the weapon over, looking for a way to load the ammo. She had seen enough television to know she had to pull back on the slide but that was a whole lot harder than the movies made it look. There was a small metal hinge on the bottom of the weapon that looked like it might accommodate the bullets (Mary wouldn't know the difference between a bullet and shell any more than Jake knew the difference between a peony and a petunia) but when she tried to jam one in, it wouldn't go.

She turned the gun up to the light and saw the copper gleam of a shell already snug in the magazine. Maybe all she had to do was pull the trigger? The small pistol which she had given to Burke had been loaded. Maybe Jake kept them all loaded?

The idea of using the gun on the man upstairs filled her stomach with salt water and turned her knees weak. Mary wasn't at all sure she could pull the trigger, even to save her own life, but knew she had to try. After a moment's hesitation she grabbed a few extra shells, stuffed them in the pocket of her dress, and headed for the stairs.

\*\*\*

Burke was on his knees, staring down the barrel of the pistol. It seemed to grow and yawn open. A cold fist was around his heart, gripping with icy fingers, and his bladder felt full to bursting. A thousand thoughts flooded his mind, most of them centered around Maddie and how she would take the news of his death. He wanted to see her one last time and tell her how much he loved her. Also, he was hoping he wouldn't piss his pants when the bullet blew his brains out. That would be an embarrassing way to go.

The Haitian said, "Last chance, mon."

"Get on with it."

The Haitian shrugged. "Have it your way."

Gadsden filled the open hatch frame, lips peeled back from sharp white teeth and his ears laid flat. He let out a deep growl, like boulders grinding together in winter and his toe nails made soft click-clacks on the polished wood deck.

The Haitian spun, levelled the pistol and pulled the trigger. The weapon coughed out three quick rounds. The shots, muffled by the suppressor, was drowned out by the blasting music from the party, but sounded like thunder claps in the close confines of the galley. Brass shells pinged off the cupboards and jingled over the floor. The first shot missed completely, smacking a hole in the hatchway, throwing splinters of wood in the air. The second grazed along Gadsden's flank. The third hit him in the shoulder.

The force of the bullet knocked him backwards, through the opening and onto the deck. A shock of bright red blood painted the doorframe. The dog twisted around, jaws snapping at the invisible hornet sting. Gadsden let out a piteous yelp and raced in a confused circle trying to reach his flank to get at the pain.

The Haitian had delt with dogs before and raced onto the deck. He was about to shoot the animal again but there was a party three boats down and someone might hear. Instead he aimed a kick at the beast's head, catching him under the jaw, and sent the dog reeling. A second kick put the dog over the railing and into the water with a heavy splash.

# Chapter Fifty-Five

Noble checked himself in the small mirror over the bathroom sink. He'd managed to procure a second-hand tux from a shop down the block called Modern Gent's Haberdasher. The sleeves showed a little too much wrist and the pants stopped just above the work boots, but it would be enough to get him through the door of the gala. He couldn't button the collar so he knotted the bowtie to keep the shirt closed.

In the movies James Bond always found excuses to wear a tux. Looking at his reflection, Noble realized this was the first time in his career with the CIA he'd required a tuxedo, and it didn't even fit right. He kept tugging at the sleeves, trying to hide two inches of white cuff. He'd borrowed Duval's razor to shave and used some styling mouse to slick his long hair back. After a moment of deliberation, he folded the Bible tract and stuffed it in his pocket then looked at himself in the mirror one last time before letting himself out of the bathroom.

The fugitive hacker was still at his computer, rat-like face bathed in the light from the monitors, clicking through a series of pages. An empty pizza box lay open on the desk.

Noble said, "How do I look?"

Duval stopped and turned. A smile jerked at his face. "Very dashing. I especially like the boots."

"Everyone's a critic," Noble commented. "Did you manage to get the ticket?"

Duval held up a forged pass printed on heavy stock from an expensive Epson inkjet. "This should get you through the door without difficulty. Don't get it wet."

Noble inspected the black background and gold ink. It was a crude forgery that Duval had created on short notice and Noble detected slight imperfections in the font and spacing. Hunt's stainless steel .45 caliber semi-automatic had been cleaned, oiled, and was in a makeshift shoulder holster constructed from a belt and old wire hanger, and was hiding beneath Noble's tuxedo jacket. He slipped the forged ticket into an inside pocket and asked, "Did you manage to rig a recording device?"

Duval held up a prepaid phone. "It's voice activated and will record up to seven hours."

"Should be more than enough."

"Just make sure you're close," Duval said. "And try to eliminate background noise."

"Easier said than done," Noble told him.

Duval shrugged. "Best I could do on short notice."

"I'll make it work," Noble said.

Duval nodded. "I'll keep working on the money trail and the deep fake. If I find out anything, I'll send the info straight to Cook and Witwicky."

"Thanks for everything," Noble told him.

"It was the least I could do," Duval said. "I still owe you for saving my life."

"Don't forget to mail those letters if..." He trailed off.

"Shouldn't be too much trouble."

Noble slugged him on the shoulder. "You're alright, Duval."

He rubbed at his arm. "Let's hope we never have to meet in person again. No offense."

Noble laughed. "None taken."

Ten minutes later he left Duval's safehouse, turned his collar up against the cold, and walked until he spotted a taxi. He gave the driver an address in the heart of London, six blocks from the gala.

# Chapter Fifty-Six

The Haitian pointed the gun at Burke's head. "Don't even think about it, fat man."

Burke had heard the dog go into the water and was casting around on the floor for his fallen pistol. His face was a grim mask of hate and his hands curled into big black fists.

The Haitian smiled. "You want to kill me, eh?"

Burke didn't bother to respond.

"Maybe in the next life." The Haitian raised his voice and called out. "Come out, come out, mon cher. I want to talk with you. Your little doggie is dead. And if you don't come out right now, your friend will die too."

"No need to yell," Mary Elise Noble said as she appeared at the top of the steps with a Remington model 920 pump action cradled in her arms. "Put that pea shooter down or I'll pull this trigger, buster."

The Haitian never even flinched. An ugly grin curled up his mouth. He said, "You ain't gonna shoot me, lady."

To her credit, Mary pulled the trigger. Only she'd neglected to chamber a round and the safety was still on. The trigger refused to budge.

The Haitian reached for the weapon with his left hand and yanked the shotgun from Mary's grasp, pulling her off balance in the process.

She stumbled, grabbed at the table, lost her hold, and went down flat on her face, hitting the floor with a hard thud.

Burke started up, intending to use the momentary distraction to his advantage. He barely reached his feet, with no time to lunge at his captor, when the Haitian, younger if not stronger, hit Burke in the chest with the butt of the shotgun.

There was a hard whack and Burke's feet went out from under him. He sat down hard, feeling his tailbone bite the floor with a rending crunch. His vision narrowed to a pinprick of light. Numbing pain turned his legs to dead stumps.

Mary whimpered and pushed herself up onto her hands and knees. She was bleeding from a small cut on her lip where she'd fallen and her nose was swollen and pink but her eyes were full of fire.

The Haitian placed the shotgun on the galley table, leaned against the counter and levelled his pistol at them. "Sit on the floor and put your backs together. Try anything and I'll have to punish you, understand?"

# Chapter Fifty-Seven

Noble felt like a rooster in a room full of swans. He was the only man in the room wearing a secondhand jacket. He had passed the ticket stand without difficulty. The pimple-faced kid in the booth hardly glanced at Duval's forged ticket before instructing Noble in a bored voice to enjoy his evening. Noble mounted sweeping steps to a grand ballroom where London's upper crust were busy rubbing elbows. The floor was pink marble and a crystal chandelier hung from the ceiling. A string quartet played a classical tune in one corner. Serving girls made their way through the crowd carrying silver trays loaded with champagne. One of the girls offered her tray to Noble. He accepted a glass with a smile. She gave him a once over and her eyes stopped on his work boots. Her brows went up. She knew right away he didn't belong. She said, "Nice shoes."

He felt his ears burning, looked down at his footwear and said, "My other shoes are at the cobbler's."

She laughed. "Try again."

"I'm crashing," he told her. "Are you going to rat me out?"

She took a moment to inspect him and then smiled. "Have fun."

Noble lifted his champagne flute. She continued on her way through the gathering and Noble went the opposite direction, in case she changed her mind. He made his way through the crowd, searching for the poison pill in the midst of all this wealth and opulence.

He found Keiser inspecting the offerings at the silent auction. The table was lined with bottles of Châteauneuf-du-Pape, a Fender Stratocaster signed by Eric Clapton, a plaque for a DeLorean, numerous leather-bound first editions by dead authors, diamond earrings, necklaces of pearl, original works of art by names Noble recognized, and none of it under lock or key.

Keiser was an overgrown bullfrog in a spotless black dinner jacket. Thin whisps of white hair clung to a liver spotted scalp and deep, fleshy bags hung under watery eyes. He craned forward in his wheelchair for a closer look at a set of jewel-encrusted cufflinks.

Behind the toad stood Wexler, six and a half feet of muscle and fiery red hair, with a patch over one eye. There was a tell-tale bulge under his coat. He spotted Noble, his one eye widened slightly, and then he bent to whisper in Keiser's ear.

The old man gave a violent start and looked up. A tick started on one side of his face. Fleshy hands went to the armrests of his chair and gripped hard.

Noble drained his champagne flute for a shot of liquid courage, felt the bubbly kindle a nice fire in his belly, set the glass on the auction table and made his way over. He kept his hands in the open. He didn't want Wexler to get jumpy and pull a weapon. A shootout in the middle of the gala would likely leave a lot of innocent people dead.

Keiser straightened up in his chair, lifting his chin in a laughable attempt to make himself taller. "Mr. Noble. What an unpleasant surprise. Do the local authorities know you're here?"

"It's about time you and I had a talk," Noble said.

"With pleasure." Keiser's face morphed into a horrible grin. "There's a private room on your right where we can have a quiet talk."

"Lead the way."

Wexler steered the wheelchair past Noble and said, "Don't try anything, Jakey boy. I'll burn you down in front of all these people."

"Give it a try," Noble said and fell into step beside the big redhead. "Find out what happens."

The three of them made their way across the ballroom to a set of a double doors. Noble walked on wooden legs with a hot ball of leaden doom taking shape in his belly. He didn't know what was behind the set of doors, or if Keiser had anticipated the confrontation. He tried to control his breathing and force his shoulders to relax.

# Chapter Fifty-Eight

Detective Inspector Stokely stood in front of a large dry erase board with surveillance images stuck to it. She wore a black ballistic vest with police emblazoned across both front and back in bright yellow stitching. A Glock 19 was on her hip and her hair was in a tight bun at the base of her skull.

A small knot of uniformed patrolmen and inspectors huddled around, holding Xeroxed pages of Wexler dressed as both a police officer and in civilian clothes. It was a hastily assembled group and they frowned down at the printer copies while Stokely spoke.

"Our target's name is Wexler," Stokely told them. She was buzzing on three cups of strong black coffee. "We like him for three murders, at least. He's former SAS so he should be considered armed and extremely dangerous. He's working for this man—" She pointed to a publicity photo of Keiser clipped from Wealth International Magazine. "Otto Keiser. He's a fat cat banker with top flight lawyers, which means we have to tread carefully. Wexler and his boss are attending a fundraising gala to feed the poor or some such thing this evening. We're going to sit on the exits, pick Wexler up when he leaves, and follow him until he's alone. I don't want anyone to move on this bloke until I say. We don't want to spook him and we can't afford any mistakes. Understood?"

The group nodded in unison.

Conagher stood on the sidelines, arms crossed over his chest and a frown on his face. He'd given Stokely permission to go after Wexler at the gala only after a long and heated back and forth. In the end, Stokely had won when she promised to take the fallout if this blew up into a media nightmare. And with MI6 involved, the fallout would be radioactive.

While Stokely laid out the plan to tail and detain Wexler in more detail, Reilly hurried up, hands on his tool belt and a flush in his pale cheeks. "Sorry to interrupt, Inspector, but we just got word; Goodfellow was spotted entering a fundraising event at The Rosewood."

"When was this?"

"Moments ago."

Stokely turned to Conagher. "We've got to move on this right now."

Conagher sucked his teeth in thought and then nodded. "Get on it."

"You heard the man," Stokely told the gathering. "We're rolling. Everybody stay on your radios. Let me know the moment you spot either Wexler *or* Goodfellow."

# Chapter Fifty-Nine

Gwen was curled up in her swivel chair, knees pulled up to her chest and her arms wrapped around her legs, listening to the back and forth between Wizard and McHale. She was praying neither man noticed the gaming laptop sitting in plain sight on the work terminal. They had arrived unexpectedly, asking for an in-depth explanation of deep fakes, and neither Cook nor Witwicky had time to hide Ben's laptop. It had a bright red outer shell with a sticker featuring an elven rouge and the words *Thieves Do It In the Dark!*

While Ezra explained the finer points of deep fakes, Gwen had quietly sipped from her coffee and nonchalantly placed the cup down on the laptop sticker, covering the cartoon character and irreverent wordplay.

"We have to give the kid the benefit of the doubt," Wizard said.

But McHale wasn't ready to give Noble a pass. He tugged at his earlobe, a worried frown on his face, and asked, "How sure are we that the recording is a fake?"

"Ninety-nine percent," Gwen told them.

"Then there's a chance it's real?"

"We found the money trail," Gwen pointed out.

"How do we know that's not been faked?" McHale asked.

It seemed McHale wanted Noble to be guilty. He was clinging to the possibility that the recording was genuine and Gwen started to suspect this had less to do with the mission in Britain and more to do with McHale's on-going efforts to drive out the old guard and replace them with fresh blood; yes men who would do the party's bidding. The thought left a nugget of fear in the pit of her belly. If McHale was working this hard to get rid of Noble, how long before he went looking for an excuse to fire her and Ezra? She worked up her courage and said, "Sir, with all due respect, it would be a mistake to operate on the assumption that this recording is genuine. It will only embolden the person who created it. Next time we pick up a transmission, it might be you talking to your drug dealer, or a prostitute."

McHale's beady eyes popped from their sockets. He looked like he'd just swallowed a dung beetle. He gaped and chortled for several seconds. "I never..." he started and then said, "but who would...? It's preposterous on the face of it."

"That's just the point, sir." Ezra jumped into the mix. "If we swallow this lie it will be open season on every CIA employee and half of Washington. Anyone with a laptop will be able to cripple our government and intelligence operations by flooding us with deep fakes. The only good option is to reject the fake, find out who created it, and punish them."

McHale didn't like being told how to respond, especially by an analyst of all people, but he couldn't counter Ezra's argument. He tugged at his earlobe some more and said, "Why did Noble bust out of the black site, injuring Hunt and our security guys in the process?"

"Hunt was undoubtedly putting the screws to him," Wizard said. "It's no wonder the kid took a powder. Right now, he's probably running scared. God only knows where he'll turn up next."

Ezra glanced at his computer screen, then did a double take. "Actually, he's at a hotel called The Rosewood."

He swiveled around in his seat and clicked an alert that had just come through. "London Metropolitan Police just sighted Noble going into a fundraising event being held at the hotel."

"Only one reason I can think of," said Wizard as he reached into his breast pocket for his heart pills. He shook one into an open palm and said, "I'd bet my baseball card collection Otto Keiser is in attendance."

"That's just what we need," McHale fumed. "A CIA officer assassinating a hedge fund manager in the middle of a charity auction."

"Noble's not that stupid." Wizard's eyes watered as he fought to swallow the pill. He pointed at Witwicky's coffee cup and snapped his fingers. She passed it over and Wizard gulped. He pulled a face, wiped tears from his eyes and said, "Knowing Noble, the kid will have a plan."

"Bully for Noble," McHale said. "Get Hunt on the phone, pronto. He needs to get to that hotel and take Noble into custody before he can make a scene. I won't have Jacob Noble, or anybody else for that matter, making a mockery of this agency."

Ezra nodded and reached for the phone.

"And tell Hunt to keep it quiet." He turned on his heel and stormed from the situation room.

Wizard said, "Tell Hunt to hurry, but tell him not to tangle with the local authorities. If he can get there before the cops, great. If not, we'll have to barter with the Brits for Noble's release."

"Do you think McHale would even bother?" Gwen asked.

"We'll force his hand." Wizard passed Gwen's coffee back and pointed at the laptop. "I'm not even going to ask what that is or how it got here."

Gwen felt her face burning. She exchanged a worried glance with Ezra and said, "Probably for the best, sir."

# Chapter Sixty

Noble's hand strayed toward his shoulder holster as they passed through a door into a meeting room with fifty felt-backed chairs and a projector screen. A slightly rancid smell hung in the air from champagne spilled on the rug earlier in the evening. Someone had left a mink stoll on the back of a chair. The lights were low and the projector still threw an image of a starving child on the screen.

One side of Keiser's face was lit by the anemic blue of the projector, the other side was hidden in shadow. A nasty grin curled his lips. "You have proven incredibly bothersome, Mr. Noble."

Noble said, "Did you really think you could frame me for treason using that deep fake and I wouldn't put up a fight?"

"On the contrary. I was absolutely certain you would put on a good show," said Keiser. "You are quite tenacious and incredibly resourceful. After Croatia, I even thought about trying recruiting you, but Wexler said you could never be bought."

"He was right," Noble said.

"So it would seem." Keiser scrubbed his hands together. "Then you went and ruined my plot to destroy the U.S. a second time when you hijacked the plane carrying my EMP. Do you have any idea how much money you cost me, Mr. Noble?"

"I hope it was a lot."

"You nearly bankrupted me." A hard, cold light danced in Keiser's eyes. He gripped the arms of his wheelchair and cranked his bulk forward. "Wexler wanted to kill you and be done with it, but I told him we had to teach you a lesson."

"So you cooked up a plan to kill Hap Chan and frame me," said Noble. "But how did you know the CIA was bringing over a defector? Who talked?"

Keiser chuckled. So did Wexler. The old toad leaned back in his wheelchair and grinned. "I've been working with the Chinese the whole time. They've known for years that Hap Chan was feeding information to America, hoping to defect."

Noble's shoulders sagged. Hap Chan had been played. He said, "Then Chan's research is bogus."

"Not at all." Keiser gave a toothy smile. "I told the Chinese the information had to be genuine in order to sell the lie. Which is why they are so eager to get it back. I'm afraid that was an actual Chinese field officer you threw off a roof last night, young man. Tut-tut. The Chinese are not at all happy about that. What did you do with the research by the way?"

"Wouldn't you like to know?"

"I most certainly would." Keiser's voice turned hard. "And I will before all this is over."

"You must think you've got me right where you want me," Noble said. "Framed for a murder I didn't commit with a fake audio recording to prove it."

Keiser spread his hands as if to say, *there you have it.*

"Sorry to disappoint," Noble said. "I put a protective detail on my mother and I've worked out the flaws in the audio. I can prove it's a fake." He patted his top pocket. "And I've been recording this conversation. The game is over. You lose."

"On the contrary." Keiser's grin never faltered. "Dealing with you has taught me one thing; always have a contingency plan."

Keiser snapped his fingers and Wexler reached inside his dinner jacket.

Noble started for his own gun but instead of a weapon, Wexler brought out a phone. He opened a photo and held it up for Noble's inspection.

A frozen weight dropped into Noble's belly. His knees nearly came unhinged. He felt an iron band closing around his chest, cutting off his air supply.

"You bastard," he heard himself say. "You *bastard*."

He was staring at a picture of Mom and Burke, tied up on the floor of *The Yeoman*.

# Chapter Sixty-One

Keiser was still talking but the words washed over Noble in acid waves. He was staring at the phone screen, staring hard at the picture of his mother and Burke. Could it also be a fake? But no. Those were his cheap plastic dishes on the galley table and his reminder to pick up dog food tacked to the small fridge.

The room spun and Noble felt like he would be sick. Fear flooded his system and mixed with anger, into a noxious cocktail that made his hands burn and his stomach freeze. His mouth worked into a silent snarl but no sound came out.

"Our little game is far from over." Keiser gripped the wheels on his chair and pushed himself closer, until he was staring up into Noble's face. "Unless you want your mother to die, you will take responsibility for Hap Chan's death, along with the two dead security people, and you will plead guilty to international espionage and treason. You're going to spend the rest of your life rotting in prison, knowing it was *I* who put you there."

"You won't get away with this," Noble heard himself say, but his words came out sounding feeble and desperate.

"I already have," Keiser said in a malicious mocking tone. "The CIA and British Intelligence have all the evidence they need. Your DNA is all over the crime scene. Not to mention the two million dollars in your account."

Noble stood, swaying on the spot. His hands clenched into useless fists.

Keiser watched him, a nasty smile showcasing yellow teeth like aged ivory in diseased gums. The old goat waited for Noble to come to the inevitable conclusion.

Either way Noble played it, Keiser won. He'd planned for every contingency—he had been one step ahead the whole way and now Noble was locked into a corner from which there was no escape. He could spend life in prison or let mom die. While he stood there trying to reorder his world into something that made sense, the wail of sirens started in the distance and steadily grew into a shrieking symphony.

Wexler cocked a hand to his ear and said in false surprise, "What's that I hear? Sounds like the coppers are on their way."

Keiser leaned back in his chair and folded his hands over his belly. A self-satisfied smile fixed firmly on his face. "What's it going to be, Jacob? Your freedom, or your mother's life?"

Heart pounding madly inside his chest, Noble heard himself say, "How do I know you'll keep your word? If I give myself up to the police, how do I know you'll let mom live?"

"My dear boy, you think I'd give up my leverage?" Keiser shook his head. "You have my word your mother will be set free. In fact, I'll make certain she gets the best possible medical care. I want her to live a long and healthy life while her little boy sits behind bars for treason."

Wexler waggled the phone. "How 'bout it, Jakey, old boy? Do I call him and tell him to ice the old bird, or do we keep her alive?"

Sirens whooped outside the front of the hotel now. Tires shrieked as patrol cars surrounded the front entrance. They'd be inside any minute.

"Time's almost up," Keiser said, enjoying the titanic struggle taking place on Noble's face. "You have to make a choice."

There was a loud commotion from the gala hall as police swarmed through the sea of attendees. Someone let out a high-pitched shriek. Others demanded to know what was going on. Noble knew he had just seconds.

"You win," he said. "I'll do it."

"You'll claim responsibility for the murders?"

Noble nodded. His mouth was a thin line and his eyes stared white hot hatred.

"And admit to espionage, fraud, and treason?"

Noble handed the phone over to Keiser in stony silence.

"I knew you'd cooperate," Keiser said with a toothy grin. "I'm going to enjoy watching you waste away in prison, Jacob. I might even send you letters."

The door to the conference room flew open with a bang. Detective Inspector Stokely, followed by half a dozen uniformed patrolmen, stormed inside.

"Jacob Goodman," Stokely shouted in a voice that echoed. "You are under arrest. Put your hands up where we can see them."

Noble lifted his hands overhead. A pair of officers patted him down, warning him not to move a muscle. They found the gun and then twisted his arms behind his back. He felt the cold metal of the cuffs and heard the bracelets ratchet into place. Noble's eyes never left Keiser. "I've got your word. You promise my mother will be okay?"

A savage grin turned up one side of Keiser's wrinkled face. "She'll be just fine, Jacob. You should worry more about yourself. You're facing serious charges."

Wexler barked a laugh. "So long, Jake. Nice knowing you."

DI Stokely holstered her weapon and hooked her fists onto her hips. "You'll be coming along with us as well, Mr. Wexler."

His face went from smug delight to shock and confusion. "On what charges?"

"Impersonating a police officer and murder."

Wexler started to open his mouth.

"I did it," Noble interrupted. "I killed Hap Chan. I want to make a full confession."

Stokely's eyes narrowed. "Are you telling me you killed all three?"

"That's right," Noble said.

The detective crossed her arms over her chest and stared hard at Noble, then shook her head. "As you like it." She turned to Wexler. "You're still facing charges for impersonating an officer. Put your hands on top of your head and turn around."

"This is preposterous," Keiser said. "This man is my employee. I can vouch for his character and his whereabouts."

"He's coming with us," Stokely told Keiser. "If we need a character witness, we'll be sure to let you know."

As Noble was dragged out by a pair of officers he yelled over his shoulder, "Keiser, I'll keep my end of the deal. I got your promise. You gave your word."

Then he was being hauled through the gala, past a sea of stunned faces, to a waiting squad car.

# Chapter Sixty-Two

Gadsden kicked with all four legs, churning salty seawater, body straining against the current, eyes wide and lungs burning for lack of oxygen. The saltwater made the bee sting in his flank hurt even worse. Gadsden did *not* like water. He struggled against the eddies of darkness trying to drag him down into the depths. The *bad man* had killed him, Gadsden knew this in the way of all animals. The *bad man* had stung him deeper than any bee sting. Gadsden knew bees because, as a pup, he'd made the mistake of sticking his nose in a honeycomb and paid the price. That had been painful but nothing close to this. This sting went deeper—the poison of this sting was crushing the life right out of him—but Gadsden had to save *the Woman,* sometimes called *Ma. Master* loved *the Woman-Ma* and had made it perfectly clear that Gadsden was to protect *the Woman-Ma.* That order was lodged fast in Gadsden's brain.

Protect *the Woman-Ma.*

So Gadsden wheeled his paws in a mad effort to reach air. His legs pushed him through silty waves. Blood leaked from his hide in inky black streamers. At last, just when he thought the water would claim him, Gadsden's muzzle broke the surface and he sucked in a lung full of balmy Florida air. His mouth was open, tongue lolling, breathing heavy, blowing water in all directions as he struggled. Paws struck the soft surface. Soon he could stand. After what felt like an hour, though in reality it was only a few moments, he was limping weakly up the beach, slogging through the shallows toward dry sand. His legs gave out once, spilling him into the surf. He laid there exhausted and weak, gasping for air.

Protect *the Woman-Ma*.

A gentle breeze dried the fur on his muzzle. His eyes were stinging from the saltwater and his chest felt like it was filled with angry bees, stinging deep inside. He wondered how long he had left. Gadsden knew *Death*. He had killed. Now *Death* had come for him. But that was okay so long as he did his job to protect *the Woman-Ma* first.

Gulls wheeled overhead, making their mocking laughter, and waves crashed on the beach. The sun was out but it was cold and the beaches were mostly empty. Gadsden pushed himself back onto his feet, stopped long enough to hack up a stomach full of sea water, then peered blearily about in search of *Home*.

He could see the marina in the distance. The current had carried him more than a half mile, though that measurement had no meaning for Gadsden. Still, he knew he'd be hard pressed to reach *Home* and give *Death* to the *bad man* before it was all over.

Head hanging and ears drooping, Gadsden struggled along the beach, leaving a trail of blood, each step was mind-numbing pain. He hadn't gone far when a little girl in a hoodie saw him.

She was crouched in the sand, scooping together a sandcastle, and she looked up. Her face lit up at the sight of a doggie, then her excitement turned to a frown.

"Hello doggie," she said in a bright voice. "Are you lost?"

She spotted the blood spatters behind him and the dark matted fur on his flank. "Are you hurt, sweetie?"

She reached out a hand.

Gadsden had no time for little people. He had to protect *the Woman-Ma*. He let out a low rumbling warning from deep in his chest and showed his teeth, to let the little person know he was in no mood to *Play*.

The girl turned on her heels and ran screaming. Her parents were eating burgers on a picnic table in the grass under the trees. The girl's mother pulled her into a protective embrace and then asked the father if they should do something about the stray dog on the beach. "Might have rabies," she said.

The father suggested the best course of action would be to call animal control and let them handle it. And a good thing he did. Had he tried to handle it himself, the angry dog would have savaged him. Instead Gadsden struggled along the beach, tongue lolling, while the father dialed emergency services and asked to be connected with animal control. Gadsden would be long gone by the time the animal control people arrived. That was also for the best because the under-paid, under-staffed people at animal control are not trained to handle Czechoslovakian wolfdogs. Pepper spray and poles are little use against a dog trained for war.

Gadsden reached the marina and had to stop near a pilon to rest when his legs gave out. He spilled into the sand, an ocean wave crashing over his body, and laid there trying to summon the strength to move.

He was close to *Home*. If only he could make it onto the boardwalks. He took a few deep breaths, tried to ignore the pain coursing through his body in electric waves, and slowly pushed himself up onto trembling legs.

# Chapter Sixty-Three

Noble was led out in handcuffs, a uniformed officer on each arm, holding him tight like he might make a run for it. His thoughts were a confused avalanche of questions without answers. At the top of the list was whether or not he could trust Keiser to keep his word. Had he made a mistake giving himself up? Was mom going to die anyway? Noble second guessed himself the whole way down the hotel steps to the jumble of cop cars jamming up the entrance. His stomach was a bundle of slippery eels coiling round and round until he felt like he'd be sick and he told the officers, "I might throw up."

"Get any on my shoes and I'll break your teeth in for ya," Officer Reilly said.

Noble recognized him and said, "You again."

"That's right," Reilly said. "Think you're pretty smart walking out of the station house, but you won't be walking away again. I'll make sure of that, even if it means I have to shoot you in the leg."

Noble knew better than to push Reilly's buttons. The young officer was ready to throw the rule book out the window. Noble allowed himself to be pulled to a waiting squad car.

A large white van with an antenna on top and BBC stenciled on the side howled to a stop outside the ring of patrol vehicles. The side door rolled open and a cameraman hopped out. Noble turned his face away and in the process spotted Hunt standing across the street, hands in his pockets and a sour twist on his face.

"Watch your head," Reilly said, putting a hand on top of Noble's skull as he started to duck into the car. Cops always did this, and it's not done out of concern but because they know most criminals resist being placed in the car at the very last moment. If you can control the head, you can control the rest of the body. Noble was halfway in, not bothering to struggle, when Stokely arrived.

"I want him in my car."

Reilly stopped and turned to her. "You haven't got a protective shield in your car."

"Put him in my car," Stokely ordered.

"All due respect, Inspector, it's against regulations. This man is a violent suspect."

Stokely was unmoved and in the end Reilly hauled Noble over to an unmarked cruiser with an open back seat. He jerked the back door open and shoved Noble inside. This time he didn't bother to control the head and Noble ended up whacking his skull on the frame.

The back seat had that new car smell. There had never been any drunks or junkies in this vehicle. It didn't smell like piss and vomit.

"Should I ride with you?" Reilly asked.

Stokely climbed in the driver's seat and turned for a long look at Noble. She studied him for several seconds in quiet and then said, "You going to behave yourself, Mr. Goodfellow?"

"Yeah." Noble nodded.

Stokely told Reilly, "I think we've got an understanding."

His hands were on his belt, his right-hand riding on his pistol grip. He sucked his teeth, clearly unhappy with the arrangement. "I'll be right behind you every step of the way, Inspector. If he tries anything I'll put him down like a rabid dog."

"You do that," Stokely told him and pressed the ignition.

It took ten minutes to get her cruiser clear of the jam. They drove in silence for several blocks before Stokely asked, "Want to tell me what's really going on then?"

"I don't know what you're talking about." Noble shifted in the seat to take his weight off his hands. Fake leather creaked. His fingers were turning numb and the metal cuffs were digging a trench in the small of his back.

Stokely peered at him in the rearview. "I think you do."

"I killed them," Noble told her. "I killed them all. I'm ready to make a full confession."

Her eyes narrowed but she put her attention back on the road. "I already know you didn't kill the Chinese man," she said. "You couldn't have. You were four blocks away when it happened getting takeaway. And I don't think you killed the two men in the house across the street either, so why are you taking the rap for murders you didn't commit?"

Noble sat in stony silence.

Her eyes went to the rearview again. "I can't help you if you don't want help, Goodfellow."

The urge to spill the whole story welled up inside. Noble opened his mouth. Maybe, just maybe, she could contact the Saint Pete police and they could save mom, but that was a long shot and mom's life hung in the balance. In the end it would never work. He had to trust that Keiser would keep mom alive as a bargaining chip. He closed his mouth with a hard snap and stared out the window, making a show of his silence.

"I'm not going to stop pulling at this thread until I've got the truth, Goodfellow. You might as well talk."

"Good luck," Noble told her.

She clicked her tongue. "Be that way then." She was about to turn her attention back to the road when something caught her eye. She blinked and craned around for a look.

"What is it?" Noble asked.

"Think a grey sedan might be following us." Stokely turned back around in her seat and focusing on the road ahead. "Friends of yours?"

"I don't have any friends."

"No matter. We've got a police escort. If they try anything—"

A black van shot from an alleyway on their right, impacted the driver's side of the cruiser with a bone-rending smack of buckling metal and shattering glass. The cruiser was thrown into a spin. Noble was not buckled in and he was flung like a ragdoll. His head kissed the side window which spider-webbed, and then he was sinking down into a deep abyss. The last thing he heard was the sharp bark of pistols.

# Chapter Sixty-Four

Noble came to in the floorboard of the cruiser, his face pressed against the nap of the carpet and his ears ringing. His head felt two sizes too big and one arm was wrenched at an odd angle. Even before he was fully aware that he was awake, his body was squirming, trying to take the pressure off the arm. He hadn't been out more than a second or two. The police cruiser was still rocking on its springs. Loud pops, like bullwhips, stabbed at Noble's eardrums. He let out a grunt of pain and struggled to push himself off the floorboard, which is tricky without the use of your hands. But Noble managed it by worming around onto his stomach and then cranking his knees under himself. He levered up into a sitting position just as a bullet blew out the rear window of the cruiser, showering him in broken glass.

"Keep your head down," Stokely shouted from the front seat. She'd been wearing her safety belt and had absorbed the impact far better than Noble. She was fighting with the belt release, cranked over in her seat trying to avoid the sideways hailstorm pelting the vehicle. "Stay down, Goodman!"

"You need to return fire." Noble had to yell to be heard over the steady flat *whack-whack-whack* of gunfire. Another window exploded, littering the cabin with deadly shards. Noble felt a warm finger of fire trace his neck and knew a bit of glass had missed his carotid by less than an inch.

Three men in ski masks piled from the black van with weapons in hand. They split their fire between the unmarked cruiser and the patrol car. Bullets hissed and snapped, punching holes in the doors and kicking up little puffs of smoke. A grey sedan, the same one Stokely had spotted, roared up behind the cruiser, boxing the police vehicle in. Two more masked gunmen leapt out and added to the chaos.

Officer Reilly and another uniformed patrolman came out of the cruiser guns blazing. Reilly had the presence of mind to open the front and back doors, creating a small safe space for himself. He leaned out around the driver's side door and fired off three rounds at the black van, punching out one of the side windows, then pivoted and sent a short barrage in the opposite direction at the grey sedan. His partner, a rookie named Hess, tried to maneuver around the car, despite Reilly's warnings, and took a bullet to the gut. He doubled over and crumpled to the blacktop, moaning loudly. The van crew finished him off with a dozen shots and Hess lay in a bloody sprawl with his eyes wide and staring.

Reilly cursed loudly, leaned out, and paid back one of the ambushers with a long peel of thunder. The gunman's head snapped back, his ski mask blossomed, and his knees came unhinged. He was dead before he hit the pavement. The slide on Reilly's service weapon locked back on an empty chamber. Smoke drifted from the barrel and Reilly was still trying to pull the trigger.

"You gotta get into action," Noble shouted. He was groping behind his back for the door handle, trying to spring himself from the back seat, unaware that the crash had bent the frame. The door would not open without the help of a good body shop. He watched Reilly and his partner taking fire and yelled, "They're dying out there."

"I'm trying," Stokely shouted back. She thumbed the belt release with both hands but it refused to budge. Her face was a white sheet of panic-stricken terror and her eyes were saucers.

"Use the seat," Noble said as half a dozen rounds ricocheted around inside the car, punching holes in the upholstery and filling the air with shredded cushion. "Crank your seat back!"

Stokely let go of the buckle and twisted around. In her panic, it took her precious seconds to find the seat controls. She levered her shoulder against the seat while jamming the button down hard and the seat cranked flat with a wrench of electronic gears. With the driver's seat laid all the way back, Stokely was able to wiggle into the back of the car and jerk her weapon from the holster.

Outside, Reilly was clawing a spare magazine from his utility belt and shouting for Stokely to keep her head low. "Stay down, Inspector!" he yelled over the cavalcade of gunfire. "You're going to be alright. Keep low and let me deal with these jokers."

It took him three tries but he finally slid the fresh magazine into place. By that time he was bleeding, unnoticed, from a wound in his shoulder. A bullet had ripped through the muscle and a dark stain was spreading down his left arm. Reilly had no clue he was injured. His adrenaline was pumping so hard he could have been missing a leg and not been aware of it until he tried to take a step. He lurched out from the safety of his vehicle, levelled his weapon at the two men sheltering behind the grey sedan, and started firing. His bullets winged off the hood, snapped against the stone brick buildings, and knocked neat holes in the windshield. But he was outgunned and couldn't defend against both directions at once.

He felt a hard snap against his neck and this time knew he'd been hit. A bib of bright red blood appeared on his uniform shirt. Reilly clapped a hand over the ugly hole in his neck and spun around to fire at the van. When he did, the two men behind the sedan popped up and hammered Reilly off his feet with a dozen shots. The young patrolman fell flat. He tried to sit up but the last of the fight went out of him and he lay still. One hand was still pressed against his neck, trying desperately to staunch the heavy flow of blood piping between his fingers, but it was only a matter of time.

In the back seat of the unmarked cruiser, Stokely was crouched, her gun in both hands. She took a few deep breaths, readying herself to die fighting. Four men in ski masks were closing in on the cruiser, weapons at the ready. It was a no win situation.

Before she could get herself killed, Noble cranked his knee up and kicked Stokely hard in the back. She slammed against the doorframe and the gun slipped from her fingers, landing with a thud in the floorboards.

Noble wrapped his legs around her neck from behind and squeezed tight. Stokely made a gagging noise and clawed at his knees in an effort to pry them apart but it was no use. Within seconds, her eyes rolled up from the lack of oxygen and her body went limp.

The masked gunmen had reached the side of the car, weapons aimed, and Noble shouted, "She's unarmed. She's unarmed."

He opened his legs and let Stokely drop to the floorboards. Sirens were screaming not far away. The masked men pointed their pistols at Noble and growled, "Don't move a muscle."

# Chapter Sixty-Five

Gadsden peeled an eye open as a fresh tidal wave of pain wracked his body. Had he fallen asleep? His doggie sense told him it wasn't yet *num-num-time* which meant he could not have been out that long. He fought to stand and limped toward the long concrete ribbon which connected the string of floating aluminum docks that strung together the marina.

\*\*\*

Conagher was sitting in his office, shades drawn, pouring a finger of good scotch into a paper tumbler. His tie was loose and his hair stuck up in places. He had bags under his eyes and a knot deep inside his gut that no amount of alcohol would loosen. He was second guessing his decision to let Stokely take a run at Keiser. The choice would come rolling back on him for sure. MI6 wouldn't be happy that one of Conagher's officers had gone poking around the case after being told to leave off. But Conagher had garnered enough good will with Scotland Yard in his thirty years on the job to weather a storm or two. Just how high up the intelligence chain this series of murders went would be obvious by how much dust MI6 kicked up in the next few hours and then Conagher would know if he could push any further or if he'd spend the next few months shinning shoes with his tongue. Either way, Conagher was at least satisfied he'd done his due diligence for the four dead bodies on his turf. He capped the bottle, replaced it in the bottom drawer, and helped himself to a large swallow of scotch. The amber liquid burned going down and the tight knot remained. He was just thinking of pouring another when there came a knock on his office door. He quickly drained the paper cup, pulled a face as he swallowed, crumpled it, and shot it at a wastepaper basket before shouting, "Enter."

A fresh-faced patrol officer stuck her head in. "We've got reports of shots fired, sir. Residents of the Clerkenwell neighborhood are calling in to report police in a shootout with masked gunmen."

Conagher was on his feet, the pleasant little buzz he had going was instantly gone, replaced by a cold hand of dread. "I want all units in the area to respond."

***

Wizard was in a meeting with the Intelligence Director about a slew of on-going operations in Ukraine. He was in his office, a bottle of heart pills open on his cluttered desk, a cigarette in one hand and an ugly throbbing in his chest that told him he'd been working too long and too hard. He unearthed a file from a tottering pile and passed it across the desk. "Those are the reports on the recruitment efforts in Kiev. It's not good. We're running out of warm bodies to use as cutouts and couriers. Everything with a pulse is being used in the war effort."

The Deputy Director of Intelligence shook his head as he skimmed the reports. He was a Harvard man with a PHD in philosophy and had been appointed by McHale. He said, "Honestly not sure why you even bother, Al. The trillions of dollars congress is funneling to Ukraine isn't going to the war effort anyways. That money is just being rerouted right back into the pockets of American politicians for their re-election campaigns. It's all just one big money laundering operation. Why put so much effort into a losing battle? Kiev has to fall eventually."

Wizard leaned back in his chair, took a drag and said, "Because it's my job to help and support the people of Ukraine in any way that I can. And until I receive orders to the contrary, that's exactly what I'm going to do."

The DDI waved a hand in front of his face. "Really wish you wouldn't smoke those things around me."

"What can your IMINT people tell me about troop movements around the Donbask region?"

"I should have a new series of satellite and drone images coming in early tomorrow. I'll send the results as soon as I have them."

There was a knock at the door. Cook's head appeared, quickly followed by Witwicky. She said, "Something's come up."

"Can you excuse me, Philip?"

The DDI tucked the file folder under one arm as he stood. "This anything I need to be made aware of?"

Wizard jammed his cigarette into an ashtray. "Not unless you want to get tangled up in a sideways mission that could be a career ender during your first month on the job."

"That's my queue to leave." The DDI shouldered past Cook and Witwicky. The pair of analysts waited until he was gone then closed the door and said, "We just got word, the police vehicle that Noble was in has been ambushed by armed gunmen. Shots were fired. At least one officer is dead and others are injured. Reports are still coming in, so this information is dicey."

Wizard said, "Get Hunt on the phone. I want information and I want it fast. Let's find out if Noble is alive, dead, or captured. We need to know what's going on over there."

# Chapter Sixty-Six

Noble was pulled from the back of the unmarked cruiser by two men. They took him by the shoulders and dragged him over top of Stokely's slumped form. She was still in the floorboard, already swimming up to consciousness. A weak moan escaped her lips, muffled by the carpet. One hand flapped harmlessly against the seat as if warding off an invisible blow.

One of the heavies grabbed a fistful of Noble's shaggy hair and forced his head down while the other man wrenched his elbows up painfully behind his back, until his muscles twanged like over-tight piano wires and the joints creaked.

The stalled cruiser strobed the surrounding buildings with blue and white light. A few brave people—or stupid depending on how you wanted to view it—leaned out their windows with their phones for viral social media content. Officer Reilly and his partner lay dead in the street, in wet puddles of blood surrounded by a litter of brass shell casings. The patrol car was full of holes and a geyser of steam hissed from the grill where one of the bullets had hit the radiator. A dog barked madly inside one of the apartments and sirens wailed, getting closer.

"What should we do with her?" One of the ambushers asked, pointing his gun at Stokely's semi-conscious form. His English was good but Noble had spent enough time in Asia to recognize a Chinese accent.

"Kill her," the leader said. He was shorter than the rest of the group, but built like a piece of farming equipment with broad shoulders and legs that looked like he spent plenty of time on the squat rack.

"No," Noble shouted. "Don't kill her. She's just a cop doing her job. She's got nothing to do with this. She hasn't seen your faces. Why kill her?"

"Maybe he's right," one of them said. "We don't need any more heat."

The leader took hold of Noble's chin and levered his face up. "You wish to save her life?"

"Yesh," Noble managed to say with his lips mashed against the man's iron grip.

The leader thrust his chin at Stokely. "Bring her along. She may be useful."

Noble was manhandled into the back of the black van. The rear seats had been removed and he was thrown down on the carpeting with enough force to make lights dance in his vision. The air went out of his lungs. Noble laid there, trying to get his breath back, blinking hard to chase away the capering fairy lights. The smell of cheap cigarettes had soaked into the carpet.

A moment later, Stokely landed next to him. They had bound her wrists with zip-ties. She was awake now and her eyes were wide with terror. Noble felt her exhale. He tried to communicate with his eyes, telling her to stay calm and they'd get out of this, but it was a lie. They'd use her as leverage and kill her when she was no longer any use to them. It might have been a mercy to let them kill her while she was still unconscious. At least she would not have suffered. Now she was in for some rough treatment. Noble already knew what the Chinese were after and they'd do just about anything to get it, which included torturing and killing a British cop. But Stokely was alive for now and where there's life, there's hope. Noble just had to keep her alive long enough to figure out some way to free her. He was already working on a plan to trade Stokely's freedom for the research when the ambushers loaded their dead comrade into the back, climbed inside, and slammed the doors.

Two of the Chinese agents crouched down with their backs against the rear doors, guns pointed at Noble and Stokely. The other two took the front seats. The dead man was on his back, blood from his shattered skull leaking out over the carpet and the hot copper smell filling the cabin. One of the Chinese pressed his pistol against Noble's knee. "Try anything and you'll never walk again."

"You're the boss," Noble told him.

The van lurched into reverse. The front bumper disentangled from the busted cruiser with a sharp twist of metal and plastic. Noble tried to slow his breathing and relax his muscles, letting the adrenaline course through his system without stalling his thinking. He needed to keep his head if he was going to keep Stokely alive. It was his fault she was tangled up in this mess. He had to do everything he could to get her out. That might mean trading his life for hers. *But where would that leave mom? Would Keiser keep his promise now that Noble had been snatched from police custody?* No way to know for certain.

They drove fifteen minutes in silence. The driver took turns at random. The sirens dwindled and eventually faded. The city sounds, horns and traffic, were replaced by a stillness that told Noble they were someplace quiet where the Chinese could do their work without worrying about prying eyes. The van slowed to a stop. The driver shifted into park and left the engine running.

"What happens now?" Stokely whispered.

"Now we trade," Noble said.

## Chapter Sixty-Seven

Fingers tangled in Noble's hair and jerked him up from the floor into a sitting position. He was thrown against the wall with enough force to rock the vehicle on its springs. His head bounced off the interior door panel. His face pinched in pain but he managed to check the grunt before it escaped. His fingers felt like throbbing sausages attached to numb hands and his knees were bent back at a bad angle so that he was sitting on his lower legs. The Chinese shoved a Sig Sauer P226 against his temple.

Stokely was manhandled into a sitting position and a gun was pressed between her shoulder blades. They had her hands zip-tied behind her back. To her credit, the Detective Inspector didn't cry out or whimper when the barrel touched her. Most people instinctively cringe when a gun dimples their flesh. Stokely took a deep breath and let it out slow. Her chest swelled and contracted but her face was a stone mask. Noble's respect for her went up a few notches. It takes real guts to be that cool under pressure.

The leader of the group settled down into the Shanghai Squat used by mainland Chinese. His feet were flat on the floor with his butt against his ankles and his elbows propped on his knees. For Noble, who had spent plenty of time in China, the Shanghai Squat confirmed their ethnicity. Chinese, Russians, and some South American islanders were the only people in the world who squatted like that comfortably.

The leader peeled off his mask and took a moment to light a cigarette. It was the bulldog from the train station. He took a long drag, studied his captives, and then shot smoke from both nostrils. The glowing ember of the cigarette blazed in the dim confines of the van. A foghorn sounded and waves lapped gently at the shore, letting Noble know they were near the banks of the Thames.

"You are Jacob Noble," the leader said, watching closely from under heavily lidded eyes. The fact he knew Noble's name spoke volumes. It meant China had made book—a CIA term used when a non-official cover operative has been identified by a rival intelligence service. It happens to most field officers sooner or later and when it does, your days of going undercover in that country are over. Most field officers try to move to a new theater of operations, but eventually a field officer has to give up the cat and mouse game altogether and either join operations at Langley or move to the private sector. The fact that China knew his identity was bad news. Who else had they shared the information with? There was no way of knowing.

"We want the information you took from Hap Chan." He tapped Stokely's foot with the barrel of his Sig pistol and said, "Let us not waste any time, Mr. Noble. You know we will do whatever it takes. We will use whatever methods necessary. Tell me simply how many bullets she must suffer before you give me what I want."

"You don't have to do that," Noble said. "I'll give you the research."

He smiled and the cigarette bobbed up. "Very good."

"But I don't have it on me."

"Then we shall go get it," the leader said. "But if you are lying, she dies."

"It's at the train station. Locker number three-one-four."

The leader threw a sideways look at one of the others. He climbed into the front seat while the other two opened the back doors and dragged the dead body out, leaving a trail of dark blood on the floor. The body landed with a thump in the gravel. They were so close to the river, Noble could smell the brine and feel the cool spray. Stokely's eyes went to the open doors and Noble could tell she was thinking about making a run for it. He shook his head.

The leader grinned at her and sucked on his cigarette. "You would not make it, officer. Co-operate and we'll let you live. You have my word."

Outside, the two Chinese agents had emptied out the dead man's pockets and started kicking his face with their boots. They stomped down until his cheek bones finally shattered with dull cracks and his nose mashed flat. Most of his teeth were broken into jagged bits and his lips shredded.

Stokely let out a horrified gasp. "Why are they stomping that poor man?"

"Make it harder to identify him," Noble explained.

The leader nodded in silent acknowledgement and watched Noble with some approval.

The Chinese agents finally used a knife to slice the dead man's face and eyes. The coroner would be left with nothing but hamburger meat.

"Barbarians," Stokely said.

The leader chuckled. "Westerners cut the genitals from their youth and think we Chinese are barbarians." He shook his head. "I believe that is what you call irony."

When it was done, the Chinese agents hopped back in the van, pulled the rear doors closed and the driver shifted into gear. The dead man was left in a puddle of blood and gristle on the banks of the Thames.

# Chapter Sixty-Eight

KEISER WAS IN THE backseat of his car, surrounded by plush leather, with a drink in one hand and a mobile in the other talking to a lawyer. The black Mercedes headed north, gliding along the streets of London like an ocean liner on calm seas. The driver had a tight grip on the wheel and wore a semi-automatic under his black jacket. He was part of Keiser's security team and the last time he'd seen his boss this incensed, Wexler had lost an eye.

"I want him out of jail before the sun comes up," Keiser was saying.

"He hasn't been arraigned yet," Thomas Rawlston said. "But the charges are serious. Impersonating an officer is no laughing matter. We'll be looking at a fairly substantial bail and he probably won't be arraigned until morning, earliest. Depending on the docket, it could be late tomorrow before he goes in front of the magistrate."

"Apparently I didn't make myself clear." Keiser rattled the ice in his glass and tried to keep his voice calm. "Get Wexler out of police custody or spend the rest of your life practicing law in Paraguay."

"I'll do my..."

Keiser didn't hear the rest. He had already hung up. He downed the last of his drink, cracked the ice between his teeth loudly, and drummed the glass against the door to get the driver's attention. "Step on it, will you, man? I've got a busy night ahead of me."

The driver put his foot down without question and the Mercedes cut through the late night traffic like a hungry shark, weaving between and around slower moving vehicles.

Keiser reached for the bottle and poured himself another. He'd already received word through his sources that Noble never made it to the police precinct. He and the police woman had been ambushed by masked men. There were two dead police officers and Noble was missing. The Inspector had gone missing as well, which meant she was probably a hostage along with Noble. And Keiser knew who had taken them. Only the Chinese would be so bold and so reckless.

Once they got the research, they'd kill Noble and the police woman. Keiser had spent a lot of time and considerable money in maneuvering Hap Chan into position to defect while making sure Noble was on the receiving end. Now Noble was going to die, if he wasn't dead already, and the Chinese would have their research back. A vast fortune down the proverbial drain. That intel was worth hundreds of millions. Keiser frowned and sipped as he thought about the complete waste of time and resources. He cursed in German. He'd wanted Noble behind bars. Now he'd have to be content with the fact that Noble was dead and no longer a threat. Which made the mother a loose end.

He dialed another number and waited entirely too long for an answer. When the Haitian finally picked up, Keiser said, "Terminate them both."

***

Mary Elise Noble was on the floor of the galley with her back against Burke and her hands tied brutally tight. Her bottom was numb, her lip was cut and bleeding, and her back ached, but that was nothing compared to the fear coursing through her in waves.

Warm sunlight pierced the windows, beading sweat on her hands and forehead. She could feel Burke's sweat soaking through her dress. He was a big man and he was drenched. And he was starting to stink.

The Haitian had roped them both together with spare rigging line and now he sat at the galley table, his gun within easy reach and the shotgun propped against the booth, eating cold leftover rice and beans out of a Styrofoam box he'd found in the refrigerator.

"Try to stay calm, Mrs. Noble," Burke whispered under his breath. His nose was broken and bleeding freely and his words came out thick and slurred. He said, "They want you alive or we'd both be dead already so keep cool and we'll find a way out of this."

"Do you really believe that?" Mary asked through trembling lips.

"Yes, I do."

"Are you scared?"

He paused before answering. "More scared than I've ever been in my life." He had to pause to catch his breath, spitting out a wad of blood onto the floor. "But where there's life there's hope."

"Hey," the Haitian spoke around a mouth stuffed with rice. "Keep quiet."

They watched him eat in silence. Mary whispered a prayer under her breath. She was asking God to save her, or at the very least make her death quick and painless. As a cancer survivor, Mary had dealt with her share of pain. She had hoped to die a peaceful death in her bed, but that didn't look likely at this point. The Haitian had them tied up at gun point and he had the cheek to eat food from the fridge, seemingly without a care in the world. And why should he? It wasn't like the police were going to come along anytime soon. No one even knew Mary and Burke were being held captive. This maniac in his leather coat could do anything he wanted with them, anything at all. He'd probably start the motor, sail them out to open waters, and dump their bodies in the sea. Hopefully she'd be dead by that point. She didn't want to drown in the crushing blackness of the ocean. She took a deep breath and it shuddered out of her in waves.

The Haitian was scrolling social media when his phone started to vibrate. He picked up, listened a moment and then said, "Consider it done."

"Bad news," Burke whispered.

"How do you know?" Mary asked.

"I just do," he said. "I'm sorry."

"It's not your fault."

The Haitian pocketed the phone, stubbed his cigarette out in the plate of rice, then went below. He was back up a moment later with a red plastic gas container. The pungent odor of petrol filled the galley. The Haitian started sloshing gasoline over Mary's legs and then her head. She let out a pitiful moan. The fumes burned her lungs and stung her eyes. She started to cry.

"You coward," Burke shouted. "At least make it quick."

"Sorry, mon." The Haitian went on pouring gas, now over Burke's head and shoulders. "Gotta make it look like an accident."

Burke pulled at the ropes, straining his massive shoulders in a useless attempt to free himself.

Mary said, "Do you know Jesus, Mr. Burke?"

He stopped struggling long enough to say, "No ma'am, but I think I'm about to meet him."

# Chapter Sixty-Nine

The Chinese parked the van outside King's Cross in an alley with easy access to Pancras Road. They switched off the engine and sat in silence. The night wore on and Noble wanted to check his watch but it was bound behind his back. It had been almost midnight when Stokely burst into the gala and arrested him. It had to be close to four in the morning now.

Was his mother still alive? He had no way of knowing. Fear was a tight knot in his throat.

The Chinese all lit cigarettes. Two sat in the front, speaking in quiet whispers. The other two were in the back, pistols in hand, staring hard at Noble and Stokely, daring them to make a move. Smoke slowly filled the van, stinging Noble's eyes. He blinked, ignoring the tears gathering on his lashes, and tried to relax.

Stokely was huddled next to him, her face tight with concentration. In a low voice she said, "What are they waiting for?"

"They're checking to see if anyone is watching the train station," Noble told her. "They have no way to know if I'm telling the truth or walking them into a trap, so they wait and watch, looking for anything out of place. I'd do the same in their position."

One of the Chinese men leaned forward and hissed in Mandarin.

"Any idea what that means?" Stokely asked.

"Loosely translates; shut up."

Noble put his head back against the wall of the van, closed his eyes and tried not to cough. The smoke was making him lightheaded and the exhaustion of the last two days was catching up. He was cold, tired, hungry, and covered in bruises. And through all the fatigue and pain, he couldn't stop thinking about mom. Was she okay? Was Burke? Every time Noble pictured them tied up on the floor of *The Yeoman* his mouth filled with hot bile and his face twisted in pain.

"You don't like the cigarette, Mr. Noble?" the leader asked.

Noble opened his eyes and said, "It's a good way to die early."

"Americans are obsessed with health." He grinned. "What's the point of staying healthy for people in our line of work?"

Noble didn't bother to answer. His mother would say something about the body being a temple. Or one of her favorites, *eat right, so you can feel right, so you can think right. Am I right?*

Time dragged by. There was a hint of grey in the black vault above King's Cross by the time the Chinese finally made their move. The leader stubbed out his cigarette, climbed into the back, and patted Stokely's pockets until he found her handcuff keys. He ordered Noble to lean forward and unlocked the cuffs. Noble massaged his wrists in an effort to get some circulation back into numb fingers. They cut the zip ties from Stokely's wrists and threw the back doors open.

The Chinese ditched their masks and pocketed their weapons. Noble and Stokely were herded from the vehicle. Cold smacked Noble's face and he took a deep breath of fresh air, enjoying the breeze in his hair, knowing he smelled like a walking humidor. One of the thugs took a tight hold on Noble's arm, pulled him close, and dug the barrel of a gun into his ribcage. "Call for help and I'll kill you. Understand?"

Noble grunted in reply.

They did the same with Stokely, a bruiser holding her arm and jamming a gun into the small of her back. Together, the group crossed the street toward the station. Once inside, Noble gave directions past the vendors and ticketing to the long term storage lockers.

"Which number?" the leader asked.

"314."

They all crowded into the aisle and the leader said, "What's the combo."

"I'll do it," Noble said and started forward.

"I'm not stupid, Mr. Noble." The leader smiled. "What's the combination."

Noble had to make them work for it. He chewed the inside of one cheek like he was thinking through his options.

There was a soft metal click as the thug holding onto Stokely thumbed back the hammer on his weapon. She stiffened.

Noble gave them the combo and, as the leader spun the dial, Noble turned to Stokely. He pressed his lips tight and pushed his eyebrows up in a silent warning, but she was too keyed up to get the message.

The lock released and the door hinged open.

There was an ear-splitting bang and a flash of light, followed by a cloud of acrid black smoke.

# Chapter Seventy

Terror clawed at the edges of Mary Noble's sanity. She was drenched in gasoline. The fumes stung her eyes. The thought of burning to death was more than her mind could bear. The idea opened a terrible rift in her subconscious that nearly unglued her. She was mad with fright and her limbs shook uncontrollably. Her bladder threatened to let go. The gasoline on her skin felt like an evil oil slick. Burke frantically pulled at his restraints, wrenching this way and that, flexing broad shoulder muscles in an effort to break free.

The Haitian emptied the fuel can and tossed it back down the steps. It landed with a hollow thud somewhere in the engine compartment. The galley smelled like a roadside filling station and Mary remembered that it's not the gasoline that ignites, it's the fumes. One good spark would set the whole place ablaze. How long would she live once the flames took hold of her? Seconds would feel like hours and every tortured second would be a preview of hell.

She opened her mouth to pray but the words didn't come out. It was just a scream inside her brain.

*God please save me. I don't want to die like this!*

She tried again to pray out loud and what came out was a song. Sitting on the galley floor, bound and drenched in gasoline, Mary started to sing a worship song, low at first and then with more conviction. She wasn't praying for deliverance any more. She knew there was nothing that could save her. She was just using the last few seconds to get right with her maker before the pain started.

The Haitian was reaching in his pocket for a cigarette and stopped. So did Burke. For several seconds both men were still and listened to this old lady, who was about to die, singing a worship song. The Haitian had killed thirty-seven people and not a single one of them had ever stopped to sing. He was gripped by a strange fantastical dread rooted in his childhood and Haitian voodoo. He was not a spiritual man but he feared supernatural powers. For a moment it was all he could do to listen to the old woman sing while a macabre terror took shape in his mind, warning him to walk away from this job and not look back. Then he reminded himself that he didn't believe in any voodoo nonsense.

He laughed, shook a cigarette from the pack and stuck it between his lips. "You're a strange old bird, you know that?"

Mary ignored him and kept singing, a little louder now despite the petrol fumes stinging her lungs.

Burke said, "You're going to hell for this, you piece of trash."

The Haitian brought out his lighter. "Say hello to the Devil for me, mon."

A shaggy wet shape exploded through the open hatch, slammed the Haitian off his feet, and the silver zippo went tumbling.

Gadsden, bloody and exhausted, tackled the Haitian. One hundred and eighty pounds of dog pinned him to the ground. Claws shredded the leather coat. The Haitian gave a terrified howl as Gadsden ripped and tore. There was a brief, frantic struggle while he tried to get at the gun in his waistband, but powerful jaws locked around his throat and within seconds it was finished. The Haitian lay dead, a bloody mangled heap. Gadsden limped over to Mary and collapsed with his head on her thigh.

# Chapter Seventy-One

Noble closed his eyes just before the door hinged open to avoid the worst of the flash but his ears were ringing from the loud thunder clap. He spun and hammered an elbow into the Chinese agent holding him, knocking the man backward into the lockers. Everyone else was stumbling around blind and deaf. The leader of the Chinese was bent over, hands over his eyes. He'd gotten a face full of powder flash from the explosion. The skin around his eyes was bright red and already forming blisters. He let out a long mewling sound like a cat giving birth.

Stokely wasted no time. She used her entire body like a battering ram against her captor. The agent stumbled and almost recovered but Stokely, swinging wild, hit him with a blind haymaker that put him down on his butt.

A thick blue cloud of smoke, smelling of singed cotton, hung in the air. People screamed and ran. The explosion had sounded like a gunshot in the close confines and now there was a general stampede for the doors. It wouldn't be long before security showed up. Noble knew he had to end this quickly and get out before the rental cops arrived.

One of the Chinese intelligence officers had his pistol out. Noble locked up the gun with both hands and lashed out with his heel. There was a nasty crunch and the agent's knee bent at a nauseating angle. His eyes opened wide. Noble wrenched the gun from his grasp and rapped him over the skull with it. His head snapped back, his eyes drifted in different directions, and he pitched over.

A second agent squinted in search of a target. He wiped his eyes, blinked, and his gaze focused in on Stokely. His finger started to tighten on the trigger.

Noble stepped forward and slammed the butt of his pistol down on the man's wrist with a bone shattering crack. The gun slipped from limp fingers. Stokely went after it on her hands and knees, coughing through tears.

The leader had finally recovered his wits and he jerked a small caliber pistol from his waistband. His face was shiny red and masked with hate.

A siren blasted throughout King's Cross. Emergency lights on the ceiling flashed bright white, adding to the confusion.

Noble closed the distance, smashing the leader against the lockers. His ears were still ringing and he was staring at the world through tears, but Noble used his whole body to keep the leader pinned while he groped for the man's wrist with his free hand. The leader tried desperately to wrench his arm free. Noble stuffed his pistol hard against the Bulldog's hipbone and pulled the trigger at point blank range.

A cacophonous boom echoed through the station. The man's face worked into a comical O. He continued to struggle for a moment and then the pain set in. He let out a shuddering breath. The strength went out of his legs and he started to sag. Noble shook the gun from his grip, kicked it away, and turned back around in time to see Stokely deliver a savage kick that laid the remaining agent out in a semiconscious sprawl. She was crouched like a jungle cat, a gun clutched tight in a white fist, finger dangerously close to the trigger, and a feral look on her face.

"You okay?" Noble had to yell over the sirens and the ringing in his ears. He slipped the gun into the pocket of his rented tux, reached into the open locker for the flash drive, then searched the leader for the van keys. The Bulldog was on the ground squirming in pain. A puddle of bright red blood formed around his hips. He was shot and bleeding but the injury wasn't life threatening, though he'd probably never dance again. Noble dug the keys from the agent's pocket.

Stokely seemed to take stock of herself, probing her chest and stomach like she was looking for hidden bullet holes, then she nodded. Her eyes were still wide and her words came out a shout. "Yeah. I think so."

"Come on," Noble said. "Let's get out of here."

He took hold of her arm and a moment later they were both sprinting the length of the station. Noble reached for her weapon and said, "Give me that."

She was still working through the shock of what had happened, not thinking clearly. In the last few hours she'd been in a car wreck, watched two cops gunned down in the street, kidnapped, held at gunpoint, and then had to fight for her life. That sort of trauma left people stunned and looking for direction but her critical thinking would soon reassert itself. Noble wanted to have her out of the station by then. He reached across, took the gun from her hand, and tucked it in his waistband. They passed a trio of guards in grey uniforms going the other direction. Noble said, "Better get over there! I think someone's been shot."

That set the guards moving faster. One of them reached for his radio as he ran and barked for emergency medical services.

Noble steered Stokely out the front entrance, across the broad expanse of sidewalk and into the alley where the Chinese agents had parked the van. He could see Stokely shaking off the mental roadblock.

She ran both hands through her hair, shook her head like she was trying to clear it and said, "That was pretty intense. You saved my life. Thank you."

"Happy to help." Noble unlocked the door and climbed in. "Hope I haven't caused you too much paperwork, officer Stokely, but this is where we part ways."

"Not so fast." She grasped hold of his arm and clambered in right alongside him. She had to climb over him to get into the passenger seat. For a moment, Noble was staring at her bottom.

"You're not getting away that easy," she said. "You saved my life, but I'm still a cop and you're still a fugitive."

Noble patted his pocket. "And I've got both guns. Now get out."

"Go ahead and shoot me."

When he didn't make a move, Stokely said, "I've got your number Mr. Jacob Noble. You're no killer. Least not if you can help it. You could have killed that Chinese thug in the train station, you could have killed them all, instead you shot him in the hip. So stop pretending like you're going to use that gun on me."

Noble started the engine and put the van in gear but didn't take his foot off the brake. "Don't kid yourself Stokely. I'll do what I have to."

She pinned him with a fierce gaze. "You're going to answer some questions, Noble."

A pair of police cruisers shot past the alley, sirens screaming.

Noble watched them and then said, "Deal, but you have to do something for me first."

Her mouth tightened.

"I saved your life," Noble reminded her.

"What is it?"

"Use your connections to contact the Saint Petersburg, Florida Police Department and have them send armed units to the North

Yacht Basin. I'll give you the slip number. There's a man and a woman being held hostage."

"What does any of this have to do with a town in Florida?" Stokely asked.

"You want answers?"

She scowled but said, "Get me to a phone."

# Chapter Seventy-Two

Tears squeezed from the corners of Mary's eyes and helped wash away some of the gasoline. The Haitian lay dead. His eyes were open and staring with a scream frozen on his face. His hands lay to either side, fingers hooked into claws. He was surrounded by a large puddle of tacky black blood slowly mixing with the petrol. Burke was still fighting to free himself and the dog lay on the floor, his muzzle on Mary's thigh, struggling to breathe. Air whistled from his nose in long tortured sighs. Mary wanted to pet him but the best she could do was stroke one side of his face with her fingertips. The poor animal must have gone through hell making his way back to the boat after being shot and kicked in the water. But he'd made it and, in the end, he'd given his life for hers. Mary had never given much thought to animals and the afterlife, but if they did go to heaven, Mary asked God to give Gadsden a comfy doggie bed and a plate piled high with bacon. He had earned it.

"You did so good," Mary managed to say through tears. "You're a good dog."

Gadsden turned his eyes on her without moving his head. He let out a weak moan and flopped one massive paw onto her thigh.

Mary had no idea how long she sat like that. She was just getting her tears under control and thanking God for a miraculous delivery when Burke finally managed to free a hand. He let out a savage curse of delight and said, "I'm out. Give me a minute I'll have you out of those ropes and we'll get the dog to a hospital. You alright Mrs. Noble?"

Mary nodded weakly. Her brain was starting to swim, thoughts seemed to skip and glide around greasy pools. She muttered that she was okay but in fact she was suffering from fume inhalation.

Burke quickly worked his other hand free, then struggled to shift the thick hemp rope over his head and shoulders. Once he was out, he turned to Mary. The dog was hurt bad but the bleeding had mostly stopped, probably because the poor beast didn't have much left. In fact, it seemed a miracle Gadsden was still alive. Burke had to remind himself he didn't believe in miracles. He hurried to free Mary from the ropes and by the time he had her hands loose, it sounded like half the Saint Pete police force was screaming up to the marina.

He was just helping Mary into a seat at the galley table when half a dozen officers in black tactical gear stormed the boat. They shouted for everyone to get down on the deck and put their hands behind their heads. Mary and Burke were too tired and exhausted to comply with that order. Burke dropped into the seat beside Mary and put his hands up over his head in surrender.

Mary waved a hand at the dead Haitian and said, "That's the one you want officers." Her words were slurred and punch drunk. "He tried to kill us."

"Dog's been shot," Burke told them. "Needs a hospital."

One of the SWAT officers knelt beside Gadsden, pressed his fingers against the dog's throat, and then spoke into the radio hooked to his tactical harness. "Got one dead and an injured dog. Going to need emergency medical. Be advised, this place is full of gasoline. We need to be careful in here or the whole boat will go up in flames."

He turned to Burke and Mary. "You folks just sit tight. We're going to get you out of here soon as we can."

"Who called the police?" Mary wanted to know.

"Funny thing." The SWAT officer was already working to stabilize the dog and talked while he ripped open a fresh bandage. He pressed the pad to the ugly bullet hole in Gadsden's side and started wrapping it with clean white gauze that turned pink instantly. "We got a call from some Detective Inspector in London, England of all places. Said there were two people being held hostage on this boat. Guess we got here a little late."

"You got here just in time," Mary assured him.

An officer took her by the arm, asked if she could stand and steered her toward the hatch. He said, "Let's get you out of here."

"What about the dog?"

"We're going to do everything we can for him."

# Chapter Seventy-Three

"Interesting place to go to ground," Stokely said as she eased into a pew next to Noble. "You know cops check local churches when they search for fugitives right? The bad guys tend to run to mom or their priest."

She had two bottles of water and handed one to him.

Noble took it and twisted off the cap. "Cops look for thugs in churches. No one looks for spies in churches."

"Maybe we should start," Stokely said. They had picked up a burner phone from a bodega around the corner. It lay on the pew between them. Stokely had used it to call the Saint Pete cops and Noble had sent a coded message to Duval.

Stokely said, "I didn't take you for the religious type."

Saint Giles is an old gothic construction on Fore Street. A row of hardwood benches marched in unison up to a raised dais with a simple wood lectern in front of a stained-glass window of Christ and his apostles. The smell of incense hung in the air. Noble was slumped in the pew, his bow tie hanging loose and his top button open. He had a dark bruise forming on the side of his head, just below the hairline where he'd taken a hard knock when Stokely's patrol car was hit. His knuckles were scraped and his bottom lip was caked in blood. He took a swig of water, reflected briefly on the fact that Stokely might have spiked it with a sleeping agent—she'd been gone long enough—and decided to risk it. He had the bible tract in one hand and said, "My mother is a born-again Bible quoting Baptist."

"You know this is a catholic church?"

"What's the difference?"

"You obviously haven't spent any time in Ireland."

Noble grinned. He knew the difference but figured; any port in a storm. He thrust his chin at the phone. "Maybe you should call."

"Patience," she said. "They'll call."

She had taken the time to clean herself up. Her hair was pulled back in a short ponytail and she'd applied foundation to a welt on her chin. It didn't cover the bruise but helped hide it. Her button-down shirt was split under the arm and her sport coat was rumpled. She knew every cop in London was searching for her and it was only a matter of time before she'd have to call the precinct. She could only play the ghost for so long. She'd have to account for all the lost time later and there were only so many lies she could tell. With two dead police officers, IA would want a full account. She'd need a rock solid story for why she hadn't reported in earlier. As of now, she planned to blame it on the Chinese. She'd say they'd been hiding and in fear for their lives. She probed the rising welt on her chin and said, "So Jacob Noble, huh?"

He grinned. "The best lies are just a few degrees away from the truth."

"And the boat in Saint Pete Florida?"

"My mother," Noble told her. "She was watching my dog for me. Keiser sent one of his bully boys to tie her up. He was going to use her to keep me in line."

"That's why you admitted to the murders," Stokely said.

Noble nodded.

"Why's Keiser gunning for you, Noble? What's his beef?"

"It's a long story."

"You owe me."

"A few years ago, Keiser tried to devalue the U.S. dollar by flooding the market with untraceable counterfeits. I put a stop to it and cost him a fortune."

She nodded understanding. "And now he wants his revenge."

"The fix is in," Noble said. He told her about the deep fake and the money in a bank account in his name.

Stokely whistled. "He sewed that up pretty tight."

"That's putting it mildly."

"Well we aren't going to let him win," Stokely said.

"I don't see how we can stop him," Noble said. "I had him on tape, admitting the whole thing, but he's got the evidence now and I'm sure he's destroyed it."

Stokely leaned over and fixed him with a hard stare. "Are you an Ameri*can* or an Ameri*can't*?"

Noble laughed out loud. He took one last look at the Bible tract, folded it and put it in his pocket. "What have you got in mind, Inspector Stokely?"

The phone rang and Stokely reached for it. A Sergeant named Donalds with the Saint Pete police department told her that the SWAT team had arrived in time to save two people. The dog was in critical condition and considered not likely but Stokely decided not to share that bit with Noble. He had enough on his plate. Donalds was very interested to know how a police inspector in London got wise to a hostage situation in Florida. She said, "The tip came in from a confidential informant. I'm sure you understand."

He wasn't satisfied but took down Stokely's name and badge number in case she was needed to answer any questions in future court proceedings, though he admitted to her that was unlikely since the suspect was dead. She thanked him, rang off and said, "The Saint Pete police have your mother sorted out. She's safe and sound. Your dog is in the hospital but they say he's going to make a full recovery. That's one less thing to worry about."

Noble flushed and Stokely realized he was fighting hard not to tear up. She put a hand on his shoulder and squeezed. He turned his attention to the stained-glass window and the large cross in the center. He whispered, "Thank you, God."

# Chapter Seventy-Four

COOK AND WITWICKY HAD the gaming lap top open, waiting for word from Duval. Gwen's elbow was propped on the desk with her head resting in her hand and her eyelids drooping. Ezra sipped from a soda can and peered at the clock on the wall. It was the middle of the night—early morning in London—and Noble had been missing for hours. Reports of the shootout between police and masked gunmen was on every British news channel. The whole country was on the lookout for *Goodman* and a missing British Inspector named Stokely. Both had been abducted at gunpoint and forced into the back of a dark van. Images taken by residents had flooded the internet and gone viral. Most were too far to make out any details and no one had bothered to get the license plate but there was a decent enough profile image of Noble to make out his rakishly long hair. It wouldn't be enough to ID him in a court of law but was enough for Cook and Witwicky. They had also learned that Wexler, the head of Keiser's personal security detail, had been taken into custody by British authorities. Unlike Noble, Wexler had arrived at the precinct, followed shortly by a lawyer claiming to represent him. Cook and Witwicky had managed to collect all this info through back channels and passed it up the chain of command to Wizard. Now it was a waiting game to see if Noble turned up alive or dead.

Ezra took another swallow of sugar-laced caffeine and set his soda aside before checking the reports coming out of London. Nothing new. Next he checked in on his video game, but there were no new messages.

The door lock chirped.

Gwen came awake with a grunt and wiped drool from her mouth while Ezra slapped the laptop lid closed.

"You can't do that," Wizard was saying. He had a bottle of pills clutched in one claw and a frown on his face. "It will be open season on our field officers all over the globe. You'll effectively shut down our intelligence apparatus."

"It's out of my hands, Dulles." McHale led the way into the situation room. He had his jacket off and his sleeves rolled up. His round glasses were riding down his bloodshot nose and his hair looked like he had combed it with a balloon. He said, "The President has already made up his mind."

"The President is a senile old goat who can't string together a coherent sentence." Wizard made sure the door closed and locked and he put his back against it. "You need to change his mind."

"It's not my place," McHale said.

"You're the Director of CIA for cripsake."

"It's done," McHale said and turned to the pair of analysts. "Any word on Noble's whereabouts?"

"None," Ezra said.

McHale frowned. "I need Hunt on the phone."

"What's going on?" Gwen asked while Ezra picked up the line and used his computer to dial.

Wizard dumped a pill into his open palm and tossed it in his mouth. "The Chinese are up in arms, making an international stink, claiming one of our people killed two of their agents."

"They admitted Hap Chan was one of their own?" Ezra asked as he listened to the phone ring.

"Why would they do that?" Gwen asked.

"Because they want Noble's head on a platter," McHale said.

"That's not what they're after." Wizard shook his head. "They want us to admit he's one of ours, which is the same as admitting we stole classified top secret research. It's tantamount to a war declaration. It wouldn't just convict Noble, it would convict the United States of espionage on the world stage."

Ezra pointed to the phone and mouthed, "Hunt."

"Put him on speaker."

McHale brought Hunt up to speed on the Chinese and their demands.

"We actually going to turn over one of our own?" Hunt asked.

"We've got no choice in the matter," McHale told him. "This comes from the very top. Your orders are to find Noble and hold him for extradition. The President doesn't want a trade war with China over one field officer."

It was a moment before Hunt answered, "With all due respect, sir, have we considered how that will affect our other field officers?"

McHale's face shaded red. "You have your orders, Mr. Hunt." He reached past Cook and stabbed the disconnect button.

"That's that then," Wizard said in rasping tones. He massaged his throat with tears standing in his eyes, trying to get the pill to go down.

Gwen hurried to hand him a cup of cold coffee.

Wizard downed the coffee and wiped his eyes. "We're playing right into the hand of the Chinese Communist Party."

McHale rounded on him. "You don't think I know how to do my job, Mr. Dulles?"

"Quite frankly, no."

McHale's face turned a deeper shade of red. "You're a legacy, Al, and you've got no shortage of friends on the Hill, but your days are numbered with this agency."

Wizard reached into his coat, casually took out his pack, stuck a cigarette in his mouth and lit it. "Tell me something I don't know."

McHale pushed past him and stormed from the situation room.

Ezra resisted the urge to do a fist pump.

Wizard pointed at the laptop. "I'm assuming you can contact Noble on that thing?"

Ezra and Gwen looked at each other and then back at Wizard. There was no sense lying. Wizard could smell a lie like a fart in a car. Ezra said, "In a roundabout way."

Wizard blew smoke. "He deserves to know."

## Chapter Seventy-Five

Noble turned the flash drive over in his hands, trying to decide on his next course of action. Mom was out of danger, which was a huge weight off his chest, but he was still wanted for murder, espionage, and treason. The morning passed slowly until breakfast time came and went and noon was fast approaching. Noble was no closer to reaching a decision and his stomach was talking to him, rumbling loudly.

Stokely sat beside him, offering up occasional reminders. "We can't hang out here all day," and "I'll have to report in soon." Mostly she encouraged him to turn himself in to the police and let the official channels sort out the mess. She promised to go to bat for him and help clear his name. Noble could tell she was running out of patience. She was a cop and cops do things by the book, but the book wasn't going to be any help here. Even if he did turn himself over to British authorities, the United States would deny any knowledge of him. Noble was a non-official cover operative which meant the cavalry would not swoop in to save him.

He closed a fist around the flash drive and his knuckles turned white. If he fled to America and turned himself over to the CIA, they'd put him in a black site and subject him to enhanced interrogation methods until they were absolutely positive he was telling the truth. That might take months and he would come out the other end a mental wreck. British authorities might be his best bet. Stokely could help clear him of the murder charges but he was still guilty of breaking about a dozen other laws. He'd probably do six months to a year in British prison, but he could do the time and come out with his sanity intact. His career with the CIA would be over but at least he'd have his health and a working brain. He was just about to say as much to Stokely when the phone rang.

Noble reached for it and Stokely said, "Speaker."

He put it on speaker and held it between them so they could both listen.

"Bad news I'm afraid," Duval said. "Just got word from our friends inside Langley. The Chinese are claiming you helped steal classified technology and that you killed two of their intelligence officials. They want your head on a platter and it looks like your president has decided to turn you over to them. China is threatening to cut off all trade with the U.S. unless you're extradited to Beijing. The FBI is reaching out to Scotland Yard and Interpol. You just shot up to the top of the most wanted list."

Noble closed his eyes and bit back a curse.

"Sorry mate," Duval offered in a dejected tone. "Is there anything I can do?"

"Mail those letters," Noble told him.

"I'll make sure they get to the right place," Duval promised. "I guess this is goodbye?"

"I guess so."

"Sorry about the way things turned out, Jake. You're a good sort."

"Thanks, Sasha. You've been a real trooper. Be sure to keep your head down and your nose clean."

"Don't worry about me," Duval said. "Your two friends at Langley and I have an understanding."

Noble managed to crack a smile. "They're two of the good ones. You can trust them."

They kept the line open for a while without talking. Neither man knew quite what to say. Finally Duval said, "Well, bye Jake."

"So long, Sasha."

He hung up and Stokely said, "Was that who I think it is?"

Noble pocketed the phone. "Yep."

"You've got interesting friends, Mr. Noble."

"I've led an interesting life."

"You talk about it like it's over."

"My back is against a wall," Noble told her. "The CIA will eventually get me and I'll be turned over to the Chinese."

"There has to be something we can do," Stokely said.

"There is." Noble held up the flash drive. "I've got it and Keiser wants it. I'm going to arrange a meeting."

"And what? Kill him?" She turned to face him in the pew, invading his personal space. "You do that and you will be guilty of murder."

"I'm going to trade the Chinese research for proof that he set me up."

"Will that be enough to clear you with the Chinese?"

He shook his head. "No, but it might be enough to make the U.S. reconsider turning me over to them."

She pushed a lock of hair out of her eyes and said, "Okay, what's the plan?"

"You going to help?"

"I'm a cop," she said. "And Keiser is breaking all sorts of laws."

# Chapter Seventy-Six

Keiser waited in the back of the car, drumming fat fingers against his thigh. Outside, snow drifted down from a flat gray sky and melted before it could pile up. Little white drifts gathered on the wipers and frost crystalized on the edges of the windows. Londoners were huddled in heavy parkas and tucked their chins as they hurried along slippery sidewalks.

The sleek black sedan was parked across the street from the police precinct where Wexler was being held. It was just past noon and Keiser's patience was wearing thin. He had been unable to contact the Haitian and Wexler should have been out on bail hours ago. He grunted his frustration and reached one pudgy, liver-spotted hand into his coat pocket for his phone when the front doors opened and Wexler started down the steps.

The big redhead spotted the waiting sedan and hesitated just a moment before crossing the street. His face was a hard slate when he climbed in next to Keiser. He didn't look at his employer. He stared hard at the seat back instead. "I didn't say a word."

"I know you didn't, my boy." Keiser tucked the phone back into his pocket and studied Wexler a long moment. "I know you better than that, and yet, you did make mistakes. You allowed yourself to be seen. They have you on camera impersonating a police officer."

Large beads of sweat formed on Wexler's forehead despite the cold. He licked dry lips. "I can make it right."

Keiser clicked his tongue. "It's too late for that. The damage is done. You're finished in Great Britain. You need to get out of the country before you have to stand trial."

Wexler's chin trembled. "What happens now?"

Keiser enjoyed watching brutes like Wexler squirm. They thought power came from lifting heavy weights and pointing a gun. Real power, Keiser knew, came from money. Money turned the levers of power more efficiently than any army ever could. Right now the big brute was wondering if Keiser planned to kill him, but Keiser had no such intentions. Wexler had been a wolf when Keiser first put him on the payroll, a strong, independent free thinker with delusions of grandeur. Now he was an obedient rottweiler, trained and disciplined. He fetched when Keiser said fetch and sat when Keiser said sit. The perfect soldier. Keiser had no plans to kill such a useful animal. He reached across and patted Wexler on the shoulder. "No need to worry, boy. There is a place for you in my organization, just not here in London."

Wexler drew in a shuddering breath. "Thank you, sir."

The phone rang and Keiser answered. "Who is this?"

"I'll give you three guesses. The last two don't count."

"Jacob Noble," Keiser said, more to himself.

Wexler sat up a little straighter and his large hands curled into fists.

"Right in one. Congratulations. You win the grand prize."

Keiser's mouth pinched like he'd just swallowed a lemon. He didn't care for Noble's cheek but he played along. "And what is the prize?"

"A meeting," Noble said. "I've got something you want."

Keiser took the phone away from his ear and put it on speaker. "I'm listening."

"Meet me at the abandoned railyard south of Clapham Station in Battersea. Six o'clock sharp," Noble said. "Just you and Wexler, nobody else. You bring proof of my innocence. I'll bring the flash drive. You get the Chinese research and I clear my name."

"And why would I do that?" Keiser asked. "Don't forget, I still have your mother. I can end her life with one phone call."

"Do you?" Noble said. "How long since you heard from your man in Saint Pete?"

Keiser didn't bother to answer. Noble had called his bluff. He obviously knew something Keiser didn't, but that wouldn't last long. He took a moment to weigh his options and said, "It might take me some time to gather all the necessary files."

"If you're one minute late I walk," Noble said. "I've got nothing to lose. I'll sell the Chinese research on the black market. If Langley thinks I'm a traitor, I might as well be a rich traitor."

"Have it your way," Keiser said. "I'll be there and I'll have the evidence you need to clear your name."

"No tricks," Noble warned. "I've got a real itchy trigger finger right now, Keiser."

"You have my word," Keiser said and then the line went dead. He turned to Wexler. "Seems you have one last bit of business in London after all, my boy."

# Chapter Seventy-Seven

"Really think they'll turn him over to the Chinese?" Gwen asked. She had just returned from a locker room on the second floor where she spent ten minutes taking a shower and twenty minutes bawling her eyes out. She took another five to put her face back together, splashing cold water on her eyes and reapplying a little foundation, before making her way back to the situation room. The thought of Jake wasting away in a Chinese prison was gut-wrenching but Gwen didn't want Ezra to know how deeply it was affecting her. Gwen and Jake had shared a kiss not too long ago. It had been a passing thing, and before she started dating Ezra, but it was still a connection that she shared with Jake. Ezra was her guy. Gwen loved him and they had a lot in common, but she carried a small torch for Jake. It was tucked away deep down, a fantasy that was fun to think about but never act on, the way some girls crush on celebrities.

Ezra looked up from his computer. "It looks that way."

Gwen dropped down into a chair. "It's not right."

"No," Ezra agreed. He had the laptop open and checked the chat box every few minutes. He pushed listlessly at his mouse and said, "I knew McHale was a bean counter and a coward, but I never knew he'd stoop this low. Turning one of our own over to the Chinese is unconscionable."

Gwen curled up in her chair, knees up to her chest, and reached for a mug half-filled with Diet Mountain Dew. She cradled the mug in both hands like it might provide some warmth. "Where does that leave us?" she asked. "We have to work for this guy. What happens when some foreign government is asking for one of us?"

"That's not likely to happen. We hardly ever leave Langley." He spoke without much conviction and one hand went to the ragged scar on his cheek.

"We've been in the field before," Gwen reminded him. "Recently."

They were both thinking the same thing; a competent Director had been shown the door over partisan politics and replaced with a weak-kneed bureaucrat who cared more about optics than the people in the field. Gwen pushed her glasses up and rubbed at her eyes. "McHale will be director for at least four years. I'm not sure I can do that."

"We just have to keep our heads down and make the best of it."

"And if Wizard requests us for another field assignment?"

"We'll cross that bridge when we come to it."

Gwen sipped her soft drink, questioning whether she could serve four years under a Director and a President for whom she had no respect. She never reached an answer. They were distracted by a message from Duval, who had managed to hack Noble's phone and picked up a conversation between Noble and Keiser.

*Noble arranged a meeting at an abandoned switching station in Battersea, 6pm. He's going to trade the Chinese research for proof of his innocence. Thought you ought to know.*

Gwen shook her head. "He's going to take another run at Keiser."

"Keiser will show up with a dozen goons."

Gwen pushed a fresh tear from her eye. "And Noble will be killed."

Ezra touched his scar. "We taking this to Wizard?"

"That will put McHale onto it," Gwen said.

"What choice do we have?" Ezra asked.

# Chapter Seventy-Eight

Noble held a bundle of Ziplock baggies in one hand while he inspected a selection of nuts and bolts. McLarens hardware store is sandwiched between a secondhand boutique on one side and a realtor office on the other. Lifeless fluorescents buzzed overhead and the comforting scent of lumber, metal shavings, and motor oil hung in the air. Growing up in a lower middle-class family, there was always something wrong with the house; if the toilet wasn't broken a sink surely was, and Jake was tasked with helping his dad fix it. He had spent a lot of time in hardware stores as a kid and the smell brought back pleasant memories. Jake smiled as he reached for a package of finishing nails.

"Something funny?" Stokely had a shopping basket in the crook of one elbow stuffed with rolls of electrical wire, kerosene and duct-tape.

"I was thinking about my dad," Noble admitted.

"My dad was always dragging me to the hardware store when I was a little girl," Stokely said. "He always had a project he was working on."

Noble nodded. "Seemed like every week when I was a kid."

"Sounds familiar," Stokely said as she shifted her bundle. "Is he gone now? You speak about him in the past tense."

"Almost ten years now."

She gave a sympathetic frown. "My dad passed six years ago. Worked right until the day he died."

"Sounds familiar," Noble said and grinned.

"Odd the things we remember about our dads." Stokely started to tell him a story about a busted radiator, then grabbed his elbow and steered him out of the aisle.

Noble glanced over his shoulder in time to see a pair of uniformed officers. He and Stokely hurried toward the back of the store and slipped down the plumbing aisle. "That was close," Stokely said. "Look, Jake, I don't know how much longer I can stay off the radar. I'm going to have to account for this time, you know?"

"Tell them I had you at gun point," Noble said. "Not like I can get in any more trouble."

"That's a criminal offence," she reminded him.

"I'm sure the Chinese will take it into account when they pass sentence on me." He forced a smile. "Look, if you want to back out, now is the time. You can turn around and walk. Let me deal with Keiser on my own."

"Not a chance," Stokely said. "The slimy bugger crashed the British economy when I was a little girl and now his henchman has murdered three people on my turf. I'm going to put him in jail."

Noble held up the nails. "I think this just about does it. You have enough in your account to cover all this?"

"I suppose you left your wallet in your other tux?"

"Something like that," Noble said.

They peeked around the corner. The officers had bought a flashlight and were headed out the door. Stokely led the way toward the register and said, "So you're a real life spy?"

"In the flesh."

"I thought spies wearing tuxedos was just a cheesy James Bond cliché. You fancy yourself double-oh-seven, do you?"

"You know what they say…" Noble tried to close the jacket but the button had come off sometime during the night. "Dress for the job you want, not the job you have."

# Chapter Seventy-Nine

Hunt bounced a scuffed tennis ball off the wall of his office and caught it on the rebound. Outside his window, the sun was half buried in the west, a red blister on the horizon, lighting the rooftops of London with a brilliant red glow. A television was tuned to BBC 1 and a phone was ringing down the hall.

Hunt tossed the tennis ball and caught it, leaving a small mark on the plaster which the next occupant would have to paint over. That was a problem for the next Chief of Station. Hunt had taken to bouncing the tennis ball as a way to keep his hands busy while his brain was working. He'd spent hours lobbing the ball at the floor, bouncing it off the wall, and back again. It drove the secretary in the next office nuts but there wasn't much she could do about it. She'd lodged a formal complaint which, because Hunt was Chief of Station, had been filed and ignored. She was an old battle-axe with blue hair and varicose veins, rapidly approaching mandatory retirement, so Hunt wasn't overly concerned with her opinion of him. He suggested she try noise cancelling headphones when she confronted him about the constant *thud-thud-thud* coming through her wall. "Or just leave out your hearing aid," he had told her.

He gave the ball one more good hard bounce before dropping it back into a cracked leather baseball glove on the corner of his desk. His hip was smarting from standing and pacing a little too long. The constant pain was a reminder of his first encounter with Noble. Hunt used his laptop to check the reports coming out of the local police precincts, looking for any news concerning Noble or the missing Inspector. He had a team of CIA staffers at the embassy monitoring traffic cams and bank transactions, and a street team out combing the neighborhoods, but no one had seen hide nor hair of Jake Noble.

"Probably halfway to Ecuador by now," Hunt told the empty office.

*Good riddance,* Hunt tried to tell himself. If Noble was out of the country, then he was somebody else's problem. He swiveled in his chair to gaze out the window at the melting sun. London was sprawled out before him, a glittering jewel hugging the banks of the winding river. Jake Noble was out there somewhere and God only knew what sort of trouble he was making. Hunt kept expecting to look out his window and see a fireball go soaring up into the sky. When it came to Jake Noble, he expected the unexpected.

Jacob Noble.

Hunt's mouth twisted into a snarl at the mere thought. Noble was a major pain in the butt, both literally and figuratively. Hunt reached for the office phone and buzzed down the hall to ask if the traffic cam crew had learned anything new. They'd spotted a tall figure with longish hair coming out of a bank an hour ago but facial analysis had determined it wasn't Noble. Hunt told them to keep at it, hung up the receiver and reached for his tennis ball, but his mobile was vibrating in his pocket. He answered after checking the caller ID, listened for thirty seconds, then stepped across the hall and opened a door.

Dunlop and Simms from the Office of Security were sunk deep in a sofa, controllers in their hands, playing a shooting game on an Xbox console. Electronic explosions erupted from the television speakers.

Dunlop seemed to be getting the better of Simms. He talked trash while Simms made a sour face.

"Cut that thing off and kit up," Hunt told them. "I've got a location on Noble."

# Chapter Eighty

Emergency medical services had drenched both Mary and Burke with a hose to wash away the gasoline before loading them in back of the ambulance. At the hospital, Mary had been tended by a pair of young nurses who checked her for a concussion before putting a butterfly bandage on her split lip and dressing her in fresh scrubs scrounged from the laundry. The top was three sizes too big and she had to hold up the pants when she walked. The nurses fussed over Mary, putting her through an exhaustive series of tests, looking for anything broken, and only agreed to release her when Mary insisted she was okay and just needed to rest.

Burke was also dressed in scrubs, only his were too small. He looked like a giant black bear shrink-wrapped inside a seafoam green bodysuit. Together they took a cab from the hospital to the vet where Gadsden was being treated and now Mary Elise Noble sat in an armchair with a large cup of hot chocolate cradled in both hands, ignoring a stack of well-thumbed magazines on a table at her elbow.

She was in a small waiting room down the hall from the emergency suit where vets were working feverishly to save Gadsden's life. The poor animal had been shot and nearly drowned. A young vet by the name of Rosenburg had come out two hours ago to inform Mary that the dog had lost nearly half the blood in his body and he had extensive internal injuries. It was a miracle he was still alive. They were doing everything they could to save him but, the doctor said, the prognosis was not good. He'd said all this with the appropriate bedside manner and the truth was not lost on Mary. The dog had overcome incredible odds and in the end given his life to save hers.

Mary considered the stack of magazines. The top issue was a fashion publication called *le Femme* and featured a man in a dress with the headline; *A Brave New World*. Mary set her cup down on top of the picture so she wouldn't have to look at it. She watched the double doors of the operating theater in silence for a while and then said, "Jake will be alright, right?"

"Jake will be just fine," Burke assured her with a smile. "That kid is one of the best I ever trained."

Mary twisted her hands together in her lap. "Think Gadsden will pull through?"

Burke frowned. "I sure hope so."

"Would you pray with me?" Mary asked.

Burke flashed a nervous grin, showing the gap between his teeth. "I'm not much for prayer, Mrs. Noble. I'm not sure how to even start."

"I'll do the praying, you just close your eyes and follow along."

Burke hesitated. His eyes went to the double doors where Gadsden was fighting for his life and he shrugged. "Guess it can't hurt."

Mary took his large black hands in her small white ones, closed her eyes, and began to pray. In the operation room, vets worked to repair a nicked artery.

# Chapter Eighty-One

The switching station at Battersea was quiet. Soft white flakes swirled down from a black vault and snow collected in silver carpets between cold metal tracks. Ice formed on top of the abandoned hulks lining the locomotive graveyard.

Noble covered over the last of their improvised explosives with snow using his bare hands. *Should have bought gloves,* he told himself. His fingers were pink and swollen but he didn't complain. He buried the makeshift bomb, checked his watch and said, "Let's get out of sight before Wexler and his buddies show up."

"You sure he'll come with backup?" Stokely asked.

"I'd stake my reputation on it."

"Your reputation as a fugitive?"

Noble grinned. "It's an easy bet."

Their shoes crunched in a thin layer of frost as they crossed the large hydraulic turn table at the center of the station. Stokely was on the tracks when Noble checked his watch again, grabbed her elbow, and pulled.

"You see something?" Stokely whispered.

"I hear the train a'comin'," Noble said.

"I don't hear any..."

Then she did. The sound built, low and distant at first, getting louder until a freight car went hurtling by on its way north to points unknown. They stood to the side, eyes narrowed, listening to the rhythmic *clack-clack-clack*. When the last car finally rolled past and the sound died down, Stokely turned to him. "How did you know a train was coming?"

"I studied the time tables," Noble said. "The next train is coming through in fifteen minutes, headed south and west. Don't be on the switch when that happens."

Wind whistled between the cars and caused snowflakes to dance in the air. Noble's cheeks were flushed. He turned up his collar and breath steamed from his mouth, forming a silver mist.

"We should have stopped to get a coat for you," Stokely said.

"Too late for that now."

"Aren't you cold?"

"Freezing," Noble admitted, but his mind was too focused on the task at hand to worry about cold. This might be his only chance to clear his name.

"How do you want to do this?"

He paused for a look about, his shoulders creeping up and his shaggy hair blowing on the breeze, then he pointed. "You set up over there on that engine. Try to get the high ground. Keep quiet and low. Wait for my signal."

"Where are you going to be?"

"I'll take a spot by the switch. I want a good field of view." Noble took Hap Chan's flash drive from his pocket. He had two; one he planned to give Wexler, and the real one, which he passed to Stokely. "You keep this."

She hesitated before taking it. "What am I supposed to do with it?"

"If I die, make sure it gets to the CIA."

She closed it in her fist and said, "You know I might just give it to MI6 instead?"

"You'd refuse the last wish of a dying man?"

"You're not going to die," Stokely said. "I've got your back."

"Thanks," Noble said. "And for what it's worth, I'm sorry I got you mixed up in this."

"When it's all over you can buy me a pint."

"Wexler will be here soon, if he's not creeping around already. Let's get out of sight."

Stokely caught his elbow, leaned in, and pecked him on the cheek. "You're alright, Noble."

"You're not so bad yourself, Stokely."

"Be careful," she said before crossing the turntable, slipping between box cars and disappearing into the labyrinth.

Noble started across the yard, searching for an alcove between cars where he would have some cover, but didn't make it halfway.

"Noble!" Hunt's voice echoed. "It's over, Noble. I don't know what kind of game you're playing, but it ends here. Stop right where you are and put your hands up."

# Chapter Eighty-Two

Wexler stopped a dark grey BMW XM at the edge of the train yard and shifted into park. He left the engine running and turned in his seat. He'd brought three members of Keiser's personal security detail, all of them former military, and all of them armed with semi-automatic AR15s. A locomotive was barreling through the abandoned hulks, making a steady rattle and clack. The team members were checking their gear and making certain their optics had fresh batteries. Wexler had handpicked every member of the group. He'd worked with them all before. They represented the best of Keiser's private army.

He said, "The guy we're after is a former Green Beret named Jacob Noble. He's probably been here way ahead of us and he's a veteran. There's no telling what kind of IEDs he's had time to rig, so watch your step. He's got a flash drive that we need intact, so don't shoot him full of holes. In fact, nobody kills Noble but me."

"Any civies we need to watch out for?" Hammersmith asked. He was a former Royal Marine who'd spent time in Afghanistan. He was balding with a face like a shovel. He'd been recruited into Keiser's security company after getting drunk and punching out a lieutenant.

Wexler shook his head. "Shouldn't meet any civilians here at this time of night, but we can't have any witnesses. Clear?"

They nodded.

Ellsworth, a massive black man with a gold hoop in one ear, asked, "This guy packing?"

"Probably something small," Wexler said. "A handgun maybe. He's been on the run for days now. Certainly won't have a rifle or any serious hardware."

"We got a hard limit on time?" Peele asked.

"We're here until we get it done," Wexler told them. "The boss isn't going to accept failure on this one, boys. We don't get that flashdrive and we might as well all slit our own throats."

Hammersmith checked the action on his rifle and said, "Let's get it done then."

They climbed out of the BMW and started across the yard. Wexler pressed the transmit button on his tactical vest and whispered, "Comms check."

"Hammer, check check."

"Big L, check check."

"Peele, check check."

"Copy. Everyone sounds good," Wexler said. "Peel and Hammer, take the south. Big L and I will take the north end. We'll meet in the middle. Keep in constant contact. Two clicks for danger close. And remember, no one kills Noble but me."

***

Noble spun around, one hand going automatically to the gun in his waistband. Hunt, along with a pair of goons from the CIA's Office of Security named Dunlop and Simms, stood at the vast turn junction. The security guys already had their weapons out and trained on Noble, hoping for an excuse to pull the trigger. Noble relaxed his hand away from the gun. "Hunt, you have no idea what you just walked into. If you're smart, you'll turn around and walk away."

"I know perfectly well what's going on, Noble." Hunt didn't bother to bring his gun out. He was content to let the Office of Security people do the heavy lifting. He stood there in a five-hundred dollar camelhair coat with his blond hair blowing in the wind and his hands stuffed in his pockets. "I told the Company it was a mistake to trust you. You finally outed yourself, Noble. Got caught with your hand in the cookie jar."

"I'm innocent." Noble backed away. He was in an alley formed by rusting box cars. "If you give me a chance, I can prove it."

"You're all out of moves, Noble." Hunt and his goons slowly advanced. "You're a traitor and the CIA knows it. They're turning you over to the Chinese. With any luck, I'll get to be at the exchange and watch you take the walk of shame. Now turn around, get on your knees, and put your hands in the air."

"You know I'm not going to do that," Noble said, looking for an opening between the cars.

Hunt shrugged, as if it was all the same to him. "We're taking you in dead or alive."

"You'll have to kill me."

"Have it your way."

The sharp *thwap-thwap-thwap* of suppressed weapons rent the winter air. Bullets hissed and snapped. Simms went down before he even knew what was happening. Slugs ripped through his body, making him dance like a puppet on a string. Bloody petals blossomed around him and he fell. He was dead before he hit the ground.

Dunlop took a shot to the elbow. A bullet ripped through the joint and spun him around. His arm bent the wrong way as his elbow disintegrated. His gun slipped from nerveless fingers. His eyes were wide and he was trying to make sense of what had happened. He bent over in an effort to pick up his weapon, but his hand no longer worked. He tried with his left instead but a second long burst shredded his chest. He made a strange gurgling sound in his throat as he fell.

Hunt clutched his thigh, let out a piercing shriek of pain, and passed out face down on the tracks.

# Chapter Eighty-Three

NOBLE THREW HIMSELF BETWEEN the cars as the shots rang out and slammed against the coupling. He hit the rusty iron knuckle with a loud *oof*. The sound was lost beneath the hard snap of suppressed automatics and the shriek of bullets. He clawed the pistol from his belt and rolled over the coupling in an effort to find cover, then scrambled beneath the cars, eyes open wide, searching for the shooters.

Dunlop and Simms were down. One was dead. A bullet had taken off the side of his head. The other was laying still, probably dead, but Hunt was still alive. The Station Chief was on the tracks, moaning softly in a semi-conscious daze. He had fallen dangerously close to Noble's first set of explosives. Noble prayed Stokely didn't panic and start dialing numbers. If she did, she'd blow Hunt to hell.

Noble scrambled forward over cold hard ground, knees scraping on gravel and his elbows clonking against railroad ties. He needed to get a sight line on the shooters.

\*\*\*

Stokely was halfway up the ladder on the back side of a steam engine when the shooting started. She yelped and nearly lost her hold. Her guts turned to liquid jelly and her legs to spring steel. She jolted up the last few rungs and threw herself flat on top of the engine, eyes wide and mouth open in a silent scream.

The three CIA guys were down, right in the center of the big turn junction. From her vantage point atop the locomotive, Stokely watched a pair of men in black fatigues and balaclavas moving along a line of dead carriages. They both had semi-auto rifles with professional-grade sound suppressors and they moved like soldiers.

Stokely watched in silence as the killers hurried along the lane between railway cars toward the main intersection. Noble had dropped down beneath a cargo hauler. He'd be easy prey for two men with rifles. Stokely took a breath and worked up her courage. Ten years in law enforcement and never once had she discharged her weapon in the line of duty. Last night was the closest she had come. But she had been dazed, trapped in her cruiser, and forced to watch two police officers brutally gunned down. She had been scared witless. Not this time. This time she had the high ground.

Pressing her weapon straight out in both hands, Stokely centered her front sight on one of the assassins. The gun clapped. An empty shell casing winged past Stokely's nose and her bullet punched the gunman in the chest.

He staggered but stayed on his feet.

Stokely pulled the trigger twice more. Fire leapt from the muzzle. Two loud whip cracks hammered her unprotected ears. The killer jerked and went down on one knee, clutching his chest. His partner dodged between rail cars. The wounded man raised his rifle, searching for the shooter. Stokely was squaring up for another shot when the man sighted on her. She pulled the trigger first, spitting three more rounds from her pistol. Two went wide, bouncing off the side of a passenger car with hard metal splats. The third drilled through the assassin's face just below the nose. His head snapped back and the rifle landed in the snow.

Stokely realized she'd been holding her breath and gasped for air. She'd just killed a man. He'd been less than a second from shredding her with a high powered rifle, but that didn't change the fact that she'd taken a life. She blinked hard several times, like she might be able to clear the image of the dead man from her eyes. But he was laying there in a pool of blood, the snow around him turning scarlet. It was a moment before she realized her pistol was locked back on an empty chamber.

She thumbed the magazine release and rolled onto her side, digging in her pocket for her spare magazine. She had twelve more rounds and then she was empty.

The second gunman emerged from between the railcars, leveled his rifle, and hammered the top of the locomotive with a long burst. The suppressed weapon spit round after round. Bullets chewed through the rusty metal roof.

With a shout, Stokely rolled to avoid the barrage and went right off the side of the engine. Her eyes popped when she felt herself go over the edge. She plummeted, landing in gravel with a crushing thud that caused lights to caper in her vision.

\*\*\*

Wexler hunkered low, reached for his shoulder mic and barked, "Who in the hell is firing? Location. Location."

He and Ellsworth were crouched against a line of empty cargo containers stacked between trains. The suppressed shots echoed around the railway yard, making it impossible to tell where they were coming from. Ellsworth took a knee and trained his weapon, searching for targets, but from his vantage point all he saw were rusted out train cars.

Several unsuppressed shots split the air. There was a short burst, a pause, and then another, longer peel of thunder. Wexler turned to Ellsworth and questioned him with a look.

The big man hiked up his shoulders.

Silver clouds boiled from Wexler's mouth as he triggered his mic again. "Peele? Hammer? Where are you and what's going on? Do you read me? Come in?"

Muffled rifle fire answered, then Hammersmith came over the radio. "Need backup straight away, boss. I'm at the big junction where they turn the cars at the center of the yard. Your boy Noble came with backup. Peele is dead. Three tangos are down and there is a third atop an engine south and east of my position. Noble ducked under some cars."

"Hold tight," Wexler said. "We're on our way."

Wexler signaled Ellsworth to cross over onto the other side of the tracks. "You take that side, I'll take this. Shoot anyone who isn't a guy with long hair."

# Chapter Eighty-Four

Noble crawled along the line of cars, through gravel and over rotting railroad ties, until he spied the intersection where Hunt lay wounded. The Chief of Station was curled up, clutching his leg. Dunlop and Simms were down. Neither was moving. Across the intersection, Noble could see a dead man in tactical gear stretched out between the line of cars. A semi-automatic rifle lay in the snow near his limp hand. Noble wanted to get his hands on that rifle but it was on the far side of the intersection. No way to reach it without being shot full of holes.

Noble eased another few feet forward until he had a sightline across the junction. He wanted a clear shot without exposing himself. He was about to call out when the caution signal lit up, blazing red, and the large iron turntable roared to life. Rusting old gears beneath the junction ground together and the tracks started to turn. A warning bell rang. A train was coming and Hunt was on the track.

"Hunt," Noble called out. "Hunt, you gotta move."

He could hear the locomotive now, getting louder by the minute. The ground beneath him started to shake. Pebbles danced between his fingers.

Hunt let out a soft moan, struggled to move, but he didn't have the strength.

Noble didn't particularly like Hunt, in fact he rather hated him. The CIA's fair-haired goldenboy had stolen Noble's girl and tortured him, but being run over by a train was a bad way to go.

He started to scramble out from under the box car and a short burst of suppressed fire forced him back down. Bullets pinged off the rusting metal with loud splats. Noble dropped into the freezing slush as a round zipped past his ear, a deadly little mosquito searching for blood.

"Stokely," Noble called out. "I need some covering fire."

There was no answer.

Noble tried a second time to break cover and nearly lost a finger to a deadly hailstorm of lead. He scooted backwards, snow soaking through his pants, until he was safe and then pulled the burner phone from his jacket pocket. The screen came to life, casting his face in a pale glow. He brought up the list of numbers, scrolled past the first—Hunt was laying on top of that bomb—and past the second, which was behind Noble, landing on the third number. The IED was planted under a small drift of snow on the opposite side of the tracks from the shooter, facing the wrong way, but it was close enough to give him a scare. Probably burst his ear drums as well. Noble hit send.

The call took a moment to connect and then an ear splitting blast rocked the train yard. Snow leapt fifteen feet in the air. Nuts and bolts peppered the side of a box car, punching ragged little holes in the thick metal plating. The explosion was not close enough to catch the shooter, but it certainly got his attention. He turned around, searching for the source of the explosion.

The junction had finished its rotation and the tracks locked in place with a soft chuffing of hydraulics. A train whistle rent the air and the headlamp etched the prone figure of Hunt in sharp relief.

Noble pushed off the ground and jolted out from under the box car, scraping his back and shoulders on the underside. He ignored the pain as he sprinted across the open intersection, pumping his arms for more speed. His heart was a race horse inside his chest. The oversized shoes slipped around on his feet. He was halfway across the junction, the train barreling down on him, when the shooter spied him and opened up with his rifle. A storm of lead chased Noble across the open space, whistling around his head and kicking up little puffs of ice.

There was no time to return fire. No time to slow down. Noble poured every bit of strength he had into his legs. His thighs burned with the effort. He'd never know it, but Noble set a personal best as he rocketed across the open ground, grasped Hunt's arm and gave a savage jerk, dragging the injured man off the tracks just seconds ahead of the train.

They had barely cleared the track when the engine went hurtling past with a blast from the airhorn. Bullets ricocheted off the engine, then trailed along the line of flatbeds loaded with cargo containers.

Noble dragged Hunt out of the intersection and along a line of abandoned box cars until he found a good spot between the forgotten hulks where he could stop and tend Hunt's injured leg.

Pretty boy's lips were turning blue and his eyelids drooped. He moaned. His hands were caked with frozen blood and his pant leg was drenched. Without a tourniquet, he'd bleed out. Noble shrugged out of his tuxedo jacket and started ripping at the sleeves.

# Chapter Eighty-Five

Stokely felt like she was riding the tilt-a-whirl. Her world kept tipping and spinning, tipping and spinning. Just when she thought the ride was about to stop and she could climb off, it would spin back up again. Queue the lights, queue the music. Round and round we go. She let out a soft moan, rolled over in the snow, and winced at a sharp flare of pain between her shoulder blades. A cough worked up from her chest, making the pain in her back worse, and a throbbing headache joined the list of hurts.

Somewhere in the distance, she heard muffled pops and then the loud scream of a locomotive tearing through the junction. The air horn gave a mournful blast.

Her world finally slowed enough that she could open her eyes without fear of vomiting. The icy train yard swam into focus. She was on her side in the gravel, snow landing gently all around her and rusted-out freight cars on either side.

First thing she did was cast about for her gun. It was nowhere to be seen. She'd lost her grip on the weapon when she'd gone off the side of the engine. She didn't know where it landed, but it couldn't have gone far.

"Come on," Stokely whispered to the darkness, a note of panic in her voice. She turned over onto her hands and knees, scanning the dark landscape. She checked under the engine and behind the wheels, and then crawled over to the other side where she stuck her head under a box car. Her bottom was in the air and one arm stretched under the gear, groping blindly, when she heard feet crunch in the gravel behind her.

"Well, well, well," Wexler said. "What have we here? The lovely young Inspector Stokely."

The air froze in her lungs.

"Come on out from under there," Wexler ordered. "Nice and slow. Hands where we can see them."

She slowly withdrew her arm and shifted around, knees scraping in the gravel, to find herself staring down the yawning barrel of a semi-automatic rifle. The muzzle looked like an open train tunnel. Stokely's bladder threatened to let go. She held onto it through sheer force of will. She didn't want the other cops in her precinct to learn she'd been found dead with wet trousers. Her whole body trembled as she raised both hands into the air. She expected to hear a loud bang before everything went black. Instead, Wexler said, "On your feet."

\*\*\*

Noble had fixed a makeshift bandage around Hunt's leg and finished it off with a tourniquet he'd fashioned from Hunt's own belt and the laces from one of his shoes. The bleeding stopped and Hunt was out of immediate danger, but he'd need a doctor soon. He was stretched out in the cramped space between two flatbed cars, head propped on a cold metal track, his face pinched in pain. His eyelids fluttered as he started to swim up from the dark abyss of shock.

"Noble," he muttered through lips that barely moved. "That you?"

"Yeah." Noble was crouched between the cars, pistol resting on the ground within easy reach, ripping his other sleeve into more bandages. "It's me."

"Why do I get shot every time I'm around you?"

"You zig when you should zag."

"Dunlop and Simms?" Hunt asked.

"Dead."

Hunt muttered a curse. Noble wasn't sure if it was aimed at him or just the situation in general.

"Where are we?" Hunt wanted to know.

"Safe," Noble said. "For now at least."

"D'you pull me off the tracks?" Hunt asked. "Last thing I remember was a train coming at me."

"I thought about leaving you," Noble admitted.

"I *would* have left you," Hunt said and then after a beat he added, "Thank you."

"Anything for a fellow officer in need," Noble said, sarcasm dripping from every syllable.

Hunt winced and reached for the tourniquet.

"Leave it alone," Noble said. "It'd be a real shame if it came loose and you bled to death."

"I'm sure you'd be heartbroken."

Noble dipped a finger into the blood and used it to mark a cross on Hunt's forehead.

"You baptizing me?" Hunt asked.

"It's for the EMS workers. I'm sure someone heard that explosion and called the police. An ambulance will be here shortly and if you pass out, I want the medical people to know you've got a tourniquet on you."

"Why you helping me, Noble?"

"This is going to shock you," Noble said, "but I'm the good guy."

"Is that right? How come you're wanted by half the law enforcement agencies in the western world?"

"It all traces back to a billionaire with too much money and time on his hands. And in a few minutes I'm going to prove that." Noble reached for the gun and stood up.

"Where're you going?" Hunt asked.

"Clear my name."

Hunt pulled a nickel plated .45 Kimber from a shoulder holster. "You're not going anywhere, Noble. I'm here to take you into custody and that's what I'm going to do."

"Go ahead and shoot," Noble said and walked away.

# Chapter Eighty-Six

Noble made his way along the line of cars back toward the junction, gun in one hand and the burner phone in the other. He went slow, taking care where he placed his feet, trying to make as little noise as humanly possible. His heart was tap-tapping at his chest and his pulse jackhammered in his ears. Air steamed out of his lungs in thick silver clouds. Noble no longer had jacket sleeves and the temperature felt like it had dropped another ten degrees. He was halfway to the junction when he heard Wexler's voice.

"Come out, come out, wherever you are."

Noble stopped and peered into the darkness, watching for any sign of movement. His back was tense and his legs felt like they wanted to run. He waited in silence, hand gripping his pistol hard.

"Noble," Wexler called again. His voice was coming from the junction. "Come on out. You and I have business to discuss."

Noble slipped between a pair of box cars and clamped the pistol between his teeth as he shimmied up the ladder. The bitter taste of gun oil touched his tongue. He belly crawled over the roof, stopped at the edge and pushed himself up for a look.

His heart sank.

Wexler and two goons stood in the middle of the junction, and they had Stokely. She was on her knees, a fresh smear of blood on her forehead where Wexler had tapped her hard with the butt of his rifle.

Her hands were in the air, fingers trembling. Wexler had a fistful of Stokely's hair and the muzzle of his weapon pressed into her back. His men held semi-automatic rifles bristling with state-of-the-art optics and muzzle attachments. All three wore black fatigues and vests loaded down with gear. They were probably sporting ballistic plates as well. Noble's pistol wouldn't be able to punch through their body armor, not at this distance.

He took the pistol from between his teeth and spat gun oil. "Let the girl go."

"What's it worth to you?" Wexler said. "You have something I want. Show yourself and we can make a deal."

Noble stuffed the gun in his waistband, scrambled down the side of the train car and up the next, where he wormed his way across the roof.

"The girl walks," Noble yelled. "Or the deal is off."

"You're in no position to make demands," Wexler shouted. "I've got your friend. If you don't show yourself, I'll blow her brains out. You have until the count of ten."

Noble had spanned the next car. He was only two cars away now.

Wexler started to count. "Ten, five, three, time's up."

"Alright." Noble slid the gun from his waistband and took a second to pull up the first number in his burner phone before pushing himself up to his knees. "I'm right here, Wexler. Let the girl go. She walks out of here and then you and I can trade. The Chinese research for proof you set me up."

"Counter proposal," Wexler said. "Give me the research. I promise to let the girl live."

"That's not much of a deal." Noble was hunched low so that if they started shooting he could quickly drop against the roof of the train and return fire. He had the phone. One of Wexler's men was practically on top of the IED. One phone call would blow him to hell, but Stokely would be caught in the blast.

"It's the only deal you're going to get," Wexler said. "I'm through talking. You're going to come down here like a good boy and give me that flash drive or you can watch me splatter her guts all over the tracks."

Wexler gave Stokely a savage jerk and she let out a sharp breath. His barrel was pressed so deep into her back, she was arched, her breasts straining against her sweater and her face twisted in pain.

"Enough," Noble said. "You win. I give up. You promise to let her go?"

"Just as soon as I have the flash drive."

Stokely said, "Don't do it, Jake."

"Shut up," Wexler growled and gave her another brutal jerk, fingers tightening in her hair until her eyebrows danced with hurt.

Noble slid to the edge of the car and dropped over the side, stumbling in the gravel and almost going down flat on his face. Lightning bolts of pain crackled up from both knees. He winced as he straightened up. He kept his left side angled away from Wexler, the phone hidden next to his thigh as he approached the junction.

"There's a good lad," Wexler said when Noble reached the edge of the junction. "That's far enough. Drop the shooter."

Noble looked down at the gun in his hand. He briefly considered trying his luck. Three men from ten yards. On a shooting range this exercise was called *el presidente*. The shooter tries to put six rounds through three targets in less than two seconds. Only these targets were wearing body armor and holding high-powered rifles. And they were waiting for him to make a move. He dropped the pistol in the snow at his feet.

Wexler said, "What's in your other hand?"

Noble lifted the phone, his thumb hovering over the send button.

Stokely's eyes opened wide.

"Throw it down," Wexler said.

Stokely wrenched herself sideways, batting the rifle aside with her elbow. She screamed, "Now," and threw herself flat.

Noble pressed the button.

# Chapter Eighty-Seven

THE CALL TOOK AN eternity to connect. Time seemed to slow and stretch until seconds felt like days. Noble heard the phone dial and the cellular signal search for a connection.

Stokely hit the ground and rolled, hands covering her face with her eyes shut tight. She had her mouth stretched wide in preparation for a scream and it probably saved her hearing.

Wexler looked from the girl to the phone in Noble's hand and an expression of dawning horror formed on his face. He started to bring his weapon up. His two goons also realized what was about to happen. Both decided discretion was the better part of valor. They turned to run.

The bomb went off with an earth-rending boom that threw dirty snow twenty feet in the air. Wexler was knocked off his feet with the force of a sledgehammer. He went down flat on his back, arms and legs flung out wide. His rifle, attached by a single-point sling, came down on his chest.

Stokely was lifted off the ground by an invisible hand and slammed back down. She let out a sound that was part surprise, part pain.

Noble staggered back a step. His ears were ringing and his vision narrowed to a fuzzy cone. There was a loud dial tone in his brain and his knees felt like they would come unhinged. He crouched and patted the ground with numb fingers in search of his weapon. The explosive at the junction had been mostly accelerant and sand. It was enough to stun but not kill. Wexler would be coming around any second and Noble had to be ready. His fingers closed on the barrel of the pistol. He came up into a crouch, pistol in both hands.

Stokely was shaking off the effects of the explosion. She had made it onto her hands and knees. Her hair was a crazy mess, like she'd just put her finger in a light socket.

Wexler gave a loud groan and struggled to sit up.

Noble was already moving. He had three targets, ten bullets, and just seconds to end the fight. He charged forward, heels crunching in the snow, and lashed out with a foot as Wexler levered himself up into a sitting position. The big redhead had both hands on his rifle when Noble's boot connected with his chest, slamming him back down. His face turned bright red. He struggled in vain to grip his weapon but Noble had it pinned to Wexler's chest.

The two goons had been knocked flat but they were back up again. One was on his feet, turning to rejoin the fight. The other was sitting on his bottom, one hand against his ear.

Pushing the pistol out in both hands, Noble trained the front sight high on the first man's chest, just below his neck, hoping to land a shot above the ballistic plate. He eased back on the trigger and felt the weapon kick. His ears were still buzzing and the pistol shot sounded like a muffled clap. He fired three shots. Two to the chest, one to the head. In the dark of the train yard, it was hard to see where his bullets landed. At least one hit the goon just below the neck and the last kicked his skull back. His feet shot out from under him and he went down hard.

Noble pivoted, taking aim at the second gunman, who was still sitting but he had his rifle up and pointed in Noble's direction. They both pulled the trigger at the same time. The semi-automatic rifle breathed fire. Bullets snapped past Noble's left ear. One actually tugged at his hair. He flinched involuntarily, heart jogging inside his chest. His own bullets found their mark. The first caught the gunman's shoulder, jerking him sideways. The next kicked up a puff of snow. The last took a bite out of the man's cheek. The side of his balaclava erupted in a shower of dark blood and gore. He dropped the rifle and put one hand to his ruined face before pitching over in the dirt.

It was over in less than five seconds. Noble waited a moment to make sure Wexler's goons were down for the count then turned to Stokely. She was alive, eyes wide and mouth hanging open. She kept patting herself in search of bullet holes but there were none to be found.

Noble said, "You okay?"

She pointed to an ear. "What?"

"You okay?" Noble raised his voice.

She nodded and gave a thumbs up.

Wexler let go of his trapped rifle, wrapped his legs around Noble's thigh, grabbed Noble's foot and twisted. He levered all his weight against Noble's leg and a moment later they were both on the ground.

# Chapter Eighty-Eight

Noble lost his grip on the pistol and landed hard in the gravel. His head impacted the cold metal track with teeth rattling force. His vision doubled, then tripled. By the time his world stopped spinning and his eyes focused, Wexler had the rifle halfway up. Noble lashed out with his foot and knocked the barrel aside.

There was an earsplitting crack. The bullet snapped past Noble's shoulder and kicked up a puff of dirt less than a foot from Stokely. She yelped and rolled away.

Noble lunged for the weapon. He grabbed hold and forced the muzzle away when Wexler jerked the trigger again. Another bullet burrowed into the earth, this time inches from Noble's foot. He and Wexler struggled for control of the rifle, but Wexler was taller and had at least forty pounds on Noble. The big redhead wrenched the rifle back and forth like an angry Pitbull. Noble was forced to hang on or be thrown aside. He clamped down with both hands and lunged forward, trying for a head butt. Wexler was faster. He brought his knee up.

Pain, exquisite and blinding, blossomed in Noble's crotch and radiated into his belly. If he'd eaten anything in the last few hours it would have come up. Thankfully his stomach was empty and instead he got a mouth full of bile. His knees turned to rubber and it was a struggle just to stay on his feet.

Wexler took advantage of the opening. He yanked the rifle from Noble's fingers and brought it straight up, smacking Noble under the chin. There was a muffled crack. Noble's head snapped back. Shockwaves of agonizing electricity crackled down his spinal column. He landed flat on his back, arms outstretched. He told himself to get back up and get in the fight, but his body was no longer taking orders from his brain. For the moment, it was all he could do to lay there sucking air.

"No!" Stokely leapt up and threw herself at Wexler, arms out stretched, fingers hooked into claws.

He swung the rifle like a baseball bat, catching her just behind the ear. She crumpled to the ground and a bright red wash of blood soaked into her collar. Her eyes rolled up, revealing whites and she slumped down in a semi-conscious daze.

Wexler straddled Noble and shouldered the rifle.

By the time Noble's body started co-operating again, he was staring down the barrel of the semi-automatic. His insides turned to ice. He put both hands up, showing empty palms.

Wexler said, "I cannot tell you how much I've looked forward to this day."

Noble knew anything he said at this point might get him shot so he clamped his teeth together and stared icy daggers.

Wexler took one hand off the weapon and pointed to the eye-patch. "I lost an eye because of you. And I lost a fortune because of you. But now I'm going to get what I deserve. Give me the research."

"You've got no plans to give it to Keiser," Noble said. "Do you?"

"To hell with Keiser," Wexler said. "That old bastard carved out my eye. I'm going to sell the technology to the highest bidder. Now hand it over."

Despite the pain and the cold, despite the fact that he was about to die, Noble managed a nasty grin. "Go ahead and shoot."

Wexler shook his head. "You haven't got it, have you?"

Noble laughed. "Think I'm stupid?"

Wexler was laughing now as well. It was a rasping, desperate sound. "You never were going to give it up, were you?"

"No."

"You're a right bastard, you know that?"

"And you're an ignorant brute," Noble told him. "Shoot me, but you'll never get your hands on that research."

Wexler slammed a foot down on Noble's chest, pinning him to the ground. "That's where you're wrong. You may not have the tech, but I'll bet she knows where it's stashed. Doesn't she?" Wexler leveled a finger at Stokely. "After you're dead, I'm going to make her talk."

Noble's mouth opened in a snarl of impotent rage and hate. He grasped at Wexler's foot in a last desperate attempt to turn the tables, but he wasn't fast enough.

Wexler pressed the barrel against Noble's forehead and his finger started to tighten on the trigger.

Five loud pops rent the air and echoed through the trainyard.

# Chapter Eighty-Nine

Noble flinched, expecting to feel bullets rip through his skull—or would everything just go black?—but neither of those things happened.

Wexler danced and jerked. Lead hornets savaged his black vest, snapping and stinging, ripping little holes in the canvas. The sound was a deafening symphony. Wexler staggered back, caught his heel on the railroad track and went over like a felled tree, landing flat on his back.

Noble lunged for the rifle, caught the barrel, and yanked it away from Wexler before he'd even hit the ground. The weapon was a comfortable weight in Noble's hands. He automatically checked the action, hauling back on the charging handle to be sure there was a round in the chamber. The rifle was loaded and ready to rock.

Noble turned.

Hunt leaned against a box car, nickel plated .45 in one hand and smoke trailing from the muzzle. He pushed away from the carriage and limped awkwardly on his good leg, crunching through the slush, to sit down next to Noble. He let out a long groan. His face twisted in pain and he gently probed the bloody bandage.

"You saved my life," Noble said.

Hunt grunted and laid back in the snow, staring up at the sky. "Don't ask me why. I should have let him cap you." A spasm of pain gripped him. He winced and then said, "Noble?"

"Yeah?"

"I hate you."

Noble reached over and patted his shoulder. "I hate you too, buddy."

Stokely was sitting up, massaging the back of her skull. The front of her coat was caked with drying blood. She looked like she'd just swallowed a grapefruit rind. She said, "We good?"

Noble started to nod, but that hurt too much. "Yeah, we're good."

Wexler was still alive. He was curled up on his side and a coughing fit wracked his large frame. The ballistic plate in his vest had caught most of Hunt's bullets, but one slipped past and made a mess of his bicep. A small puddle of blood was forming around him, soaking into the snow. His eye was a narrow slit, hurling poison daggers at Noble. He said, "This changes nothing. You're still going to jail. You got no proof we set you up."

"Got all the proof I need," Noble told him. He was on his knees checking Hunt's bandage. "This was never about the deep fake. I knew you'd never bring the evidence with you. It was about you."

Wexler's face twisted in confusion.

Stokely, still holding the back of her skull, said, "We don't have to prove Noble's innocent. We just have to hand you over to the CIA and let them sweat the info out of you."

"Everybody breaks sooner or later," Noble said. "You're going to tell them everything you know."

Wexler looked from Stokely to Noble, then to Hunt. His chin bunched up like a little boy about to burst into tears. He shook his head, at a loss for words. His eye fell on something in the snow. Noble followed his gaze and spotted the butt of his fallen pistol half buried next to the tracks.

Wexler lunged.

"No!" Noble shouted.

Wexler brought the gun up, pressed the muzzle against his own temple, and squeezed the trigger. The side of his head blew off in a shower of gore, spraying the tracks with a macabre tapestry.

It was all over in a moment. Wexler lay dead and any proof Keiser had orchestrated the whole affair was dead with him.

Sirens sounded in the night. In another moment, the train yard would swarm with police and EMS. Noble went down on his knees and closed his eyes.

Stokely put an arm around his shoulders, pulled him into a hug and whispered, "We'll figure something out."

# Chapter Ninety

Mary Elise Noble had Matthew Burke's large black hands clasped in her frail white ones. She'd prayed for the dog, and herself, and even prayed for the boat—God forbid anything happen to the boat, Jake would never forgive her—but mostly she prayed for Jake.

Burke, for the most part, sat in quiet contemplation. Listening to Mary pray had a calming effect on him. He didn't know if it was the sound of her voice, God, or maybe just the power of belief, but as she prayed, he felt the knot in his belly start to unwind. He had several days of police interviews to look forward to—he'd need to concoct a few lies to satisfy the investigators—and a wife who would be worried sick. Mary's prayers were helping to take the edge off. For that he was grateful. He even offered up his own half-hearted prayer. He hadn't really done any serious praying since he was a boy sitting in a sweltering church in Savanna, listening to a Baptist preacher talk fire and brimstone. But he prayed now. He asked God to take care of Noble and, if at all possible, the dog as well.

His mind wandered. He was thinking longingly of a Hawaiian pizza and a cold margarita when the door to the operating theater swung open and the vet emerged in a smock daubed with blood. He took a moment to strip out of his gloves, then pulled his mask down around his neck.

Mary and Burke turned to him, still holding hands.

"Good news," the doctor said. "Looks like your dog's going to make it. He's not out of the woods yet, so to speak. He lost a lot of blood but he's stable. We've got him sedated and we're going to keep him overnight at the very least. He's going to need a lot of help over the next few weeks."

They thanked the surgeon and when he was gone, Mary covered her face with her hands and broke down crying. Burke wrapped a thick arm around her narrow shoulders and pulled her into a tight hug. "Let's get you home."

"I want to see Gadsden first."

Burke smiled. "I suppose we can do that."

# Chapter Ninety-One

Wizard stood with his hips against his desk, a cigarette burning in one hand, staring at the black and white photo of Keiser tacked to his wall. Smoke drifted up in lazy loops toward the air vent. The clock on the wall was slowly ticking round toward ten. The sky outside was black. Yellow arc sodiums made pale haloes in the snow-covered parking lot beyond his office window. His secretary had gone home for the evening and the seventh floor was mostly deserted. Wizard put the cigarette to his lips, took a long drag, and shot streams of smoke from both nostrils.

He was on his third pack and he'd drank two pots of coffee. His head was buzzing. He had spent the day arguing with McHale over the president's decision to extradite Noble to the Chinese and he hadn't gained even an inch. Xi Jing Ping had threatened to cancel any and all trade negotiation with the United States if Noble wasn't turned over. America needed toilet paper, so Noble was going to China, and that was that.

Wizard scratched an eyebrow with a nicotine-stained fingernail and muttered a curse.

There was a knock at the door.

Wizard's brow pinched. He twisted around and growled, "Enter."

Cook and Witwicky filed into his office looking tired but excited.

"What did you find?" Wizard asked.

Cook held up a sheaf of printed pages. "We found the leak," he said. "One of the dead security guys in the safehouse, an agent by the name of Pauls, had a younger brother injured in a motorcycle accident earlier this year. The medical bills were piling up and the family had no way to pay. Last month the family suddenly had a windfall. Looks like most of that money came through one of Keiser's shell companies."

Wizard circled around behind his desk and parked his bottom in his swivel chair. "Kieser bribed him with money for the kid's medical bills."

Witwicky nodded. "That's how Wexler knew about the safe house."

"And then double crossed Pauls," Wizard said, "tying up loose ends."

"Now we can prove Noble is innocent," Witwicky said.

"I'm afraid it's no longer that simple," Wizard told them. "The Chinese want a scapegoat and the President has determined it's going to be Noble."

"Sir," Cook began, "we have to officially protest Noble's release to the Chinese government. It's tantamount to murder. Not to mention the fact, that it would be playing right into China's hands. We'd lose all credibility on the world stage."

Witwicky had tears in her eyes. "Noble's innocent."

Cook nodded. "If the Director won't reconsider, then we're both going to resign in protest, and we'll go to the press. We'll tell them everything."

Wizard lit a fresh cigarette off the end of the old one. "You finished?"

Neither analyst knew what to say. Witwicky tortured her hands together while Cook frowned and crossed his arms.

"Get the hell out of my office," Wizard told them. "Don't let me hear you talk about quitting again. And the next time you threaten to go to the press, I'll have you both arrested for treason."

The color drained from Witwicky's face. Her shoulders sank and she started for the door. Cook stood his ground. The scar on his face was stark white and livid against his flushed cheeks. He stuck his jaw out and Wizard could tell he was looking for the right words to say.

Wizard narrowed his eyes and watched Cook through a veil of blue smoke. He said, "You've got guts kid, but this is a fight you can't win. Go home. That's an order."

Cook allowed himself to be dragged from the office by his girlfriend and Wizard was alone again with his thoughts. He turned toward the wall of news clippings and red string, toward his arch nemesis. Minutes ticked slowly by, the clock on the wall counting off the seconds with loud clonks of cheap gears. Wizard reached a decision and picked up the phone.

Matthew Burke answered after six rings, his voice thick with sleep.

"Did I wake you?"

"Been a rough day," Burke said.

"So I heard. How's the dog?"

"He's going to make it."

"Good," Wizard said. "You still in contact with our mutual friend in Israel?"

There was a long pause. Burke said, "You know about that?"

"I been doing this a long time," Wizard told him.

"I'm still in contact with her," Burke admitted. "She's been working with the Rabbi."

Wizard stared out the window at the parking lot. "We're going to need her help."

"Off the books?" Burke guessed.

"Off the reservation," Wizard admitted.

"If you're planning what I suspect, we'll need a lot of capital. Operations like that aren't cheap."

"I'll come up with the money," Wizard told him. "Can I count on your help?"

"Jake is like a son to me."

"Good. I need all the help I can get," Wizard said. "I'll contact you soon with more details."

He hung up, crushed out his cigarette and turned back to the wall of newspaper clippings.

# Chapter Ninety-Two

Noble stood on the tarmac in front of a private hangar in a seldom used corner of Heathrow. A 747 rumbled overhead, shaking the ground beneath his feet. He was wearing a thick wool overcoat, which used to belong to Stokely's father, and handcuffs. The snow of the last few days had turned to a heavy wet fog that plastered Noble's hair to his skull.

Stokely was on his right, one hand clutching Noble's elbow. Six stitches walked across her forehead just below the hairline. She had dressed in her best pinstripe suit with her hair pulled back and her shield clipped to her coat lapel. She'd been Noble's constant companion the last three days and had to fight tooth and nail to be present at the exchange.

Hunt stood on Noble's left. He was leaning heavily on a cane. He was there to make sure the exchange went smoothly and he told Noble as much in clipped tones that didn't invite any questions.

"This is so wrong," Stokely said to no one in particular. She had bright spots of color in her cheeks and her eyes were rimmed in red. She took a handkerchief from her pocket and dabbed away tears.

A private plane had touched down and was slowly taxiing toward the hangar. Noble waited in silence.

"I want you to know I did everything I could to stop this," Stokely said.

"I know," Noble told her. "There was nothing you could do."

"It's not right." She shook her head.

The private jet slowed to a stop in front of the hangar.

Noble tried to offer her a smile, but it came off looking more like a sad grimace. He was fighting to keep his own waterworks in check. As a covert operative, there was always the chance you'd be rolled up by an enemy intelligence outfit, but he never thought his own country would arrest him and hand him over to the Chinese. He said, "It's not your fault."

"I'm so sorry, Jake." She kissed him on the cheek. "I really am."

"You'll talk to my mother," Noble asked. He'd spent three days trying to come up with the words and in the end just told Stokely to make sure his mom knew that he loved her. What else was there to say really?

"I'll do it in person," she promised.

The door of the craft whirred open and a pair of Chinese military officers, one man, one woman, bundled in long green coats descended. Their eyes were half veiled by their military caps. They stopped at the bottom of the steps, waiting.

"It's time," Hunt said in a tight voice.

"I suppose it won't hurt to let you have this." Stokely took the battered and folded Bible tract from her pocket and passed it to Noble. She'd underlined Psalm 23. He gripped the glossy brochure in both hands.

Hunt took his elbow and motioned him toward the plane.

It was the hardest thing Noble ever had to do, just to get his feet moving. Putting one foot in front of the other seemed a monumental task and once started, it was the beginning of the end. Noble desperately wished he could freeze time. Instead he found himself walking across the blacktop toward the waiting plane. He tucked the Bible tract into his pocket, squared his shoulders and fixed a cold stare on his face as he passed the waiting Chinese agents and started up the steps. He turned for one last look at Stokely, at freedom, before a small Chinese officer with a high pitched voice herded him onto the plane using shoves and harsh words. Noble barely noted the fact that the belligerent officer was using Cantonese rather than Mandarin.

# Chapter Ninety-Three

Otto Keiser relaxed on the leather sofa of his penthouse apartment in Bern, Switzerland. He had a champagne flute in one hand and his arm around a beautiful redhead. She rubbed the inside of his thigh. Her name was Elizabeth something or other. She'd been sent by an agency Keiser used regularly. She had arrived at his door in a slinky green dress and heels. A pair of security men had checked her purse before showing her into the apartment. Keiser had greeted her and asked her to pour them both a glass of champagne before laboriously transferring himself from the wheelchair to the sofa where they'd be able to sit together.

Tonight was a celebration of sorts. He'd failed to procure the Chinese research and he'd lost a valuable employee, but he'd eliminated a thorn from his side and managed to keep his own hands clean in the process. He sipped his drink and congratulated himself on a job well done.

The redhead let out a purr, trailed kisses along his neck, and started to unbutton his shirt. She kept calling him Daddy, which Keiser didn't care for, but she was enthusiastic which went a long way. He felt himself starting to respond to her, set his glass aside, and took hold of one silky smooth thigh.

She flicked her tongue against his earlobe and Keiser said, "You're a wild one."

"You have no idea," she whispered as she straddled him on the sofa.

Her emerald green dress rode up, revealing a pair of matching panties. She raked her fingernails down his bare chest, leaving red marks.

Keiser was groping her bottom and ignored the first small stab of chest pain. It had been a long time since he'd been with such a spirited woman. He was pushing her dress down over her shoulders when the shockwave hit. He grunted and one hand went to his heart. The first real note of panic formed on his face. An invisible anvil settled on his sagging man boobs and sweat beaded on his forehead. The weight of the girl wasn't helping. He tried to tell her to stop, to get off him, but that was too much effort. She didn't seem to realize he was in pain.

Her thighs squeezed his belly painfully hard. Another tremor of pain hit like a tidal wave. Keiser croaked out a soft wheezing note, tried to push the girl off and, when that didn't work, he reached for his mobile phone on the coffee table.

***

"You won't be needing that." Eliška Cermákova plucked the cellphone from Keiser's hand and tossed it under the sofa. "I'm afraid it's far too late to summon an ambulance."

The fat old toad made another gagging noise. His face was turning beet red and he pointed at his chest, trying to croak out words but he couldn't get enough air. Large beads of sweat trailed down his cheeks.

"You are going into cardiac arrest," Eliška explained.

Still not understanding, Keiser motioned frantically toward the front door of the apartment. Eliška followed his gaze. "Oh, they won't be able to help you. In fact, no one can help you. You'll be dead in a matter of minutes."

He tried again to push her off, but his strength was failing. Eliška took his wrists and pinned them behind his head. She was still squeezing his belly with toned thighs, cutting off his air.

Keiser struggled in a useless attempt to throw her off. His face went from red to an alarming shade of purple. A vein stood out like a thick python on his forehead and his eyes bulged. He managed to rasp out, "Who ... you?"

Eliška leaned in close and whispered. "Jake Noble sends his regards."

Keiser's face morphed into a twisted mask of rage and hatred. His body tensed. For one incredible moment Eliška thought the old fart might actually manage to throw her aside, but it was just his death throes. The last of his strength drained away. He made a few feeble choking noises, jerked violently, and then lay still.

When it was over, Eliška quickly stripped off his clothes and dropped them on the floor in a pile before carrying his champagne glass to the sink. She poured the poisoned bubbly down the drain, rinsed the glass, and returned it to the coffee table. She gave a few loud moans of sexual frenzy in case the security guards outside the door liked to listen in, then took wet wipes from her purse and ran them over any surfaces she had touched. She went on performing while she cleaned, finishing with a rousing series of ecstatic screams. When she was finished, she checked Keiser's pulse just to be sure. He was stone cold dead. His eyes were rolled up in his skull and his mouth hung open.

Eliška ripped open a condom from her purse, dropped it on the Persian rug, then slipped her heels back on, slung her clutch over her shoulder, and let herself out of the apartment.

If anyone bothered to investigate, they'd conclude the old goat had hired a prostitute, had a little too much fun, and been hit with a crippling heart attack after she left. Case closed.

In the hall, the security thugs eyed her up and down, open curiosity on their faces.

Eliška smiled, covered her lips with one finger and whispered, "He's sleeping."

"Sounds like you know what you're doing in there," Müller said.

She was on her way to the elevator and said, "I'm a *killer* in the sack."

Schneider smiled. "I hope you didn't give him a heart attack."

They both laughed.

The elevator doors opened. Eliška stepped inside the car, thumbed the button for the ground floor and blew a kiss to Keiser's security detail as the doors rolled shut.

**The End.**

## Can't Wait for More Jake Noble?

Sign up for the Jake Noble Fan Club and get, SIDE JOBS: Volume 1, The Heist for FREE! This story is available exclusively to my mailing list.

**SIGN UP**

**Please take a moment and leave a review on Amazon**. Readers depend on reviews when choosing what to read next, and authors depend on them to sell books. **An honest review is like leaving your waiter a hundred dollar tip.** The best part... It doesn't cost you a dime.

WILLIAM MILLER JOINED THE United States Army after 9/11. He is an ardent supporter of the Second Amendment, collects firearms and spends a lot of time at the range. He loves to travel and learn new languages. When not writing, he can be found rock climbing, playing guitar and haunting smoke-filled jazz clubs. He is currently at work on the next Jake Noble thriller. Follow him on Instagram @AuthorWilliamMiller, Facebook, and at www.LiteraryRebel.com

# Also by William Miller

**THE JAKE NOBLE CHRONICLES:**
NOBLE MAN
NOBLE VENGEANCE
NOBLE INTENT
NOBLE SANCTION
NOBLE ASSET
NOBLE STORM

**THE MACKENZIE AND COLE MYSTERIES:**
THE DEVIL HIS DUE
SKIN IN THE GAME

**NON-FICTION:**
CRAFTING FICTION VOLUME ONE: HARD-BOILED OUTLINES

Turn the page for a preview of The Devil His Due, a thrilling murder mystery by William Miller.

The apartment building was fifteen floors of art deco construction and arched windows. A fire escape clung to the front like a scaly black insect. Police and paramedics were already on scene by the time I arrived, and a crowd had gathered across the street. I double-parked my beat-up '67 Mercury Cougar in back of the CSU van and the engine died with a series of soft ticking sounds. They had called me in on my day off, so I knew it must be important. I had been with the NYPD for fifteen years now, the last four spent on patrol, riding around in a black-and-white, busting petty criminals and responding to domestic disturbance calls. Before that I spent seven years as a detective, gold shield and all. How I went from detective to walking a beat is a long story for another time. I won't bore you with the details.

The driver's side door of the Mercury cranked open with a shriek of rusting hinges, and a blast of cold air put spots of color in my cheeks. It was a blustery October day. Halloween was just around the corner and gusting winds sent dry yellow leaves skittering along the sidewalks. I swung the door shut with a bang, turned the collar of my coat up against the chill, and climbed the front steps. A uniformed officer in a rain slicker gave a chin jut of recognition. "You've never seen anything like this."

"Bad?" I asked.

"Hinkey," he said.

I let myself into the lobby. The original elevator was still in operation. The door was a collapsible brass grate guarding an open shaft. I climbed inside the box and thumbed the button. The car rose with the twang and pop of steel cables. Another uniform greeted me up on four, where yellow and black crime scene tape draped the apartment door like parade bunting. I flashed my shield and the officer waved me through.

The overpowering stench of singed flesh and rotting eggs hit me like a sucker punch. Tears filled my eyes, and I resisted the urge to cover my nose. It took me a moment to identify the smell—brimstone.

A body lay on the floor of the apartment, eyes wide and mouth stretched in a silent scream—a terrified grimace frozen on a pretty face. She was dressed in a man's white button-down and cotton panties. Angry red blisters covered every inch of exposed flesh. Her arms and legs were contorted in what medical examiners call the boxer's stance. It happens when people die in a fire. The arm and leg muscles cramp, leaving the victim looking like a boxer with his arms drawn up and his knees bent, ready for action.

A few feet away, burned into the polished hardwood floor of this stylish Upper East Side apartment, was a pentagram. Tendrils of smoke still drifted up from the hottest points of the star.

The patrolman was right, *I'd never seen anything like this.*

The rest of the apartment was a hive of quiet activity. Half a dozen CSU techs in white space suits took samples, bagged evidence, and snapped photographs, but I noticed they moved a lot slower than normal and there was none of the usual crime scene banter. They worked in hushed silence and, when they had to talk, they whispered. There was a strange feeling in the air, like too much static electricity, or maybe that was just my nerves. Either way, I felt like an interloper here, a trespasser on the scene of some unholy ritual. I realized the small hairs on the back of my neck were standing on end.

I gave a shudder, worked my shoulders around, trying to throw off that creepy feeling. Then I noticed her.

A brunette in corduroy slacks and a cable-knit sweater was examining the door, her nose less than an inch from the busted lock. Chestnut tresses were pulled back in a loose ponytail, held together by a brightly colored scrunchie that clashed horribly with her outfit. And I'm not exactly Calvin Kline. She gave me the impression of a gangly ballerina trying to hide imagined flaws beneath the oversized sweater. She wasn't wearing a badge or a gun, so she wasn't a cop, and she wasn't covered in plastic, which ruled out CSU. If I didn't know better, I'd think a civilian had wandered into the crime scene.

I said, "Can I help you?"

Her gaze flicked to me and then back to the lock. She shook her head. "No."

I gave her a hard stare which she ignored and then I propped a hand on my belt, the tips of my fingers resting against my shield. It's a pose that normally commands respect from the civilian population, but the ballerina ignored me, crossed the apartment and picked up a stack of unopened mail on the kitchen counter. I opened my mouth to read her the riot act but I was interrupted.

"Officer Cole. Nice of you to join us." Lieutenant DeSilva emerged from the back bedroom with a notepad in one hand and a stub of pencil behind his ear. He looked like something out of a Hollywood vampire movie, tall and thin with white-blonde hair combed straight back from a high forehead. His eyes were the color of faded denim and his chin tapered to a point.

"Our victim's name is Britney Westin," he said. "Landlord confirmed her identity. Twenty-eight. Single. Lives alone. Parents have a house in the Hamptons." He waved his notepad at a framed copy of *Le Femme* magazine hanging on the wall. "Our vic was the managing editor at the magazine."

I hunkered down next to the body of Britney Westin. She had been a good-looking woman, but death wasn't kind. It never was. I said, "So what are we thinking? Some kind of cult killing? Bad guys break in, kill our victim, and burn a pentagram into the floor?"

"Try again," DeSilva told me. "Door was locked and chained from the inside. We had to break it down."

I twisted around for a look. The frame was splintered. "Who called it in?"

"Upstairs neighbors noticed the smell. Fire department was first on the scene. They kicked in the door when they didn't get a response." DeSilva spread his hands. "They found this."

"Could the killer have come in through the fire escape?"

DeSilva shook his head. "All the windows are locked. No sign of forced entry."

I took a moment to let that sink in before turning to the medical examiner. "Cause of death?"

Tippy Lewis was a big man with heavy jowls and a bulbous red nose that whistled every time he exhaled. "Your guess is as good as mine," he said. "All I can tell you right now is that her heart stopped."

"What caused these burns?"

Tippy shook his head. "I don't know yet, but they're localized."

"Meaning?"

"The heat source didn't burn her clothing or the floor beneath her."

I looked again at the body. The button-down shirt was untouched by fire. A wash and a dry and it would be ready to wear, though you'd never catch me in it. "Hinkey," I said. "Time of death?"

"Between nine thirty and eleven," Tippy said. "I can narrow that down more once I've got the labs back."

"She died at approximately ten forty."

I looked up at the sound of the voice.

It was the gangly ballerina in the corduroy slacks and cable-knit sweater. She joined us at the edge of the pentagram, dropped onto her belly, put her face an inch from the charred wood, and sniffed.

I said "How can you be so sure?"

"Simple," she said. "The upstairs neighbors noticed the smell and called the fire department at ten fifty-one. Given the extent of the burns and the size of the apartment, I'd estimate it took roughly ten minutes for the smell to migrate upstairs. I can also tell you she died instantly, or close to it."

"What makes you say that?"

"Otherwise she would have called for help or fled the apartment. I'd place time of death no sooner than ten forty. Ten forty-five at the latest."

Tippy scanned the apartment and admitted the logic with a shrug.

I turned to the lieutenant. "Who is this?"

"Mike Cole, meet Special Investigator Jessica Mackenzie of the FBI." DeSilva drew out the syllables. "Mackenzie's going to be running point. You are to assist her in any way you can."

MACKENZIE THRUST HER HAND out. "Nice to meet you."

She was still flat on her belly with her arm stretched across the smoldering Satanic symbol. She had a good firm handshake but didn't meet my gaze. Her attention remained fixed on the pentagram. She gave my hand a perfunctory pump before going back to her examination. As we watched, she pinched charred soot between gloved fingers and sniffed.

"Phosphorous and nitrate," she muttered to herself before pushing up to her knees. "Doors and windows all locked. No sign of forced entry. No sign of a struggle. And a perfectly symmetrical pentagram burned into the floor. We know Ms. Westin wasn't subdued; there are no signs of restraint on the body, and the pentagram is still warm to the touch so it must have been made shortly after Ms. Westin was killed. It would be difficult for a human, especially one who had just committed murder, to draw such an exacting circle on the floor. The killer would obviously be worried about witnesses."

I saw where she was going with that line of thinking and said, "What's your theory, Mackenzie? Did the Devil do it?"

"You joke, but there is ample evidence to support the existence of the paranormal," Mackenzie said.

"Put out an APB," I told the room at large. "Horns. Tail. Pitchfork. Answers to the name Beelzebub."

Everybody laughed, including DeSilva, but it was a nervous laughter and died quickly, like a shuttle that fails to get off the launchpad.

Mackenzie said, "There are more things in heaven and earth, Horatio, than are dreamt of in your philosophy."

I turned to DeSilva and cocked a thumb at the door. "Can I talk to you in the hall for a minute?"

We ducked the crime scene tape and I lowered my voice. "You called in the FBI?"

"She called us actually."

"And you invited her onto our case?"

DeSilva looked through the door at the blistered remains. "Are we seeing the same picture?"

"Granted," I said, "it's a mess, but we don't need federal help. Reinstate me as a detective. I'll take the case."

"You know it's not that easy, Mike. You want your gold shield back, you're gonna have to earn it."

"Haven't I been punished enough?" I said and shook my head. "I been on patrol for the last four years."

DeSilva said, "The only way you're going to be reinstated into the detective bureau is to prove to me that you're not a risk to yourself or a liability to this department. Is that clear?"

"Fine," I said, "but do I have to prove it riding shotgun for the feds? Give me a partner and I'll close this case without FBI help."

"There's nobody to partner with you."

"What about Bremmer?" I asked. "He's not riding with anybody."

DeSilva shook his head. "He refused."

"He'd rather ride a desk than work with me?"

"You're radioactive, Cole. Nobody wants to work with you."

"Unbelievable," I said to myself.

DeSilva thrust his chin at the body on the floor. "That's unbelievable. This is office politics."

I hauled up a heavy sigh from somewhere deep in my chest and let it out with a shake of my head.

DeSilva said, "Look, it's simple, Cole. Help Agent Mackenzie close this case and you'll be reinstated as a detective at your old pay grade. Fail, and you go back to walking a beat. The choice is yours."

I propped my hands on my hips, took in some air, and let it out slow. If I had to help the FBI close a case to get back on the murder boards, that's exactly what I'd do, but I said, "I want that in writing."

"The paperwork will be on my desk by end of watch."

"How did the feds even get wind of this?" I asked.

DeSilva hitched up his shoulders. "I have no idea. She arrived right after me and requested an NYPD officer to aid her investigation into the . . . incident."

"I notice you didn't call it murder."

"Until I have a cause of death, it's an incident," DeSilva said.

"Don't tell me you buy her theory about the Devil."

"I don't know what to believe. I've never seen anything like this in all my years on the force." DeSilva sucked his teeth and stared at the body. "If the media gets hold of this, it's going cause a panic."

"They won't hear it from me," I said.

DeSilva motioned and I followed him back inside.

MACKENZIE WAS HOLDING A framed picture. In it the victim was smiling alongside three other girls. The photograph was old and starting to fade. At the bottom, scrawled in black marker, were the words "The Pact."

I cleared my throat. "Welcome to the team, Agent Mackenzie. Happy to be working with you."

*Working* with *you*, I said, *not* for *you*, because I wanted her to know I wasn't taking marching orders from a fed. She gave a distracted sort of nod without looking up from the photograph.

"So what's the FBI's interest?" I asked.

"The FBI isn't interested," Mackenzie told me. "I am."

DeSilva and I traded a look. Mine said "What have you gotten me into?" His said "Good luck with this one."

"What was that?" Mackenzie asked.

"What was what?" I said.

"That look?" she said and cocked her head to one side. Her brow pinched. "You looked at him, he shrugged, and you nodded. What does that mean?"

"It doesn't mean anything," I told her. *Was she dressing us down?*

Mackenzie blinked a few times, like she was trying to decide what to make of it. After a minute, she let it go and told one of the techs to admit the photograph into evidence, then stripped off her gloves.

"We'll want to canvas the neighbors. See if anyone saw or heard anything. I assume you have uniformed officers doing that already?"

"Standard procedure," DeSilva assured her. "They'll let you know if they turn up anything."

"Good." Mackenzie nodded. "The victim had sex with someone last night. I want to know who."

"How do you know that?" I asked.

"Fresh flowers on the table along with a used condom in the bathroom trash."

My eyes went to the low table in front of the leather sofa where a dozen long-stemmed roses stood in a cheap plastic vase. It was the kind of bouquet you pick up last minute from a corner bodega. The petals were still thick and red and the arrangement had yet to be placed into a nicer vase. First thing most women do is move flowers into a more expensive container. A look around the apartment told me Westin had money. She'd have at least one or two old vases around that she could put the flowers into, but she hadn't gotten the chance. I said, "Okay, the flowers are fresh, but you can't possibly know how long the condom has been in the trash. It could have been there for days."

"I found a crumpled receipt from a store at the end of the block where the condoms were purchased," Mackenzie told me. "Dated yesterday. The roses are apology roses. Britney Westin recently made up with her lover."

"Did you find the apology note?"

"That part's admittedly conjecture," Mackenzie said. "It's my understand that men bring flowers when they want to apologize."

"Only time my wife ever gets flowers," one of the techs commented.

Mackenzie said, "I also want to know what sort of medical problems Britney Westin was having."

I said, "How do you know she was having medical problems?"

She pointed to the kitchen. "There's a stack of medical bills on the counter along with the results of numerous tests."

Tippy Lewis grunted his way to the kitchen and paged through the stack of mail. "She's right. Seems Britney Westin was having a load of tests done. Most of the bills are from a specialist in cardiology."

DeSilva turned his attention back to the corpse. "Could a heart condition do this?"

Tippy opened his mouth to speak but Mackenzie beat him to the punch. "Most certainly not."

Tippy stared daggers at the FBI agent and said, "No cardiac condition I've ever encountered would result in burns like this, but I won't rule it out until I get her on the slab."

I pointed to the pentagram. "No heart condition did that. She was murdered. We just have to figure out how. When we know how it was done, we'll be one step closer to knowing who."

"Assuming there is an ordinary explanation," Mackenzie said. "We'll explore every avenue until we have exhausted all possibilities. Mr. Lewis, make this autopsy your top priority. Do it first thing, please."

Tippy Lewis smacked the stack of medical reports down on the counter. "Sure, I'll just rearrange my entire schedule. All those other cops waiting on cuts can just wait a little longer."

The sarcasm was lost on Mackenzie. She said, "Thank you. I've seen everything I need here. Do you have a car, Officer Cole?"

"A car?" I questioned.

She nodded and clarified, "An automobile."

"Yeah," I said. "I've got a car."

"Good. We'll start with the parents. I want to notify next of kin before it goes out over the wire."

"What happened to your car?" I asked.

She shook her head. "I don't drive."

"Of course you don't." I fixed DeSilva with a look.

The lieutenant grinned and shot finger pistols at the pair of us. "This looks like the beginning of a beautiful friendship."

**Grab a copy and start reading today!**

Made in the USA
Middletown, DE
27 January 2024